THE LAST
SAXON KING

A JUMP IN TIME NOVEL
BOOK ONE

ANDREW VARGA

IMBRIFEX BOOKS

IMBRIFEX BOOKS
8275 S. Eastern Avenue, Suite 200
Las Vegas, NV 89123
Imbrifex.com

THE LAST SAXON KING: A JUMP IN TIME NOVEL (BOOK ONE)

Library of Congress Cataloging-in-Publication Data
Names: Varga, Andrew, 1969- author.
Title: The last Saxon king : a jump in time novel / Andrew Varga.
Description: First edition. | Las Vegas, NV : Imbrifex Books, 2023. |
    Series: A jump in time ; book 1 | Audience: Ages 12-15. | Audience: Grades 7-9. |
    Summary: When sixteen-year-old Dan Renfrew accidentally transports himself to
    England in the year 1066, he learns he is a time jumper, descended from a long line of
    secret heroes who protect the present by traveling to the past to fix breaks and glitches in
    the time stream.
Identifiers: LCCN 2022016128 (print) | LCCN 2022016129 (ebook) |
    ISBN 9781945501821 (hardcover) | ISBN 9781945501852 (paperback) |
    ISBN 9781945501838 (ebook) | ISBN 9781945501845
Subjects: LCSH: Great Britain--History--Anglo-Saxon period, 449-1066--Fiction. |
    CYAC: Time travel--Fiction. | Harold II, King of England, 1022?-1066--Fiction. | LCGFT:
    Historical fiction. | Novels. Classification: LCC PZ7.1.V39635 Las 2023 (print) | LCC
    PZ7.1.V39635 (ebook) | DDC [Fic]--dc23
LC record available at https://lccn.loc.gov/2022016128
LC ebook record available at https://lccn.loc.gov/2022016129

Jacket designed by Jason Heuer
Book Designed by Sue Campbell Book Design
Author photo: Andrew Johnson
Typeset in Berkley Oldstyle

Printed in the United States of America
Distributed by Publishers Group West
First Edition: March 2023

For Pam, Leah, Arawn, and Calvin

Ða com Wyllelm eorl of Normandige into Pefnesea on Sancte
Michæles mæsseæfen,
sona þæs hi fere wæron, worhton castel æt Hæstingaport.
Þis wearð þa Harolde cynge gecydd, he gaderade þa mycelne here,
com him togenes æt þære haran apuldran,
Wyllelm him com ongean on unwær, ær þis folc gefylced wære.
Ac se kyng þeah him swiðe heardlice wið feaht mid þam mannum þe
him gelæstan woldon,
þær wearð micel wæl geslægen on ægðre healfe

Then came William earl of Normandy into Pevensey,
on the eve of St. Michael's mass.
Soon after they were on their way, they constructed
a castle at Hasting's-port.
This was then made known to king Harold, and
he then gathered a great force, and came to meet him at the
estuary of Appledore.
William came against him unawares, before his people
were set in order.
But the king nevertheless strenuously fought against him with
those men who would follow him.
There was great slaughter made on either hand.

Anglo-Saxon Chronicle Manuscript D, Worcester Chronicle,
entry for year 1066
Anonymous Monk, eleventh century

CHAPTER 1

As I stood staring at the display of new video games in the store's front window, a security guard appeared behind me in the reflection. He hovered just a few steps back, rhythmically slapping a large black flashlight into the palm of his hand. "Whatcha doing out of school, kid?" he asked in the accusing tone that all mall cops use with teenagers—the tone that implied he already knew I was up to something, even though I was just standing there minding my own business.

I didn't make the slightest movement to acknowledge his presence. "I'm homeschooled."

"Well, shouldn't you be at home, then?" He smacked his flashlight into his palm with a meaty thump.

"My dad gave me the day off."

The tip of the flashlight poked me in the shoulder. "Look at me when I'm talking to you!"

Sighing, I turned to face him. His name tag read *Jenkins*. He was slightly taller than me and a few years older—probably at his first real job. He wore the standard mall cop uniform: shiny black shoes, dark pants with a crisp white shirt, thick belt with all sorts of useless gadgets, and a huge chip on his shoulder. Instantly his eyes dropped to the tattoo on the inside of my right forearm. He took a step back and pointed his flashlight at the four-pointed star within a circle. "That gang ink?" he asked suspiciously.

Was this guy for real? We were in the world's most boring mall in the world's most boring neighborhood. The only gangs here were the hordes of senior citizens who walked the halls every morning for exercise.

I decided to be nice to Jenkins and not tell him how stupid he was. I mean, with all the useless stuff my dad was teaching me at home, I was probably gonna end up stuck as a mall cop myself one day, and Jenkins might be my boss. "No. It's a family tattoo," I explained. "I've had it for as long as I can remember. My dad has the same one."

"You're lying, kid."

I rolled my eyes and shook my head. All this hassle because I was staring at some stuff in a store window that I couldn't afford anyway. I wouldn't even be at the mall except Dad had given me twenty bucks and told me to get out of the house for a few hours because someone was coming over for a meeting. And since it was pouring outside, my options had been kind of limited. I'd already spent most of my cash on lunch and a movie, and I probably had at least another hour to kill before I could go back home. No matter how much it pained me, I needed to suck up to Jenkins before he tossed me out into the rain.

"Look," I said, "I'm not a thief or in a gang. I'm just hanging out." Jenkins opened his mouth to say something, but I cut him off. "I know you don't believe me, but I can prove it. I'm on file here. Come on, I'll show you."

Without waiting for his response, I began heading for the mall administration office. After a moment's hesitation, I heard his shoes squeaking across the tiled floor behind me.

The office was in the darkest corner of the building, right next to the bathrooms. I strode confidently through a door marked Security

Personnel Only and into a cramped, stuffy room with a ratty armchair, a coffee machine, and two filing cabinets. I pointed to the bulletin board near the door, pamphlets and memos splattered across it with no sense of order. "You'll find me under 'Special Notices.' Look for Daniel Renfrew."

Jenkins grunted and pushed aside some papers on handwashing. He found my sheet and removed it from its thumbtack. "Daniel Renfrew," he read. "Sixteen. Homeschooled. Occasionally wanders the mall and rarely buys anything. Harmless but sometimes lippy. Father is Professor James Renfrew of SUNY…" He skimmed over the rest of the details and looked at the photo paper-clipped to the sheet. It was from about eight months ago, when I'd had my first run-in with a mall cop. After a long explanation and a call to Dad, management had agreed to keep me on file to avoid further hassles. I hadn't changed much since that picture had been taken. It showed a teenager with dirty-blond hair, an unsmiling face, and bored blue eyes. Not one of my better looks.

Jenkins held it up in line with my face, his eyes narrowing as he scrutinized the two like some border control officer on the lookout for terrorists.

After a few seconds, he tacked my sheet back on the board. "I guess you're free to wander around," he grumbled. "Although I have no clue why you'd want to spend time in this dump. I get paid to be here and I can't wait to leave. You should be outside, hanging around with your friends and meeting girls."

I snorted as I left the office. What a tool. Did he seriously think I'd be wasting my time here if I had friends or girls as an option?

Working at the mall was probably the most soul-crushing job imaginable, but at least Jenkins wasn't alone all day every day. That was homeschool for me: stuck in my room in front of the computer learning the official school-board-approved curriculum off the internet. And then even more hours spent doing the extra assignments Dad would pile on me before he left for work. Conjugating Latin verbs. Memorizing lists of ancient kings. Writing reports about forgotten battles or long-lost empires. A high school diploma wasn't good enough for Dad—he was dead set on turning me into a history geek like him.

Hell, even our summer camping trips to the Finger Lakes devolved into opportunities for him to sneak in a few extra lessons. Normal people went camping in RVs or at least tents. Dad's version of camping involved making a lean-to out of branches, creating a fire with flint and steel, and shivering all night long under an itchy wool blanket. He said it allowed us a fantastic opportunity to truly experience the outdoors like our ancestors had. What a load of crap. All I ever experienced were backaches and hypothermia.

I couldn't count the times I'd begged him to free me from home-school prison and send me to an actual school, where I could learn from real teachers and make friends or maybe even join a club or a team. Each time, I got the same arguments. *Teachers don't teach you how to think; they teach you how to follow. Blah, blah … Schools have become infested with drugs and gangs, leading to an unsafe educational environment. Blah, blah … The world's greatest inventors, philosophers, and leaders all had an education that focused on classical language and history.* And, of course, his trump card: *All Renfrew men have been educated this way.*

Whatever.

The usual afternoon mall crowd strolled around me: shopping moms, retired folks with nowhere better to be, salesclerks on break. Not a single girl my age. If this was really how all Renfrew men had been educated, it amazed me that our family line hadn't died out ages ago—all this studying left pretty much no time for anything that even remotely looked like a social life.

The only thing that made Dad's history obsession slightly bearable was the physical education portion of the curriculum. For most kids, PE meant suffering through dodgeball or writing essays on nutrition.

But I got daily training in hand-to-hand combat and medieval weapons. Over the years, I'd learned to fight with swords, axes, knives, bows, and even a bunch of weapons that most people had never heard of, like the bola and the atlatl.

It was hella fun, but what good was that skill set going to do me? My résumé was going to be a joke. Work skills: None. Education: Obsessive focus on history. Hobbies: Using an atlatl. *Next!* I let out a long sigh, drawing curious glances from the older couple walking past me.

This royally sucks.

Wandering around was stupid. I should just go home and play Xbox. Who cared if Dad had a meeting? It wasn't like I didn't know how to behave around adults.

The main entrance of the mall suddenly loomed in front of me again. How many times had I already passed it this afternoon? Five? Six? Should I go for another pointless loop of the halls and make it seven?

Then I realized the rain had stopped. That was definitely a sign from the universe telling me to go home, sneak through the back door to avoid Dad's guests, and then creep downstairs to get in some quality gaming time.

I pushed through the double glass doors. Overhead, the clouds were gray and the air was heavy with the smell of worms and moisture, but I was glad to ditch the mall—nothing exciting ever happened there. The food was mediocre. The stores were lame. And I'd never met a single girl there, or even had one smile at me. Not that I'd know what to do if I actually met a girl. *Hi there, I'm Dan. Want to see my atlatl?* Probably not the best pickup line.

Hold it …

Was that why Dad had kicked me out today? Had he actually brought a woman home? That would explain why he'd been acting weirder than usual the past few weeks. He'd snuck in late at night. He'd called in sick to work a few times. And whenever I came in the room while he was on the phone, he would start whispering. A girlfriend was the only logical explanation for all his secret agent crap.

All right, Dad!

I began walking faster, practically running. If he had brought someone home, I wanted to check her out before she left. Mom had died so long ago that I could barely remember her. It'd be awesome if Dad had actually found someone. Not that he was a bad parent or anything; he'd done a half-decent job on his own. We lived in a pretty nice house. The fridge was always full. I had shelves of video games and all the streaming services. But if he actually had someone else to pay attention to, maybe he'd stop trying to ram history down my throat every chance he got.

I tore around our corner and came to a screeching halt—Dad's Audi sat alone in the driveway.

Crap …

She'd ditched him already. The poor guy probably tried to impress her by making her lunch. One sniff of his authentic medieval leek soup would send anyone running. So much for my new mom.

What do I do now?

A good son would go in and try to console his dad over his failed date. But sneaking in and playing Overwatch was way more fun and a lot less awkward.

The crash of breaking pottery interrupted my deliberations.

What the … ?

Was Dad chucking plates around? Did his date go *that* badly?

Someone cried out, followed seconds later by the clang of metal striking metal. It sounded like … a sword fight?

My back stiffened and I could feel the blood drain from my face. Was Dad in trouble?

CHAPTER 2

I raced for the front steps but stopped halfway across the lawn. *What the hell am I doing?* If a sword fight was going on in there, barging in unarmed was a great way to get stabbed. Dad must have told me a thousand times: *Never rush into a situation—always assess what's going on first. Then find your opening.*

Crouching low, I snuck around to the back door. With shaking hands, I inserted my key and cracked the door open. The rapid peal of metal striking metal was louder now. There was no mistaking that sound—a sword fight was going on in my living room.

Suddenly, the flurry of blows ended, bringing the fight to an ominous pause.

"You cannot win, James," a deep voice said. "Give me the device."

"I can't," Dad replied, his words coming out in tired gasps. "Your plan is monstrous. I'd rather die than contribute to it in any way."

"Do not make the same foolish choice as William and Julian."

"You didn't …" Dad groaned.

"They gave me no choice. But you can avoid their fate. If you refuse to pledge allegiance to me and the cause, then at least surrender the device and I will spare your life."

"Please, Victor," Dad pleaded. "Think of what you're doing. You still have time to stop all this madness."

I tiptoed through the kitchen and peered around the doorframe into the living room. The place looked like a bomb had hit it. Books and papers littered the floor, the glass coffee tabletop had shattered, and a large gash split the fourteenth-century tapestry hanging by the window. Dad was backed up against the far wall, next to the front door. His white dress shirt was slashed across the sleeves and chest, with ever-expanding bloodstains turning the shirt from white to red. He gripped a saber in one hand, and in his other, held close to his chest, he clutched something that looked like a metal baton from a relay race.

Victor had his back turned to me. He was slightly taller than Dad, with perfectly styled black hair fading to gray over the ears. He wore a pin-striped dark blue suit, and in his right hand, pointing at Dad, he held the Spanish rapier that usually hung next to the bookshelf. "I do not think you have much fight left in you, my old friend," he said.

Victor advanced toward Dad, the rapier in guard position. A fist of panic whacked me in the gut. Dad looked tired, all the color drained from his face. He couldn't win this fight.

Should I call the cops? No, they'd take too long.

Scream for help? Who'd respond? Mrs. Jennings and her cat?

There was only one option—*I* needed to save Dad. And I had one chance to do it.

Sucking down my fear, I grabbed the ancient Sumerian clay statue from the corner table. "Dad!" I screamed as I hurled the statue at Victor's head.

I felt like an idiot the moment the word left my mouth. I'd meant it as a shout of encouragement to Dad, to let him know that help was on the way. Instead, Victor whipped his head around, locked eyes with me for an instant, and then, with reflexes that seemed way too quick for an old guy in a fancy suit, he ducked. The statue flew over his head, smashed into the wall, and exploded into a shower of dust and clay fragments.

My momentary surge of adrenaline fizzled away, and I stood there unarmed.

"This just became more interesting, James." Victor chuckled. "Maybe your son will be able to encourage you to do the right thing."

"Leave him alone!" Dad cried.

Victor ignored Dad and turned his rapier toward me, glaring at me with arrogant eyes. "Come here, boy," he commanded. "Now! Or your father dies."

I scanned the room for anything that could serve as a weapon.

Dad leaped forward and slashed at Victor. "Daniel! Run!"

Victor spun and parried Dad's saber, knocking it aside. Before Dad could recover, Victor plunged the rapier into his chest. Dad's eyes went wide and his mouth gaped. The saber fell from his hand and clattered noisily to the hardwood floor.

"No!" I wailed, my eyes blurry with tears.

Dad sank to his knees, his face twisted in pain, the rapier still stuck in his chest. His eyes closed for a second and he drew in a deep breath. With his last bit of strength, he tossed the baton toward me. It flew across the width of the room, bounced a few times, then rolled to a stop at my feet. "Hold the rod ..." Dad wheezed. "Say the bedtime rhyme."

Victor wrenched his rapier out with an irritated twist and his eyes zeroed in on the rod. "Do not touch it, *Daniel!*" he ordered, placing extra emphasis on my name—as if I would obey just because he'd used it.

A thousand thoughts raced through my mind. Could I call the cops before Victor reached me? Should I take the rod and run? Should I try to bargain for Dad's life?

Every course of action seemed destined for failure. And why would

Dad want me to say that stupid rhyme? It was just some gibberish he and I would recite when I was a kid, just before I went to sleep. How could that possibly help? That seemed like the most useless thing for me to do right now.

I bent and snatched up the rod. It was heavier than it looked and felt cold to the touch, as if it had just come out of the fridge. It wasn't actually round, more like hexagonal or octagonal, like a giant pencil, with strange markings etched into it.

Victor held out his left hand, the sword still gripped in his right. "Toss me the device, Daniel. There is still time to save your father."

Dad slumped against the base of the far wall, his once-white shirt now almost completely red. His hands hung by his sides and his chin rested on his chest. He struggled to raise his head and look at me. "I love you ... Say the rhyme ... Fix what's wrong ... Trust ... no one."

"Don't leave me, Dad!"

Victor took a step back and lowered his sword to the floor. "I mean you no harm." He raised both hands. "Just give me the device and I will leave. Then you can save your father."

"Say the rhyme!" Dad gasped.

"Why, Dad?" I cried, desperate to do *something*. "How is that going to help?"

He didn't answer, but when I saw the pleading in his eyes, it spilled out of me. "*Azkabaleth virros ku, haztri valent bhidri du.*"

In the fragment of time that it took for my heart to beat once, the markings on the rod started glowing with a fierce intensity that lit up the room.

Victor yelled, but time seemed to slow down so that his word stretched out as "Noooooooooo!" The glow from the rod increased until the room was bathed in light so bright that I had to shut my eyes to its glare.

CHAPTER 3

The floor vanished from beneath my feet and I felt weightless, as if I was floating in space. The brightness continued hammering against my eyes, forcing me to keep them tightly shut, so I flailed my legs and arms, desperately reaching for a floor or a wall or … anything, but felt nothing. I might have been moving, but there was no wind or sound to let me know for sure.

What the hell is happening?

Just when I stopped fighting the air and let myself float, I felt a strange sensation of motion, as if I was in an elevator that was slowing down before reaching my floor. Something solid materialized beneath my feet, and the scent of pine filled the air. A gentle breeze carried the sound of moving water.

I opened my eyes hesitantly, cautious of the harsh light.

"No way!" My own voice startled me. Through the purple spots floating in front of my eyes, I could see I was standing on the bank of a river in the middle of a forest. Reeds and bulrushes hugged the shore to my right; to the left was a mix of sand and pebbles. The rain clouds were gone, and the sun shone brightly, but a cold shudder ran through me.

Where am I?

A wave of dizziness knocked me to my knees. A second later, my stomach heaved, and the remains of my lunch splattered across the grass. I fought through the nausea and, with shaking legs, forced myself back to my feet. Later I'd try to figure out how the hell I had teleported from my house in the suburbs to the middle of nowhere. But right now, Dad needed my help. I reached into the back pocket of my jeans and pulled out my phone to call the police. The screen lit up. *No service.*

Damn it! I was in the middle of a freakin' forest; why would there be service? I opened the map and waited for it to tell me my location, but a little processing icon appeared and just kept spinning.

"Come on, you stupid phone."

I raised it high above my head and turned around in slow circles, praying for even a single bar.

Nothing.

Something super-weird was going on. How could GPS not work? It always worked. If it couldn't find me, where the hell was I?

My hands began to shake, and my breath came in short, panicky gasps. Dad wasn't the only one in deep trouble.

Easy, Dan.

Flipping out was the worst thing I could do. Dad had always taught me to stay calm and think my way out of a situation.

I took off my shoes and socks and sat down by the river's edge, letting my feet dangle in the water. Its chilly bite brought a welcome shock to my system.

First question: Where am I?

The trees looked similar to the forests near my house—a mix of pine and deciduous. Something struck me as odd about these trees, though: some of them were already changing color. And the air had a coolness to it that I didn't remember from this morning. This seemed like a forest in early fall. But how? It was early June.

Maybe I was going at it the wrong way. I kept assuming that the stupid rod had taken me someplace, but what if it had knocked me out and I was dreaming all of this?

I pinched myself hard on the arm. Other than a stab of pain and a small red mark on my skin, nothing happened. I was still there next to the river.

Okay, not a dream. But how had I ended up in the middle of nowhere? Had the rod put me to sleep? Had Victor kidnapped me and dumped me here?

Nope. Victor had wanted that rod, and I still had it with me.

The rod.

I turned it over in my hands, hoping to find an answer. It was hexagonal and divided into six equal-length segments, with strange symbols covering each face. If the symbols were a type of writing, they came from an alphabet I'd never seen before. The rod was made of a dull metal that looked ancient and was covered in pits and scratches. I tried to twist one of the segments of the rod and it spun stiffly around, like the side of a Rubik's Cube.

I spun the segment back to its original position. What was I supposed to do with this thing? It was too big to fit in the pocket of my jeans, so I put it in one of my shoes sitting next to the riverbank. Whatever this thing did, I couldn't figure out how it sent me here, so it was time to switch to Plan B: yelling like a fool for help.

"Hello! Hello! Is anybody out there?" My words flew across the water and echoed in the distance. I waited for a response.

Nothing.

I tried again, even louder, my howl driven by the fear and desperation welling up inside me.

The echoes of my cry faded, and all I heard in response were the calls of birds and the sighing of wind in the trees.

I threw my head back, cupped my hands around my mouth, and bellowed one last time. "Hellooo! Is anybody out there?"

"Shut up, you idiot!" hissed a voice from behind me. "Someone will hear you!"

I whirled around, my heart pounding. Someone had found me, but he didn't seem pleased about it. I scanned the forest for him but saw only trees and more trees. "W-w-where are you?" I asked.

"I'll ask the questions." The voice had a muffled quality to it, so I couldn't tell if the speaker was young or old or spoke with an accent. "Who are you?" It seemed to be coming from a thick clump of trees about twenty paces ahead of me.

"I'm Dan ... Dan Renfrew." I took a step toward the trees.

"Don't move!"

I froze. *What the hell is going on here?* "Umm ... do you have a phone I could use? Mine's not working."

"You brought a *phone*? Are you stupid or something? Like it's not bad enough that you're wearing those clothes and shouting in English like a complete moron. Are you trying to get yourself killed?"

Dread settled over me like a cold fog. This wasn't a hiker or a park ranger here to rescue me. "Uh ... if you just point me to the nearest road, I'll leave you alone," I said as I retreated a step back toward my shoes.

The brush rustled and a figure emerged. He was about my height and wore soft brown leather boots, gray pants, a loose-fitting tunic, and a drab-green cloak with the hood pulled up, leaving his face in shadow. In his gloved hands he held a bow with an arrow nocked and aimed straight at me.

I inhaled sharply and threw my hands in the air. I lost sight of everything except the bow and the dull steel arrow pointed at my chest. The bow looked to be handmade of laminated wood—not one of the fiberglass or composite bows you usually see. And the arrow that was nocked and pointed at my chest? It had a wood shaft, with real feathers for fletching. Even its steel tip looked to be hand-forged.

Great ... Some deranged Robin Hood wannabe was about to shoot me, and I'd just spent my last moments admiring his bow. "Please," I pleaded, my stomach twisting in knots, "don't kill me."

"Whose side are you on?" the archer barked.

"Side? What side?"

"In the war."

"What war?" I asked, my voice cracking. "I have no clue what you're talking about. Please! You have to believe me." I held my breath as the archer stood there silently, his arrow not wavering.

"How'd you get here?"

I hesitated. The truth would make me sound delusional. "I don't really know," I said finally.

"Don't lie to me!" the archer snapped. "Where's your jump device?"

"Please!" I cried. I was seconds away from pissing myself from fear. "Nothing you're saying makes any sense. I don't know about a war. I don't know what a jump device is. Can you just let me go so I can find a phone? I need to get back home and save my dad."

The archer lowered his bow slightly so that it pointed at my groin instead of my chest. "Your jump device is a short metal rod covered in symbols. You could only have gotten here if you had one, so where is it?"

I eyed the archer warily. How did he know about the rod? Was he in league with Victor? My hands balled into fists as I remembered Victor's triumphant sneer as he stabbed Dad. No, if the archer was in league with Victor, I'd be dead already. So how did he know about it? I thought about denying that I had it, but his agitated tone changed my mind. "It's in my shoe." I pointed to my pile of stuff.

"You left it in your *shoe*?" he asked incredulously. "Where it could easily fall in the river?"

"Uh … I guess?" I shrugged. "Why?"

The archer sighed loudly. "You really don't know what's going on, do you?"

"No. I don't. One minute my dad's getting stabbed by some guy with a sword, and then suddenly I'm here and you're pointing an arrow at me."

The archer raised his face skyward and shook his head slowly, as if upset with the universe. "Awww, hell," he muttered, "a newbie."

"A newbie? To what?"

The archer motioned to my shoes. "Get your jump device and put your shoes on. And hurry!"

I backpedaled to the riverbank, not daring to take my eyes off him, then fumbled to pull on my socks and shoes. Right now my only goal was keeping this nutjob happy so I didn't find an arrow buried in my chest.

When I stood up, the archer looked me up and down and nodded. "Your life depends on you following every last instruction I tell you. One—don't say anything. Two—don't stop running until I tell you to. Understand?"

Every part of me was shaking so much that I couldn't even speak. I could only muster the weakest of nods.

"Good." He pointed to an overgrown path through the trees that led away from the river. "Now go!"

I tore off down the path, panic driving my every step. *Where am I? How did I get here? Can I still save Dad?*

The questions kept piling up, but I didn't know if I would live long enough to find the answers.

CHAPTER 4

Trees and bushes whipped by in a blur, slapping me on the arms and legs as my feet pounded the trail. My churning breaths echoed heavily in my ears. Behind me the archer glided silently through the forest, like a ghost. Every few seconds, I peered over my shoulder to see if I had somehow ditched him, but he was always there, keeping pace with me—a constant threat.

"Stop!" he commanded as the path veered off around the foot of a small hill. "We're heading up there." He motioned with his bow to a cluster of cedars at the top.

I began scrabbling through the underbrush, picking my way up the slope. From a distance the clump of trees had looked like an impenetrable wall of trunks and branches. But up close, a narrow gap appeared.

"Through there," the archer directed.

I squeezed between two trunks and found myself in a small clearing, no more than a few paces across. A low fire burned in the middle, with a rabbit roasting on a spit above it. Judging by the amount of ash, this fire had been here for less than a day. A wool blanket lay on the ground next to it, and water skins rested in the shade beside a leather backpack.

No tents. No sleeping bag. Some poor animal cooking over the fire. I sucked in my breath—it looked just like the type of camp Dad and I had always made.

The archer pointed to the far side of the fire. "Stand over there."

I glanced warily around the clearing, looking for some way out. There was only one—the way we came in—and the archer now blocked it. I was trapped.

I moved to the far side of the fire and put my hands up. "My dad has some cash," I pleaded. "He'll pay to get me back unharmed." *If he's still alive.*

"Put your hands down!" the archer snapped. "Trust me; I'm not going to hurt you."

"Trust you?" I sputtered. "You kidnapped me at bowpoint, have done nothing but yell at me, and I can't see your face. Hell, I don't even know your name."

For a few seconds he didn't respond. "My name's Sam," he finally grumbled, his voice still weirdly muffled. "Now, I need you to hand over your shoes and clothes."

My stomach lurched, and if I'd had any lunch left in me I would have puked again. Was that his plan? Steal my stuff, murder me, and bury me where no one would ever find my body? "Don't kill me," I begged. "Just let me go. I won't tell anyone about you. I promise."

"I'm not going to kill you," he snapped. "If I wanted to do that, I would have done it back by the river ... or any time in the forest."

"And how is listing all the places where you might have killed me supposed to make me trust you more?"

Sam exhaled loudly and shook his head. "Look, I could have just sat here in my little clearing and eaten my lunch. You're lucky I heard you yelling like a fool and went to save you."

"Save me?" I snorted. "You're trying to steal all my stuff! If you want to save me, give me a working phone so I can call for help and get home."

"Just stop arguing and give me your clothes."

"Come on!" I pleaded. "Can't you just take my wallet and phone?" I tossed the two items over and they landed in the dirt near Sam's feet. "I don't have much cash, maybe a buck or two in coins, but I can get you more. And I won't tell anyone."

A groan escaped Sam's lips and he clapped a gloved hand to his hooded brow. "Seriously? You have coins too?" He shook his head. "Of course you do."

"Uh … sorry?" I said, hoping to calm him down, even though I had no clue why he'd be getting upset over coins.

"Do you have any other metal on you?" Sam asked. "And I don't just mean jewelry—I need to know every last bit of metal. Metal zippers, aluminum foil, soda cans, anything?"

I thought for a second. "My jeans have a metal zipper. But that's it." Even though the guy could clearly see my arms sticking out of my T-shirt, I held them up to show I wasn't wearing any bracelets or rings.

"And what about that metal rod in your hand?" Sam asked.

That hit me like a punch in the face. "No," I growled. "You can't have it. My dad fought with his life to protect this." My eyes narrowed and I took a step back, scanning the clearing for a possible weapon. A few small rocks and some dry sticks lay on the ground, but nothing within reach. I clenched my fists and rose lightly on the balls of my feet, ready to fight my way out of here.

Surprisingly, Sam nodded. "Good, at least you learned that much." To my relief, he also lowered his bow. "Now, I'm going to give you some instructions that you need to follow. They're going to sound strange, but if you want to live past today, you better follow them. I'm not the bad guy here. I'm trying to help you. Understand?"

I nodded, although I didn't believe a word he said.

"Good. Now take off your clothes, including your socks and shoes, and toss them on the fire."

"What? You're stealing my stuff to burn it? What's the freakin' point?"

"Do you *ever* stop talking?" Sam snapped. "Just put your damn clothes on the fire. If anyone sees you in them, you'll be dead." He motioned with his head to the backpack lying by the fire. "You'll find a change of clothes in there. We're about the same size, so they should fit."

As long as he had the bow, he made the rules. Without taking my eyes off him, I checked out the backpack. It certainly wasn't something you'd find in your local camping store. It was completely made of leather, with what looked like animal gut binding the seams together. I opened it cautiously, expecting to find a severed head or a bundle of dead squirrels. To my surprise, it held a pair of gray pants, a dark blue tunic, and a long cloth belt. Maybe Sam wasn't a deranged murderer after all.

I took out the clothes then stopped. How was I supposed to do this? I doubted Sam would let me leave the clearing and get changed out of his sight.

If I chose modesty and turned my back, I wouldn't be able to watch him. And right now that bow of his was the most important thing in my life.

Without ever breaking eye contact with him, I stripped naked.

"Ugh … No …" Sam said as he raised a hand to shield his eyes. "You can keep the underwear. No one should *ever* be seeing those."

Hastily I yanked my boxers back up and then changed into the new clothes. Apparently, I'd be going barefoot.

I picked up the rod and grudgingly dumped my pile of old clothes onto the fire. The flames licked greedily at them, and soon oily black smoke billowed from the rubber soles of my running shoes. Sam added some more dry sticks to the fire and the flames rose to an intense heat. In seconds the smoke stopped, although the smell of burnt rubber lingered in the clearing. As I stared helplessly at the fire, watching my stuff turn to ash, Sam tossed my phone and wallet into the blaze.

"Hey! You can't burn those! My ID is in there!"

Sam snorted. "Trust me. ID is the last thing you need here."

The finality in his tone sent a shiver through me. He kept saying to trust him, that he meant me no harm, but I was no fool. If I ever wanted to see my home again, I'd have to fight my way out of here. But with what?

My gaze drifted to the fire between us. The dry ends of some of the sticks lay within reach. If I hit Sam across the face with a burning stick, that should buy me enough time to run.

"Do you know where you are?" he asked.

Trapped in a forest with a madman. "Not a clue."

"Sit down," Sam ordered. "What I'm about to tell you will save your life."

Warily I sat next to the fire, my eyes never leaving Sam. At the right moment, as soon as he dropped his guard, I'd leap up, grab a burning branch, whack him in the face, and run like hell.

Just as warily, Sam sat across the fire from me. This close, I could finally see under his hood, sort of. He wore a scarf across his nose and mouth, leaving only his eyes visible, although they were still in shadow. He put his bow down on the ground and drew out a long knife from a sheath at his waist. "No funny business." With the point of the knife, Sam began scratching circles in the dirt. "From what I've figured out, we're somewhere in medieval Europe," he said.

Medieval Europe? Was he unhinged, or was this some sick game of his? Either way, I'd have to be careful how I responded. "Where in Europe?" I asked, trying to sound sincerely interested.

"Not sure," Sam replied. "I overheard some villagers talking about going next week to the market in Eoforwic, so I figure we're close to there, but I have no idea where that actually is. As for the *when* ... Judging by the amount of daylight and the position of the constellations, we're probably in the month of September. But I still haven't figured out what year."

My mind latched onto one word from all of Sam's crazy talk. *Eoforwic?* As in, the old Anglo-Saxon name of York, England? Nobody had called it that in a thousand years. Why would Sam say that? What game was he playing?

An awkward silence fell across our little clearing, interrupted only by the crackle of branches on the fire. Sam clearly was waiting for me to respond, but what the hell could I say? "Oh, that's, uh, interesting," I finally managed.

Sam's head snapped up and he leveled the knife at me. "Damn it, Newbie! I can tell you think I'm nuts, but I'm not! We're in medieval Europe!"

"Whoa! Whoa! I believe you!" I blurted, my eyes not leaving the knife.

For a few tense seconds, Sam kept it aimed at me before finally lowering it. I let out a small sigh of relief—I'd bought myself a few more minutes of life. Almost as important, I'd figured out something about Sam. He honestly believed he was in medieval Europe and was trying to live the part. That explained the clothes, the backpack, and the handmade bow and arrows. Now I just had to make sure his fantasy didn't include killing me and wearing my skin as a poncho.

"So … how'd you get here?" I asked casually, hoping he'd slip up and tell me where the nearest highway was.

"Same as you," Sam said. "I held the rod and said all that *Azkabaleth virros ku* stuff."

I startled back. "How do you know that rhyme?"

"That's none of your business," Sam barked. "And, since I'm the one with the weapons, I'll be the one asking the questions." He waved his knife at me again. "I don't trust you, or your story. It can't be a coincidence that a completely clueless newb just happens to land so close to me and then starts yelling like an idiot so everyone around can hear."

A nagging doubt wormed its way into my head. What if Sam *was* telling the truth and I had somehow time-traveled?

No. There had to be another explanation. Something more … possible. But I'd never find it here in this clearing. I needed to get away from Sam. "If you don't trust me, you should let me go," I suggested.

Sam snorted. "You really think you're ready? Do you have even the slightest idea how to behave in history?"

"Of course I do." I'd seen a ton of time-travel movies—they all shared the same basic ideas. "You just have to make sure you don't do anything that can affect the future. So no smacking bugs. No talking to people. Don't worry. I got it."

A short, muffled sound, which I could only assume was a laugh, came from under Sam's hood. "You know nothing. History doesn't get messed up just because you swat a mosquito or I decide to have rabbit for lunch. What you really need to worry about is that little metal rod, which you so stupidly left sitting on a riverbank. That's the most important thing in your life right now. Lose it, and you're stuck here forever. And always keep it next to your skin," Sam added. "When it's touching you, it acts as a translator."

Translator? Yeah … right … It was doing an awesome job of translating English into English for me. I bit back my comment and just nodded like I was taking mental notes of everything he said.

"If you want to live longer than a day," Sam continued, "you really have to learn how to blend in. You can't stand next to a river, shouting like an idiot, dressed in modern clothes and holding a phone. You'll get yourself tossed into a dungeon, burned at a stake, or even just killed on the spot."

"Got it. Act natural."

"No!" Sam shook his head. "Act medieval! Are you listening to anything I'm saying?"

"Of course I am." I had heard every insane word that had spewed out of Sam's mouth. I didn't believe a single one, but I had listened. "The rod's a magic translator," I repeated. "Learn to blend in. Act medieval. I think I got everything."

Sam didn't say anything for a few seconds; he only looked at me from the shadows of his hood. Finally, he shrugged. "I can see by that stupid look on your face that you don't believe me, but you know what? I don't care. If you're too dumb to recognize the obvious, I'm not going to waste my breath." Sam stood up, moved to the side of the clearing, and pointed with his knife to the gap between the trees. "You're free to go."

A spark of hope glowed in my chest. Was he actually letting me go, or was this some kind of trick? I took a hesitant step toward the exit to gauge his reaction, but Sam didn't budge.

"Are you planning on leaving today?" Sam asked. "My lunch is burning."

I took a few more steps and made it to the opening. I turned to face him and began slowly backing away from his hidden clearing.

Sam shook his head and glanced skyward. "Good luck, Newbie." He chuckled. "You're going to need it."

I backed through the gap in the trees, and once I felt there was enough distance between me and Sam, I turned to race down the hill. I ran in a zigzag, ducking behind every tree and bush as I kept imagining one of Sam's arrows suddenly striking me right between the shoulder blades.

When my feet finally reached the path at the bottom of the hill, I tore off in a dead run. My bare feet seemed to hit every rock and twig lying in the way, but I just grimaced and kept running, not daring to look back. I had to get away from Sam.

CHAPTER 5

The trail widened the farther I traveled, and I zipped along, brandishing the rod in my hand like a baton, my feet slapping against the hard-packed earth. My lungs heaved, but I didn't slow down. I wouldn't feel safe until I was positive Sam would never find me.

When I caught sight of a few puffs of smoke curling through the trees, my fear turned to excitement. Were those campfires ahead? Cottages?

I whipped around a bend and right into the path of a girl in a dark green dress coming the opposite way. I tried to dodge her, but my shoulder clipped her, knocking her to the ground and sending me stumbling along until I crashed into the brush framing the path. As my right leg banged into a large rock, the rod Dad had sacrificed himself for sailed out of my hand and tumbled end over end, landing somewhere in the underbrush.

My shin was on fire from the huge bloody scrape running up it, but I staggered to my feet to help the fallen girl. She was about my age and pretty in a wholesome, country-girl sort of way, with startling blue eyes and long golden hair done up in a simple braid. I reached a hand out to help her up, but she scrambled out of reach.

"I'm sorry for knocking you over," I said, my breath coming in gasps. "I didn't see you."

My words didn't have the soothing effect that I expected. The girl leaped to her feet and scampered away from me, her eyes darting around like those of a caged animal. She kept glancing behind me, toward the distant smoke. She was clearly afraid of me, but I had no idea why.

I raised my hands to show her I meant no harm. After Sam, I was desperate to talk with someone who wasn't crazy. But her clothes were giving me a bad feeling. Her long-sleeved, ankle-length dress hung loosely on her frame and was belted at the waist with a simple strip of cloth. The clothes weren't ugly: in fact, she looked pretty good in them. But they weren't remotely modern—she looked like she belonged at a Renaissance fair.

Wait. Is that what's going on? Had I stumbled into a Renaissance campground? That would explain Sam, the girl, and basically everything.

The girl still stood there staring at me, her feet spread wide, ready to bolt.

"I'm Dan," I said, giving her a friendly smile as I kicked aside ferns, trying to find the metal rod.

She mumbled something in reply.

"Sorry," I said. "I didn't catch that."

"Hwaet cwethest thu?"

Whoa! She doesn't speak English. Just my luck to find the one foreigner at the fair. But her words still sounded oddly familiar. Were they German? Dutch?

"Do … you … speak … English?" I said, articulating each word slowly and loudly like a lost tourist. "I … need … help."

The girl's eyes widened as if she was in a horror movie and just about to scream. *"Hwelce spraece sprecest thu?"*

Things were definitely not going well here. This girl was clearly petrified of me. I needed to calm her down and—

The glint of metal caught my eye. "Hang on," I called over my shoulder as I stepped deeper into the undergrowth beside the path.

She wasn't waiting, though. With a panicked look on her face, she tore past me. *"Ic cythe thaes tunes heafodman ymb the!"* she yelped.

"Wait!" I yelled back.

She kept running.

I couldn't let her go—she was my ticket out of this forest. But I couldn't leave the rod either. "Stop! Please!" I yelled frantically, hoping that if she couldn't understand my words, she'd at least understand the desperation in my voice.

In the distance, now almost completely hidden by the trees and bushes in between, I saw her stop. *"Andswara me! Hwa eart thu?"* she demanded.

I picked up the rod from where it had landed and turned to face her. Her words sounded so familiar. Almost like English, but not quite. "Can ... you ... please ... repeat ... that?" I asked slowly, trying to make myself understood despite the language barrier.

What the hell? Somehow, my words didn't come out in English, they came out in some weird language that sounded like what she was speaking.

"Answer me!" she responded. "Who are you?"

It took all my willpower to keep my mouth from hanging open. She was still speaking her language, but now I understood her as if I'd been speaking her language all my life. The smallest shred of me marveled at how this short piece of mystery metal could translate things so effortlessly, but the rest of me cringed. Magic translators didn't exist, but I obviously had one. And if Sam was right about the rod, was he also right about everything else?

I shook my head stubbornly. No. There was no way I'd traveled through time and wound up in Anglo-Saxon England. There had to be a logical explanation. And I hoped this girl could provide it. But first I needed to calm her down so she didn't run off screaming to her village.

"I'm lost," I explained. "I need help."

Approaching a few steps closer, she eyed me warily. "You were speaking a different language at first. Where do you come from?"

"From far away." I stepped back onto the trail and held up my hands in a calming gesture. "I'm sorry I frightened you, but I'm lost, hungry, injured, and I just want to get back home."

Her tough demeanor softened slightly. "I will bring you to the leader of my village. He will certainly be able to help you."

In a daze, I began following her along the path. She still didn't seem to trust me, as she remained far ahead and glanced back frequently to make sure I didn't get too close.

After a few minutes, her village came into full view: about fifteen small, low houses with thatched roofs and wood walls scattered around a little church. A few young kids ran between the huts, playing games or chasing the chickens that roamed freely, but everyone older was hard at work. In the distant fields, the men were busy pulling in the harvest, while inside the village, women worked outside their homes boiling laundry, weaving, or tending to small vegetable gardens. The men were dressed similar to me in knee-length tunics and leggings, while the women wore long dresses similar to the blond girl's.

No phones. No cars. No modern clothing. Everyone speaking perfect Anglo-Saxon without a trace of hesitation.

An aching knot formed in my stomach. This wasn't a Renaissance fair.

A woman looked up from weeding her vegetable patch and saw the girl and me approach. She brandished her rake and rushed toward us. "Sunngifu," she yelled, "get away from that strange boy!" She turned to one of the kids, who had all stopped playing and were watching us intently. "Aelfric, go tell your father that a stranger has come to the village. Now!"

The boy dashed off toward the fields as if his life depended on it.

"There is no need to fear him, Mother," Sunngifu said. "He is just a boy I found in the forest. He is hurt and lost, and he needs our help."

"Lost? Bah! He is probably a runaway slave," Sunngifu's mother spat. "No matter, your father and the other men of the village will decide what to do with him."

I barely paid attention to their conversation. I knew that I probably should, because I was most likely getting into more trouble, but right now all my focus was on stopping myself from hyperventilating. I was in an actual Anglo-Saxon village, speaking a language that no one had used in a thousand years. My mind had pretty much run out of excuses, but I tried one last question—one last attempt to prove Sam's story about time traveling wrong.

"Excuse me," I said to Sunngifu. "I banged my head pretty badly after I left my own village, so I've forgotten some things. Could you please tell me what year this is?"

She smiled at me as if I'd said something funny. "It is the first year of King Harold Godwin's son's reign."

King Harold Godwinson. I remembered him from the lists of dead kings Dad had made me memorize. Born 1020, elected to the throne in 1066, reigned less than a year. My entire body slumped as my last shred of denial died—I had somehow traveled back in time to England in the year 1066. And the potentially hostile villagers surrounding me were the least of my worries.

I was stuck in history with no clue how to get back home. What the hell had Dad gotten me into?

CHAPTER 6

A dozen or so men in filthy clothing rushed toward me with rakes and shovels clenched in their fists. They looked like a peasant mob from a Frankenstein movie; all that was missing were the flaming torches. My brain screamed *run*, but I was too stunned by the reality of my situation to move. I had actually traveled through time and was now standing in an Anglo-Saxon village. So much of my life suddenly made sense. The way Dad kept disappearing on "work trips" for a few days and returned all banged up and with some lame excuse about falling down the stairs. His obsession with teaching me history—forcing me to learn dead languages and memorize lists of kings and long-forgotten events. All the training in weapons. But why hadn't he told me anything about all of this?

In seconds, the hostile farmers had surrounded me, snapping me out of my stupor. They kept a safe distance, holding their farming tools in front of them like weapons. My eyes darted around wildly, expecting them to attack me at any second. *Okay, Dan. Be cool*, I told myself. *It's just like the security guard at the mall. You can talk your way out of this.*

I tucked the jump device into the back waistband of my pants, making sure the metal kept in contact with my bare skin so I could understand them. "Hi! I'm lost," I said. "Can you help me?"

A tall bearded man stepped forward. He was probably about Dad's age but seemed like one of the older men in the village. His light-colored hair and beard were both streaked with gray, and his face bore the lines of someone who had worked in the sun all his life. His confidence marked him as one of the village leaders. "Who are you and where do you come from?" he demanded, keeping his shovel pointed at me.

My name's Dan and I come from the future would probably get me a face full of shovel. I needed to think of a suitable Anglo-Saxon name— fast. "Umm, my name is ..."

Frodo? Bruce Wayne? Napoleon? Come on! What's an Anglo-Saxon name?

"It's ... it's..." Finally I remembered a name from a history book Dad had forced me to read. "Leofric!"

"And where are you from, Leofric?" he asked.

Good freakin' question. "I'm from, uh, from ..." Sam's comment about our location sprang to mind. "I'm from Eoforwic!"

Disbelief registered on the men's faces, and I cringed inwardly. Eoforwic must be farther away than Sam had realized.

"You have wandered very far," the villager said, his voice thick with skepticism. "How did you not find your way home?"

"Uh, I was gathering fallen branches ... for firewood." I scrambled to think of a believable excuse. "A boar chased me and I ran away, and then, um, then I ... fell into the river. If it wasn't for a log floating nearby, I would have drowned." I made sure to make my voice sound all panicky at this point, which wasn't hard, considering how much trouble I'd be in if these villagers didn't believe my story. "I don't know how long I floated, but I finally managed to get to shore somewhere near your village. My shoes were gone, taken by the current, so I dried myself in the sun … and then I met Sunngifu on the path. And that's how I'm here."

Not bad. Not bad at all. If they handed out an Oscar for the Best Spontaneous Lie in a Life-or-Death Situation, I would have just won it.

Shovel guy didn't say a thing. His blue eyes studied mine, as if searching for the truth. His gaze made me feel increasingly uncomfortable. But I knew if I pulled away, I'd be branded a liar.

"Look at the poor boy, Osmund," one of the women said, breaking our staring contest. "He is scared and tired. Let him stay the night. We can set him on his way home tomorrow."

"I do not trust his words, Aelfgifu," the man said. "We should send him away immediately."

"Where is your kindness, Osmund? He is just a boy. What harm can he do?"

Osmund lowered his shovel but didn't look pleased. "So be it. But I will not have him staying in anyone's home. He can shelter in the church."

I breathed a huge sigh of relief. I had a place to stay, and the horde of suspicious villagers weren't going to kill me—yet.

They led me to the church, a small wood structure about the size of a two-car garage. No stained-glass windows, no bell tower, just a rectangular building with a simple cross over the entrance. Osmund opened the door and waved me in. I ducked under the low door frame and stepped into one large room with a straw-covered floor and no pews. A wooden altar at the far end was the only furniture. A slit above the altar let in a weak beam of sunlight, leaving the rest of the room shrouded in darkness. Since I was seemingly the only entertainment in town, everyone now crammed around the entrance to watch me.

"You can sleep here." Osmund pointed to the floor. "My wife will bring you a blanket and some food."

"Thank you," I said.

The villagers stood there, not saying anything and yet not leaving either. They looked at me expectantly, as if waiting for something to happen. "Umm … how may I repay you for your hospitality?" I ventured.

A faint smile crossed Osmund's lips. "No payment is necessary. However, if during the rest of the day, you find the quiet of the church not to your liking, we could use the help of a strong lad like you to pull in the harvest."

Usually the choice between an afternoon of hard work and lying around getting some sleep would be a no-brainer, but this was Anglo-Saxon England. I had to change how I did things if I wanted to survive here. One of the last things Dad had said to me was *Fix what's wrong.* He knew he was sending me back in time, so he must have been confident that I could figure out what he meant by that. Clearly I needed to go out, explore, find something wrong, and then fix it so I could go home. I had no clue where to start, but the answer definitely wasn't in this church.

"I'd be glad to help," I replied.

I tromped off behind the men into a field covered with rows and rows of cabbages and, after some introductions and a quick lesson on what was required of me, got to work.

Not that I could focus on harvesting cabbages. All I could think of was the fact that I was in Anglo-Saxon England in 1066. Why hadn't Dad ever told me he was a freakin' *time traveler*? He'd spent sixteen years of my life cramming my head full of some of the most boring crap imaginable—at any point he could have said, "By the way, Dan, I'm teaching you all this stuff because I time travel." But no—he kept it all a secret. Had he been waiting for me to turn eighteen? Did he think I was too incompetent to trust with the knowledge? Whatever his reasons for holding back, he'd screwed up royally, because now I was stuck here in an Anglo-Saxon field, dumping stupid cabbages into a stupid basket and wondering how the hell I could get back home.

I should have listened to Sam. He'd tried to tell me what was going on. Part of me wanted to sneak away from the farm and see if I could find him again. I doubted I could, though—I hadn't paid attention to any of the landmarks that would help me get back to his hiding spot. I was stuck here until I either figured things out on my own or he came to find me.

As I bent down to cut another cabbage, a shadow fell over me. One of the older village boys stood in front of me with his thick peasant arms crossed. He had blond hair, blue eyes, and a dumb-looking grin. "You are too slow," he sneered. "Your basket is almost empty while mine is full already. In your own village, do you sit with the women and sew while the men work in the fields?"

The villagers laughed, but I held my tongue. There was nothing to be gained by arguing with someone a thousand years in my past, especially when he was not wrong about my terrible cabbage-harvesting skills.

One of the boy's friends took up the taunts. "He is too scared to answer, Wulfric. Maybe if we arm him with some sewing needles, he will find his courage."

My ears burned as the laughter ramped up, but I still said nothing.

Wulfric walked up to me and shoved me in the shoulder. "Why do you not say anything? Do you think you are better than us just because you come from the city?"

"I don't want trouble." I kept my eyes focused on my work.

Wulfric kicked my basket aside, spilling the few cabbages I had harvested. "Come. Show me how tough you city people are."

The men of the village were watching the exchange out of the corners of their eyes but continued working. I wasn't from their village. They didn't care what happened to me.

"I don't want to fight you," I said as I got up from my crouch. "I just want to help with the harvest." Wulfric was a bit shorter than me but bulkier. Years of hard work in the fields had given him layers of muscle that I didn't possess.

"Not want to fight? Any man of honor should be prepared to fight to protect his home, his family, or himself. Only cowards and weaklings refuse to fight. So which one of those are you?" Wulfric motioned with his hands, encouraging me to throw the first punch.

A quick elbow to his jaw would end his bullying, but how would that affect the future? What if Wulfric's great-great-great-great grand-child was a famous inventor or explorer, and me knocking him out set back the course of human history by hundreds of years?

As I stood there playing out the possibilities, Wulfric launched a huge right hook at me. Years of martial arts training with my dad kicked in and I knocked his arm aside with a rising block and coun-tered with a lunge punch. Wulfric's nose cracked under the impact, and he fell backward to the ground, blood streaming from his face.

The stomp of footsteps behind me warned me of another attack. I sidestepped and jammed my elbow backward, catching Wulfric's friend in the stomach. As he doubled over in pain, I caught his face with a rising back fist. He crumpled to his knees, gasping for breath.

I stood between the two fallen farm boys, hoping our little contest was finished.

It wasn't.

Another of Wulfric's friends raced at me, his shovel raised over his head. I kicked at the dry soil to send a spray of dirt at his face. He ducked, giving me enough time to swing my rake up in front of me like a quarterstaff. Wulfric's friend swung wildly at my head. I ducked under the attack, then struck him twice in the ribs with the handle of my rake. He crumpled over and I kicked him in the knee, knocking him to the ground.

"Enough!" Osmund yelled as he moved in to separate us. "Back to work! The harvest must be pulled in before the first frost. We don't have time for any ..."

His voice trailed off as he looked to the edge of the field where the forest started. The steady clomp of hooves warned of a horseman approaching. Seconds later, a rider appeared along the trail, heading toward the circle of peasants. Dust covered his brown riding cloak and his horse panted as if finishing a long ride.

The horseman reined in his mount at the edge of our little group. "I bring ill tidings," he declared. "The king's foul brother Tostig has returned to these lands, and he brought an army of Northmen with him. They have defeated the Eorls at Fulford and taken Eoforwic! At this moment, King Harold is rushing north with his troops to repel the invaders, and he has called for all local lords to aid him. Lord Orm demands that the village of Torp sends two men to serve him and his warriors as they go to support the king."

Angry muttering spread among the farmers.

Osmund raised his hands for silence. "We will send two men," he assured the rider. "Where are we to meet?"

"Tomorrow at Tada. And now, I bid your leave. I must inform Lord Orm's other holdings." The messenger spurred his horse and galloped off along the path.

"Two men!" a farmer exclaimed. "How does our lord expect us to bring in the harvest when we are two men fewer?"

"The fields will be done," Osmund said. "If we work harder now, then the loss of two men will not be felt as much."

"But which of our men shall go?"

"I shall," said Osmund. "And Beorn should go as well."

"Beorn! You cannot take Beorn. With you and he both gone, we will be short two of our strongest men for the harvest. Take one of the boys in his stead. Lord Orm only needs you to fetch water and chop wood and take care of his horses while he and his men sit on their asses. There is no sense in sending two men for that task."

"Aye," said another farmer. "Take Leofric. He said he comes from Eoforwic, so he should want to help our king take back his city from those filthy Northmen. And he has shown that he has no skill at hard work, so his effort will not be missed here."

Osmund put a hand on his chin. "Well, Leofric, what say you?" he asked, looking straight at me.

For half a second, I wondered what exactly he wanted. Then it hit me—*I was Leofric*. And I'd just been volunteered for the Anglo-Saxon army.

CHAPTER 7

All eyes were on me, and at that moment I finally understood why the time-travel thingy had dumped me so close to this village. The flow of history wasn't going to be fixed by me digging up cabbages. But joining King Harold's forces as they rushed off to fight an invading army?

"Yeah, I'll go with you," I said, though I could muster little enthusiasm.

Osmund clapped his hand on my shoulder. "Good. Now let us see that the village's weapons and armor are in good order before we return to the harvest."

He turned to a short man in a green vest. "Beorn, see that Wulfric and his friends do a man's portion of work, for they fight like women."

This comment brought chuckles from the men and angry glares from the three guys I had thumped. I ignored them and followed Osmund back to the village.

He led me to an enclosure that held the village's herd of plow oxen. We walked alongside the split-timber fence to a small wooden building at the back. Light spilled in when he opened the shed door, revealing a room cluttered with yokes, harnesses, hand plows, feed bags, and farm tools. At the back of all this gear, two well-used hunting spears and two round wooden shields leaned against the wall. Osmund gingerly stepped past all the clutter and tossed me a shield. "Check that the straps are still in good order," he instructed as he eyed his own.

"They are," I said after a brief inspection. But that was about the only thing in good shape. The wood was warped and cracked and rattled every time I rapped my knuckles against the shield. One good hit would probably shatter this sucker. I had no clue why Osmund was even bothering with checking the shields when all we were going to be doing was acting as servants for Lord Orm and his warriors. But I wasn't about to ask—that might lead to me being stuck harvesting stupid cabbages again.

"You fought well with your hands," Osmund remarked. "Can you do as well with a shield and spear?"

"Yes," I said quietly, my thoughts drifting back to all the hours I'd spent sparring with Dad. The rush of adrenaline. The feeling of victory when I'd sneak past his guard and get in a hit. The way we'd sit exhausted on the ground afterward and chat about nothing.

"Are you well, Leofric?" Osmund asked, looking concerned.

"I'm okay," I muttered.

He placed a hand on my shoulder. "Come, show me your skill."

He led me to a clearing beyond the shed and stood facing me, his shield in guard position, the spear raised high.

I lifted my own shield and held my spear overhead. For a second, neither of us moved. Then Osmund jabbed weakly at my head, as if testing my reflexes. I raised my shield to block his thrust and his blade bit into the wood. I jabbed back, but he blocked my attack. We continued like this, trading tentative blows, neither of us attacking too hard.

"Enough of this fighting like children," Osmund decided finally. "Let me see how well you can really fight."

You sure about that?

How would he handle the trick that Dad always fell for? I jabbed at Osmund's head. He moved his shield to block, and I quickly swept my spear low and smacked him hard on the side of the knee. He lost his balance for a fraction of a second and his shield dipped. Before he could recover, I whipped my blade up and stopped it just under his chin.

Gotcha!

Although he wasn't nearly as good as Dad at fighting, I still felt a small flush of victory.

Osmund dropped his shield on the ground, releasing a puff of dust from the dry soil. "I yield," he said, smiling. "You fight well, Leofric. Very well." His eyes narrowed. "I've seen you in the fields, and you are no farmer. And you fight too well for a man from the city. So what are you?"

Good question.

Until today, I'd always thought of myself as a normal-ish teenager. But Dad had apparently been training me to be a time traveler like him. So if I had all the skills of a time traveler, but none of the knowledge, what did that actually make me?

"Honestly, I don't know," I replied.

"No matter. With your skill, there will be a place for you in the line when we fight the invaders."

"When we *fight*? Wait! I thought we were just supposed to fetch water and stuff like that, and leave the real fighting for everyone else."

Osmund shrugged. "We must always be prepared. The Northmen already defeated one army. If they prevail again against the king, then all must be willing to put their lives on the line to defend our lands— even you."

No, nonono, nope …

I couldn't fight. It was bad enough that I'd beat up Wulfric and his friends. What if I ended up stabbing my own great-great-great-great-great grandfather? Or, worse, what if he stabbed *me*? Following Osmund into battle seemed like my best chance of figuring out how to get myself home, but there had to be some way for me to avoid any actual fighting.

Osmund banged his spear against his shield, interrupting my thoughts. "Again," he said.

We practiced until the sun went down and the men returned from the fields. With both of us tired and sweaty from a hard day's work-out, Osmund and I returned our equipment to the shed, and then he led me back to the church. A single candle burning in a wall sconce illuminated a woolen blanket spread on the straw-strewn floor, with a clay mug and a steaming bowl next to it. "You are free to stay here in our village until Eoforwic is freed," Osmund said. "You may not know much about harvesting cabbages, but you fight well, and Torp is lucky to have you. Will you be missed at Eoforwic?"

I was getting to like Osmund; he seemed to be a genuinely good guy. I was glad that for once I could stop lying and tell him something that resembled the truth. "My mother died when I was young, and I don't even know if my father is still alive." A lump formed in my throat and my eyes felt gritty with tears. "So no, no one will miss me."

Osmund placed a comforting hand on my shoulder. "If there is no life left for you in Eoforwic, then maybe you could make a life here. Think on my words." He nodded at me once, then turned and left the church, closing the door behind him.

I traced the outline of the tattoo on my arm with a finger. What would happen if I didn't fix the time glitch—would I be stuck here in Torp forever? Did Dad really think I was smart enough to figure things out here and get back home safely, or had he been so afraid of whatever Victor planned in our present that he thought it was better to just lose me to the past?

Sighing, I reached for my dinner: a slab of brown bread and some boiled grains that looked like barley. To my surprise, the clay mug contained a murky-looking beer that had an almost breadlike taste. It was a bit on the watery side and much weaker than the beer Dad occasionally brewed at home. The food itself would probably get zero stars on Yelp, but my stomach was growling after a long day, so I didn't care. I ate in silence, my only entertainment the shadows on the wall created by the lone flickering candle.

After I ate, I made a pile of straw in a corner. It smelled of must and the fields but would protect me from the cold seeping up through the packed-earth floor. I spread out the blanket on top of the pile, blew out the candle, and lay down. Darkness enveloped the room and I stared into it, trying to figure out answers that just weren't there. I felt myself drifting off to sleep, until the creaking of the church's wooden door brought me instantly alert.

CHAPTER 8

"Newbie, you awake?" came a familiar muffled voice.

"Sam!" This morning I had been ready to dismiss him as crazy, and I had tried my hardest to get away from him. But now hearing his voice again was like hearing from my best friend. "I'm here in the corner," I said. "Let me see if I can get this candle lit."

"No! No lights!" he said sharply.

"Oh, right. Sorry. I'm still getting used to the whole 'act medieval' thing. By the way," I added, just to show that I wasn't completely useless, "I figured out where we are. England, and it's 1066."

"England, huh? That makes sense," Sam said. "Did you figure out anything else?"

"Yup," I said, a touch of smugness in my tone. "It's September, and we're about two days before the Battle of Stamford Bridge. King Harold is rushing north with his army to confront the Vikings who are camped out near Eoforwic. Me and one of the village headmen are going tomorrow to meet up with him."

"Wow, Newbie. Well done," Sam said without a hint of sarcasm. "I guess you finally believe me, about the whole time-travel thing, huh?"

"I do. I just can't believe my dad never told me about it."

"Yeah, that's weird. My dad didn't tell me much either, but at least he taught me the basics."

"Like what?" My ears perked up. "Tell me! I'm so clueless it's not funny. I don't know a damn thing."

"Well, you know that tattoo on your arm? It's the mark of a time jumper. The job has been passed down from father to son for generations. Every time jumper wears that tattoo."

"Generations?" I asked. "How many?"

"I don't know. But I'd guess at least a thousand years or more. The jump devices are really ancient."

"And what do 'time jumpers' actually do? One of the last things my dad told me was to fix what's wrong, but I have no clue what that means."

Sam sighed, and I could hear the straw rustle as he sat down on the floor just inside the church door, with his back resting against the wall. "Here's how my dad explained it to me. Think of time like a river, forever flowing. Your existence in time is like a leaf on that river. You move downstream, swept along by the current. But just because the leaf passes a certain spot doesn't mean the river stops flowing over that same point, you just get farther and farther away from it. And, just like water dislodges pebbles from a riverbed, the stream of time sometimes nudges events out of place. If it's a small event, then the time stream just kind of fixes itself, and nothing happens to us in the future. But if the time stream nudges a big event out of place, it's like a tree falling across the river and making the water flow in a different direction—and your leaf is affected. So it's our job to kind of clear the river of jams and fix things so that history returns to its normal flow."

It made a certain kind of sense, as long as you could believe in magical gizmos that let people jump through history, a concept my mind was still having a hard time dealing with. "So what's a big event and a small event? Because this morning I punched out three guys who were trying to push me around."

A short, muffled laugh came from Sam. "Don't worry; that's nothing. This is my fifth jump, and from my experience it's only the *really* big events that mess up the future. You know, things like a king dying at the wrong time, or the wrong side winning a battle. So this battle you're heading to is the perfect spot for the glitch."

I nodded but then realized I couldn't be seen in the dark. "So how do these time-travel thingies even work?"

"I don't know the actual science. I just know that they're tuned to the time flow. They get cold when there's a glitch in history, and saying the words makes them transport you to that glitch. Once the blockage is removed, the rods get warm again, and you can go home."

"There's no other way to get home?"

"There is, but I don't know it. So if we don't fix the glitch, we're stuck here."

That figured. Nothing about jumping through time seemed simple. For about the thousandth time today, I wondered if Dad knew what he was doing when he sent me here. "You said 'home.' Where are you from?"

"Nope. Not happening, Newbie," Sam said. "That's on a need-to-know basis, and you don't need to know."

"Can you at least tell me *when* you're from?" I pleaded.

"Same as you. All time jumpers live in what we call the present."

"*All?* How many are there?"

Silence. It hung there awkwardly, an almost living thing in the darkness. I didn't know why Sam was ignoring my question, and I was about to ask it again when he spoke.

"I still don't fully trust your story, Newbie. But if you really are brand-new to all of this, then I'll have to let you know some stuff. Because if you don't learn a few important things, you'll probably end up dead."

Any fatigue I might have felt from today fled. I sat up and gripped my blanket. "What's going on?"

"Do you remember when I met you this morning and I asked you whose side you're on?"

"Yeah. And I still don't know what you meant."

"You're not going to like this, but there's a war going on between members of the time-jumping community. A lot of them are dead because of it."

I was struck by the horrible image of Dad slumped against the wall with the expanding bloodstain on his white shirt. "No ... My dad." I buried my face in my hands.

"Yup. If what you told me about him is true, then I'm sorry, but he just became another casualty of this war."

"You think I'd make up my dad being stabbed?" I snapped.

"Hey, I'm just being careful about who I trust and what I believe," Sam replied matter-of-factly. "It's the only way I've survived so long. But you seem truly clueless, so I feel kind of obligated to help you. After all, the bad guys won't be happy with just taking out your dad. They'll be hunting you down too—and I've seen too many good people die."

The air inside the little church suddenly seemed oppressive. I just wanted to run away from the church and the village and England and ... everything. This wasn't fair. I knew nothing about time-jumping—why should I be a target?

I shuddered and shrank down into the straw. "How do you know about this war?" I asked. In the quiet of the church, my voice sounded scared.

There was a long pause. When Sam finally spoke, his voice was heavy with sadness. "My dad told me on the day he died. He had just come back from a jump and had three arrows in him. We tried to save him, but it was too late. He held on long enough to tell us what he could about the rift in the time-jumping community and to warn us to be careful."

"And what are they fighting over?"

"I don't know."

I had so many questions I wanted to ask, but they were all jumbled up inside my head. At last I managed to blurt out one. "You said *we*. Who else was with you?"

"My brother," Sam replied, his voice barely audible. "He was my only friend after my dad was killed, but he didn't last long—just a few months. Hit and run. The cops never found the guy who did it, but it was no accident. He was killed because he'd taken Dad's jump device and started using it."

"I'm sorry."

I heard the whisper of shifting cloth. Sam had stood up. "I'm going now," he said, "but I'll check in on you every now and then. I seriously hope everything you told me so far hasn't been a load of crap, Newbie, and that you really are one of the good guys. There are so few of us left, and I need all the help I can get."

"Wait! Is there any way I can protect myself?"

"Find out who doesn't belong in this world, and kill them before they kill you. That's the only way."

The door creaked open, and the light of the night sky beyond illuminated Sam's shadowy figure. He slipped outside, leaving me alone.

I lay in my bed of straw and stared into the darkness, trying to make sense of everything I'd just learned. Somehow I had to find out what was wrong with history and fix it—while not getting killed in battle or murdered by some unknown time jumper.

Sleep was a long time coming.

CHAPTER 9

A hurried pounding on the church door jolted me awake. "Leofric! Dawn has come. We must join the king!"

I blearily opened my eyes to see a pale light filtering in through the church's one small window. It was past sunrise, but probably not by much. "I'm coming," I groaned as I shrugged off my blanket, bit back the shock of the cold air, and dragged myself to my feet. Stalks of straw fell from my pants and tunic as I shuffled over to the heavy door and wrenched it open.

Osmund stood outside with a steaming bowl in his hands. "Break your fast, then meet me at the shed," he instructed as he shoved the bowl into my grasp.

Without waiting for my response, he rushed away, leaving me to my breakfast: simple oat porridge with a drizzle of honey across the top. I shoveled the warm spoonfuls down while trying to figure out how badly I'd mess up the time stream if I taught these Anglo-Saxon peasants how to make pancakes.

The sun was just peeking over the treetops when I arrived at the shed, but the village was already wide awake. Men gathered their tools for a day of farming while children milked goats or searched for chicken eggs. A few people said good morning or nodded to me as I passed. Volunteering to help out the king's army as they fought against the Vikings had clearly increased my worth in their eyes.

Osmund and I grabbed our spears and shields and then headed to the center of the village, where the villagers had gathered to see us off. Osmund's wife and children gave him hugs and kisses, while many of the villagers said farewell to me. Even Wulfric, his nose swollen and both his eyes black, clapped me on the shoulder and gave me a nod of support.

We finished our goodbyes, and then Osmund handed me a large bundle made from a tied-up blanket. "Food for our journey," he said as he swung a similar one over his shoulder.

Sunngifu stepped hesitantly forward, her eyes cast to the ground. The morning light reflected off her hair, making it look even more radiant than before.

All right, the hero is about to get a kiss from a beautiful maiden.

"For you," she said simply as she passed me a pair of shoes.

"Th-thanks," I stammered. This was way better than a kiss. The shoes were made of crude leather and looked a few sizes too big, but anything was an improvement over tramping around barefoot.

I put on my new footwear and then slung the food bag over my shoulder. It felt light, maybe containing only a loaf of bread and some vegetables. The village clearly didn't expect us to be gone for long.

Osmund kissed his wife one more time. "Ready?" he asked me.

I nodded. "Ready."

With a final wave to his family and the other villagers, Osmund headed for the path that ran alongside the river, and I followed close behind. The sun poked through the canopy of leaves, adding a golden luster to the green and making the path look almost magical.

Osmund didn't say anything as we walked along, which was fine with me. He was probably twenty years older than me, and a thousand years in my past, so we didn't exactly have a lot in common. He seemed content to just whistle to himself as we trudged down the path.

We continued this way for a long time, until Osmund finally called a halt at a spot where the river became wider but shallower. "We cross here." He stripped off his shoes and placed them, along with his food, on top of his shield. He then waded into the river, carrying all his gear above his head.

I took off my shoes and followed him into the slow-moving current. The cold water stung my calves, and with each step the water inched higher until it lapped with excruciating chill at my stomach.

Osmund stopped at the midway point. "Do you know which way Eoforwic lies from here?" he asked, with an almost amused tone to his voice.

Oh crap …

He was testing me. I looked around, praying to see anything that might even remotely hint at where my supposed hometown was. But the thick forest surrounding the river gave no hints. Time for me to make something up. "It's that way," I said with false confidence, pointing to the south. I had a one in four chance of being right.

"No, Eoforwic lies over there." Osmund gestured to the east.

"Well, I did get kind of turned around when that boar was chasing me," I began, scrambling for some way to keep my story going. "And then when I fell in the river, the current really—"

"Do you see which way the river flows, Leofric?" Osmund interrupted.

I didn't need to look. I could feel the current pushing against me. "Yeah, the river flows that—" I stopped myself. The river flowed south, away from Osmund's village and not anywhere close to Eoforwic. He'd known all along that my story about falling into the river and floating to his village was a complete lie.

A faint smile spread across Osmund's face. "All men have secrets,

Leofric. In that, there is no shame. Serve the king and his warriors well, and whatever secrets you hide about your past will be overlooked."

He pushed ahead to the far bank, where he put his shoes back on and started walking off along another path. I stood waist-deep in water for a few seconds, watching him recede into the distance, my cheeks tingling with the flush of embarrassment. How many others in the village had realized I was lying? If I ever returned, how many would be laughing at me behind my back?

I forded the river and ran after Osmund, not sure what to say. Finally I decided to say nothing. My lies had gotten me into trouble in the first place; more would only make things worse. Osmund nodded when I fell in step beside him, and we continued our journey in silence.

By noon, we'd caught up with the king's army at the city of Tada. Thousands of warriors from the surrounding countryside had arrived before us, and now they camped out in the fields and clearings along the road. The best-equipped had shields and chain-mail armor and carried axes or multiple spears, while some wore only leather armor or padded vests and brought crude shields just slightly better than the useless kindling Osmund and I carried. All sat in little clusters around fires and laughed or drank or talked about their desire to get the fight over quickly so they could return to their homes. Only a few men had tents—most had just brought along blanket bags, like me and Osmund.

Osmund glanced expectantly at each group of men we passed but always continued on. "Lord Orm and his warriors must be closer to the town," he said by way of explanation.

We proceeded down the road and within minutes reached the edge of the city—although calling it a city was pretty generous. It was maybe twice the size of Osmund's village. Here the number of tents increased, and the topics of conversation changed. Scars marked hands and faces, and the discussion was all about past battles and the coming fight. The armor changed too: not a single crappy shield or padded jacket anywhere. Every one of the warriors within the city wore a suit of chain mail and carried a large, sturdy shield.

"Who are these guys?" I asked.

"The king's housecarls," Osmund said, a note of admiration in his voice. "His loyal and trusted retainers who follow him to every battle."

As we walked past these professional warriors laughing and joking while sharpening their weapons, I became filled with a strange mixture of fear and excitement—I was in the middle of a freakin' Anglo-Saxon army preparing for battle. Had Dad felt the same rush of adrenaline when he traveled back in time?

At the center of the housecarl camp, next to the stone church, a huge striped tent towered over the tents around it, large enough to hold thirty men. Above it two flags flapped listlessly in the weak breeze: one bore a gold dragon, the other a crude image of a fighting man.

"Is that King Harold's tent?" I asked.

"Aye." Osmund pointed to the flag with the fighting man on it. "That is his personal banner; it has flown over many fields of victory before he became king. Let us hope that in the coming battle it will fly victorious again."

Just a few minutes to the east of the king's tent we found Lord Orm and his men. Orm must have been one of the richer guys in this part of England, because he brought a huge group of warriors with him, all equipped with chain-mail armor, shields, and strong spears. Some even carried long, two-handled axes.

After the briefest of introductions, where Orm barely acknowledged our presence, Osmund and I were put to work. Luckily, tons of other peasants had arrived to help from Orm's other villages, so the work wasn't unbearable. We stocked up on firewood for the night, unsaddled and watered the horses, put up tents, and basically did everything so that Orm and his companions could sit comfortably around the fire eating and drinking. Not that I was complaining. Being waterboy to a bunch of warriors was a hell of a lot better than having to fight. I just wanted to figure out the time glitch, fix it, and then get out of this place.

Once we finally finished all our chores, Osmund and I found a spot near a fire among the other farmers, away from the center of the camp and close to the forest. "Keep your food close," Osmund said as he placed his bag on the ground, opened it, spread out the blanket, and then arranged his supply of food at the foot of his blanket and his spear and shield on either side. "You do not want animals to take it in the night."

A growing sense of unease stirred within me as I began setting up my gear like Osmund. Last night in the church had been cold; how much worse would it be sleeping outdoors with only the warmth of the waning fires to keep away the cold of the night? My eyes drifted up to the sky, scanning for clouds. A few in the distance looked dark and heavy. Rain would be the completely terrible icing on an already-bad cake. In anticipation of a night spent freezing and possibly soaking wet, I wrapped my blanket around myself and leaned toward the fire.

As I nibbled on a dinner of bread and raw leeks, Osmund tapped me on the shoulder. "I go to speak with my good friend Caedmon. Will you come with me?"

"No, I'm good." I knew Osmund was only inviting me to be polite. He'd have a better time without me around.

I watched as he walked over to his friend's fire. Caedmon leaped up and gave him a big hug and they soon began laughing and telling stories to each other. When I glanced around, all the other farmers seemed to be enjoying themselves as well. They strolled around the camp or lounged by fires, sharing food and telling jokes. No one else was huddled alone by the fire looking like he was suffering from the flu. Embarrassed, I shrugged off my blanket and stood up. I needed to stop behaving like a pampered brat and start acting like the guy who had to save history.

Before I could give much thought to what that might entail, the blare of a horn interrupted my thoughts. I was looking around, trying to figure out where the sound had come from, when Osmund grabbed me by the arm and pulled me along after him. We followed a tide of men to the center of the camp, all staring ahead toward the lofty peak of the king's tent. If the king himself was there, I couldn't see him. The horn sounded again, and suddenly a blond head rose above the crowd. By the cheering, I figured this must be the king. He looked close to my dad's age, with shoulder-length hair kept away from his face by a gold circlet.

"Brave warriors," he began, and instantly the crowd hushed. "I was chosen as your rightful king by the Witan, those wise lords and priests who have always given good counsel in the past. My evil brother Tostig and that swineherd Hardrada of Norway do not trust the choice made by the leaders of this land, and they wish to take the kingship from me. They have already burned Skarthaborg and killed many of the men who fought for Eoforwic." The king paused as angry mutters rippled through the crowd.

"News has come to me that the enemy have left Eoforwic and split their forces. Some have gone east to receive supplies and hostages as tribute. The rest are at Riccall, waiting by their ships. Now is the time to strike! We shall attack my foul brother and his men at Riccall, while their forces are weak, and we shall burn them out of their boats!"

All around me, men raised their weapons high, yelling their support, while I stood there numbly with my mouth hanging open. Dad had taught me about King Harold and the battles he needed to fight to keep his crown—Riccall wasn't one of them. According to history, King Harold had ignored the troops at Riccall and instead attacked the forces waiting to the east of Eoforwic, totally destroying them at a bloody battle known as Stamford Bridge.

I'd found the time glitch. But how could I make things right again?

CHAPTER 10

No time to think it over. If I wanted to get home and save Dad, I needed to get Harold to change his plans now, before the army started marching. I began shoving my way through the press of peasants, warriors, and housecarls, trying to reach the king. It was like trying to swim through the tide. For every step I gained, I lost two as the mass of men pushed me back.

Finally, I got within shouting distance of the king. He stood in front of his tent, at the center of a group of housecarls. I stood just at the edge of this group, waiting for my chance to speak with him privately.

"Rest well," the king urged his men. "The fighting shall be heavy tomorrow, but the fate of England depends on us." He raised an ale horn in salute to his men and drank deeply from it, the warriors around him cheering lustily for their king. Wiping his lips with the back of his sleeve, Harold turned around and walked toward his tent.

I was about to lose my chance.

"You can't go to Riccall!" I yelled, my desperate voice barely louder than the clamor around it. "You need to attack the Vikings to the east of Eoforwic."

On a subtlety scale of one to ten, yelling at a king would rate a negative six. I'm sure someone with more experience in time-jumping would have figured out a better way to approach the king, gain his ear, and then get him to decide on his own that he needed to head for Stamford Bridge. Unfortunately, that person wasn't here, so the fate of history rested in my incompetent hands.

The king heard me, at least. He stopped and turned in my direction. His blue eyes bored into me, and his lips curled in a dismissive sneer. "Kings do not seek the advice of farmers when it comes to war." The men around him laughed, and King Harold entered his tent. My extremely brief audience was over.

My shoulders slumped as I bowed my head in defeat. I'd failed big-time. What would happen if Harold didn't fight at Stamford Bridge? That one battle had changed history—my dad had made me write an entire report on it. Harold so utterly crushed his brother Tostig, and Tostig's Viking allies, that this battle was considered the end of the Viking age. If Harold lost, or never even showed up, would the Vikings become rulers of England? What would that mean for the future of Europe, and the world?

I returned to the little campsite I shared with Osmund. The fire crackled and I watched as the flames slowly devoured the scraps of wood. *How would Dad handle this situation? What would he say to King Harold?* I needed to figure out an answer soon—history depended on me.

"Your brow is heavy with thought," Osmund observed. "Do not fear about the battle tomorrow. The king has many warriors with him, and they fight for their homes. We shall win."

"It's not the fighting I'm worried about—it's the location. I have a bad feeling about fighting at Riccall. I think we should fight to the east."

Osmund sat across from me and dangled the end of a branch over the fire. "You may be right. Indeed the east may be the better path. But

the king has decided we are to fight at Riccall, and that is now our fate."
He poked his stick into the fire, sending a flurry of sparks skyward.
"A wise and peaceful man learns to accept his fate, while a foolish and
angry man tries to change it." He tossed the stick fully into the fire.
"Now get some sleep, so on the morrow we may both face our fates well
rested." He lay down and drew his blanket over himself.

Around the camp, other men began turning in as well, but I
couldn't sleep. My mind kept racing through different strategies to get
the king to the right battlefield. I sat there staring at the fire, watching
it slowly die as the sky darkened and the moon and stars emerged.

I probably sat there for hours, my mind jumping from one doomed-
to-fail plan to the next. When my eyelids finally started drooping, I
realized I was the only one in the camp still awake. The fires had all
died down, leaving only red glowing pits of embers behind.

I rose to take a leak before trying to sleep. I walked quietly past
countless snoring men and found a thick tree just outside the camp.

As I stood there in the darkness, relieving myself, I heard a footstep.
"Who's there?" I asked nervously.

No answer.

I fought back a tendril of fear and peered over my shoulder. I saw
nothing except the dark outlines of trees against the starry sky, but I
knew someone was there. I stood silent for a moment, listening, but
only the whisper of the breeze through the branches came to my ears.

Slowly I exhaled and relaxed, but then a twig snapped behind me
and I whirled around. A dark figure lunged at me, a glint of steel in
his hand. In panic, I flung my arm up to block the strike but was a
split second too late. The attacker's knife plunged into my left shoulder,
sending a blaze of pain down my arm. I fought the urge to clutch my
damaged shoulder and instead punched out with my good arm. My fist
collided with a face. The attacker grunted, and his blade flashed in the
moonlight for another strike. "Help!" I yelled as I jumped to one side.

"They will not save you, boy," came a low voice from close behind me.

There were two of them!

I dove to the side. My shoulder slammed into the ground and needles of pain seared into me, but I didn't care. If I stopped moving, I was dead. My two attackers cursed and stumbled after me, putting themselves between me and the camp. Adrenaline sent me racing into the forest, branches and bushes whipping at my face and body.

Behind me, twigs and leaves crunched under my assailants' feet. The noises got louder by the second; they were gaining on me.

A tree stump appeared out of nowhere and slammed into my shins. I face-planted, my legs feeling like someone had taken a baseball bat to them. As I spat dirt from my mouth and pulled myself to my feet, one of my attackers leaped at me and knocked me down again before landing on top of me. A knife flashed in his hand, and I grabbed hold of his wrist as the blade plunged toward me, stopping its descent just a hand's width above my face. He leaned over the knife, putting all his weight behind it. It edged slowly downward, moving closer and closer to my throat. I wriggled under him, trying to throw him off.

Twigs snapped nearby as the second attacker appeared from the darkness.

"Help!" I screamed.

The first guy jerked his arm and slammed his elbow into my jaw so hard that bright spots filled my vision. As I lay there partially stunned, he wrenched his knife hand free from my grasp. A triumphant snarl crossed his lips as he grasped the knife handle with both hands and raised it above his head.

Suddenly, an arrow thudded into his chest, and he fell sideways off me, collapsing in the underbrush.

The second attacker rushed toward me. I leaped to my feet, prepared to fight for my life but, as if by magic, another arrow pierced his throat and he crumpled to the ground.

"Newbie," came a loud whisper from deep in the forest. "If you want to live, run toward to my voice."

I looked back at the camp, where fires flared as men rose and tried to figure out what had woken them. At this distance, I could see only their silhouettes against the flames, while I was as good as invisible to them in the darkness of the forest. I could either go back to the safety and warmth of the campfires where Osmund and thousands of other armed men would protect me. Or I could follow Sam.

I took a first step toward the fires but then stopped to look at the men who had tried to kill me. Both wore simple tunics and breeches and looked just like any of the hundreds of other peasants supporting King Harold's army. More could be hiding in the camp and I'd never know.

I turned away from the campfires and began stumbling through the forest. About thirty paces away from the fallen bodies of my attackers, Sam stepped silently from between the trees, practically invisible in the darkness.

"You saved my life," I gasped. "Thank you."

"You got lucky, Newbie," Sam grunted. "Your screams woke me and you ended up running in the right direction. Anywhere else and you'd be dead."

A simple *you're welcome* would have made me feel better. But Sam was right: I'd gotten lucky ... again.

"Are you hurt?" Sam asked.

"Yeah. One of them stabbed me in the shoulder and I think it went pretty deep. But everything's kind of numb right now from shock so it's hard to tell."

"Damn it," he sighed. "All right. I'll have a look at it back at my camp."

He led me through the woods to a spot behind a hill and well out of sight of the king's gathering. A ring of stones marked where a fire had been, with a blanket and backpack lying next to it.

"Take your tunic off and sit down," Sam said, pointing to a spot next to his fire pit. "I want to see your arm." He tossed a few twigs on the coals, and a feeble orange light spread around us.

I gingerly sat down and tried to pull my tunic off over my head. Every move of my left arm sent new waves of pain shooting through my shoulder. I gritted my teeth and, with one huge effort, tugged the bloodstained tunic off, leaving me shirtless in the cool night air. By the light from the fire I could see a huge gash across my left shoulder, blood still seeping from it.

"That doesn't look good," Sam observed. "If I don't patch it up, it'll get infected, and you could either lose the entire arm or die."

I nodded as I couldn't say much else. The shock and adrenaline were beginning to wear off, and the pain was increasing.

"Here, take a few mouthfuls of this." Sam passed me his water skin.

I expected water but instead tasted the warmth of red wine. After a few gulps, I passed the skin back to Sam, whose eyes locked with mine. "I'm going to wash and clean your wound, and then I'm going to have to sew it shut," he warned. "This is going to hurt like hell, but you have to keep quiet. No matter what happens, don't scream—understand?"

I nodded.

Sam rummaged through his backpack. "Damn it! I have just enough gauze to bandage you up. Do you have anything clean on you that I can use to wash the wound?"

"No."

"Nothing? Where are your first-aid supplies?"

"Where would I get first-aid supplies? I just have what you gave me. And after two days of farming and hiking with Osmund, none of it's even remotely clean."

Sam's gaze shifted a few times between the gauze clasped in his hands and my wound. Finally, he shook his head and exhaled slowly. "Well, Newbie, you were bound to find out sometime." His voice was thick with resignation.

"Find out what?"

Sam pushed back his hood, revealing long red hair tightly pulled into a ponytail. His arms obscured his face for a second as he bent his head forward and reached around to untie the knot that secured the cloth around his face. Then he snapped his head up and glared at me defiantly, as if challenging me to say anything.

Full lips. A small, rounded nose. High cheekbones. Piercing eyes.

"You're a girl!"

CHAPTER 11

S am soaked her scarf with wine. "Nothing gets past you, does it, Newbie?"

Without the scarf around her face, her voice had lost its muffled quality: clearly feminine now, although laced with sarcasm.

"Why do you hide your face?" I asked. "Someone who looks as good as you should—ow!"

She had wrung her scarf out to get rid of the excess liquid, and slapped it straight on my shoulder. "Sorry," she said, though the smirk on her face said otherwise. "This is going to hurt," she warned. "You ready?"

I gritted my teeth. "Ready."

She dabbed at my wound, sending spasms of pain through my whole arm. "You really want to know why I hide my face?" Sam asked as she began wiping the blood and dirt away. "Eighteen months ago, on my first-ever time jump, I didn't hide who I was. I kind of knew what to do because I always spied on my dad and brother when they trained, and I'd heard all their stories. So I thought I could do it just as well as they could. I was so dumb." She sloshed some more wine onto the cloth, wrung it out, and returned to my shoulder. "I ended up in medieval Spain, outside a small village. Within minutes I ran into a drunken soldier. It was late at night and no one else was out. He threw me into the bushes and tried to rip my pants off." Her face grew hard at the memory. "I managed to bash him in the head with a rock before he could get too far … and then I ran." Her lips drew tight as she shook her head. "And that was my welcome to time travel. That's when I realized I would always have to hide who I was and keep to the shadows if I wanted to survive. Men have it so much easier."

"Easier?" I grunted. "The king wouldn't even talk to me because I'm a peasant. And look at my shoulder—I've been stabbed!"

"Boo hoo, poor Newbie," Sam said without a trace of sympathy. "Try being a woman in medieval times. There are worse things than being stabbed. That's why all time jumpers are male—women get the short end of the stick throughout history—everywhere, every time."

"But you're female. You're a time jumper."

"Only because I snatched my brother's device after he was killed. Neither my dad nor my brother ever expected me to take over for them." She stopped wiping my wound and picked up a stick from the ground. "Bite on this," she instructed.

"I'm not really hungry," I replied.

"You really are a newb, aren't you?" She reached into her pack and pulled out a small leather case. By the light of the fire, she threaded a large needle. "You think that cloth hurt? Just wait until you feel this." She waved the needle in front of my face. "Now bite down on that stick so your screams don't wake up the entire forest."

What followed was the most painful experience of my life. Every moment was its own separate agony as the needle repeatedly dug through my flesh. I felt each tug, each pull of the thread, as the stitches went in. My jaw ached as I bit down on the stick and sawed at it furiously with my teeth.

I don't know how long it all lasted, but after what seemed like an eternity, Sam cinched the last stitch tight and cut the end off the thread with her knife. "All done."

I leaned to one side and spat the stick out of my mouth, trying to get rid of the gritty taste of wood and dirt. My shoulder did look a lot better. The bleeding had stopped, and ten stitches spanned the ragged cut, about a hand's width in size, running from my collarbone to my armpit.

"Well, I think you're going to live, Newbie." Sam unfolded a small wax-paper packet and smeared a dab of what looked like antibiotic cream over the cut. Despite the throbbing pain in my arm, I couldn't help noticing her gentle touch. It was rare for me to be near a pretty girl, never mind have one actually talking to me—taking care of me, even. I hoped I wouldn't say or do anything stupid to blow this moment.

She finished dressing my wound with the gauze and then returned her first-aid kit to her backpack. "Why'd you get attacked?" she asked as she sat back down by the fire. "Did you do anything to attract attention?"

I put my bloodstained tunic back on and sat down across the fire from her. "Well, I figured out what the time glitch was, and I tried to fix it."

She let out an exasperated sigh. "What did you do?"

"Nothing," I muttered, and looked away. I couldn't admit to Sam that I had forgotten all her warnings about being careful and had instead drawn huge attention to myself.

"Come on," she insisted. "Tell me."

"Fine," I grumbled. "I tried to talk with the king, but he was surrounded by his troops and other people, so I kind of shouted to him that he needed to change his plans for tomorrow." I raised my good hand in a silencing motion. "You don't need to tell me how stupid that was."

Sam nodded but said nothing.

"What do I do now?" I asked.

"Rest the night here," she said, "so I can make sure your wound isn't going to get infected. If everything is okay in the morning, go back to the camp and try again to talk to the king."

"Go back? Are you crazy? That's the last thing I want to do. I almost died in that camp. What if someone else tries to kill me?"

"No time for wimping out. If you don't fix the glitch, we'll both be stuck here forever. And who the hell knows what's going to happen to history."

My stomach twisted into knots. "And you're relying on *me* to fix it? You go—you're the expert."

"But I'm also a girl. Think of how little respect *you're* getting from them. It'd be even worse for me."

I let out a long, ragged sigh. Sam was right; it would have to be me. At least I knew Osmund, and I looked similar enough to the other farmers. She'd never fit in. "Do you think I'll get attacked again?"

Sam chewed on her lower lip for a second. "I hate to say it," she said quietly, "but there's probably a good chance of that. It isn't normal for someone to be randomly attacked, especially someone who clearly has no cash on them, like you." She waved her hand in the direction of the forest. "Those guys I killed weren't time jumpers, but I bet they were hired by one."

I groaned and put my face in my hands. "You really think there's another time jumper somewhere here?"

"Yeah, that makes the most sense."

"Then why don't we just let him fix the glitch? We can hide in the forest and keep ourselves safe until he does."

"Because I could be wrong; we might be the only ones here. The only way to make sure we get home is to fix this glitch ourselves."

I lay back on the cold ground, staring up at the night sky. If I didn't go back to the camp, I'd be stuck here forever. But going back could mean my death.

"I'm scared," I said quietly. I'd never admitted that to anyone before, and I felt weak doing it now. But I was near my breaking point. I didn't know if I had the strength to keep going.

"You can do it, Dan. You have to."

I couldn't help but notice that she'd called me Dan. Somehow being called by my real name gave me strength. I closed my eyes and concentrated on her last words. They actually made me feel less panicky. Were all men suckers like me for a pretty face? As the wine and fatigue pushed me toward sleep, I resolved that tomorrow I'd go back to camp, get the king to head east—and try not to get killed in the attempt.

CHAPTER 12

A gentle nudge on my arm stirred me from my sleep. "Dan. It's time to get up."

Where am I?

Feet? Frozen.

Back? Aching like I'd slept on a pile of rocks.

Neck? Sore with a cramp that would probably never come out.

Only camping could make me feel this bad.

I opened my eyes. In the dim gray of the near dawn, the forest had a ghostly look to it. The tree trunks were dark slashes disappearing skyward, and mist obscured the forest floor. Sam crouched beside me, her hand resting on my arm.

"Hey." She gave me a warm smile.

"Hey," I replied groggily. I sat up and groaned as pain flared through my wounded arm.

"How's the shoulder?"

"Still hurts like hell, but it feels better than yesterday, I guess."

Sam knelt beside me and pushed the sleeve of my tunic aside to inspect the wound. Her fingers skimmed across my skin, lightly prodding, but not hurting me. "The cut's swollen and bruised, but doesn't look infected. Just take it easy with this arm for a few days."

I didn't respond. I couldn't. Her face was only inches from mine, so I could see her features clearly for the first time. She was really pretty. No—scratch that—she was beyond pretty: she was beautiful. Green eyes, fiery red hair, and a dusting of freckles on her nose and cheeks. She was probably about my age, but her eyes had a haunted look to them, as if she had seen things way beyond her years. I'd only been time-jumping for three days now, and I already hated it more than anything. I couldn't imagine the toll that five time jumps had taken on her.

She rolled the sleeve of my tunic back down and then pulled a small loaf of bread from her backpack. She tore it down the middle and pressed one of the halves into my hand. "Here. You need to eat." She tossed her water skin on the ground beside me. "Sorry it's not much."

"Don't worry. This is great." I ripped off a piece of bread and popped it into my mouth. Who cared if all Sam had for breakfast was bread and water? With her I felt safe—which was something I hadn't felt once since arriving in this miserable time period.

"Um," Sam said, "that bread and water was supposed to be more of a take-out meal, not a casual dine-in sort of thing. After all"—she pointed in the direction of the Anglo-Saxon camp—"King Harold is over there, and we *are* kind of stuck here until this time glitch gets fixed."

Damn.

Nothing like my stupid obligation to save history to ruin my one moment of tranquility. I grudgingly pulled myself to my feet. Should I thank Sam again for saving my life? Shake her hand? Stand there awkwardly like some idiot who had no clue how to behave around a woman?

"Get your butt moving, Newb!" she said as she jabbed a finger toward Harold's camp. "History's waiting!"

With a flush of embarrassment stinging my cheeks, I ran into the forest. It looked a lot less threatening now than it had last night, and I had an easier time avoiding branches and random stumps. But what would I say when I got back to camp? Yesterday it had been a struggle just to talk to the king, and then he ignored my feeble warnings; would I even get close enough to speak to him today? And, if the chance did arise, what could I say to change his mind?

I ran through the trees, trying to remember everything Dad had told me about King Harold and the events leading up to the Battle of Stamford Bridge. I knew that Tostig, Harold's brother, was a cruel and ruthless man who'd been banished from England by King Edward the Confessor in the fall of 1065 on Harold's advice. Tostig spent the next few months sailing to Flanders, Scotland, and Norway, trying to find allies to help him win the crown that his brother ended up taking in January of 1066 when King Edward died, leaving no heirs. Tostig eventually gained the support of King Harald Hardrada of Norway, and together they attacked England that September, trying to overthrow Harold. Which brought me to where I was now, running through a forest in northern England, wondering how any of that information could help me convince King Harold that he was heading the wrong way. I arrived back at the camp to find Osmund and the rest of the peasants packing up all the gear of Lord Orm and his warriors.

"Hi, Osmund," I said.

"Leofric!" he yelled back, a wide smile on his face. "I knew you would not run away." His smile faded as his gaze settled on the blood-stained sleeve of my tunic. "You are hurt."

"I'm fine," I said.

"You do not look fine. You have been injured. Who did this to you?"

A small crowd of men gathered around, eager to hear what had happened to me. I took a deep breath and prepared to tell my story.

"While everyone was asleep last night," I began, "two men attacked me in the forest and—"

"Two men attacked you during the night!" Osmund interrupted. "And yet you are still alive? You truly are a lucky man."

"Luck had nothing to do with it," I said. "A hunter heard my screams and shot both the guys attacking me. If not for him, I'd be dead."

Osmund scanned the faces of the men now listening to my tale. "Where is this hunter?" he asked.

One of the men snorted. "You believe these stories of murderers and hunters? Why would anyone want him dead? He is just a peasant boy. More likely he grew scared of the coming battle and stabbed himself so he could run back to his mother."

"I'm telling the truth," I insisted.

"Bah!" Another man waved his hand dismissively. "I will not waste my time listening to a coward's tales."

I looked around at their faces. Clearly, not a single person believed me. How could I get King Harold to change his plan if I couldn't even get a bunch of peasants to believe something that had actually happened? I was coming to the rapid conclusion that in the great medieval pecking order, farm boys ranked just above goats. "Osmund," I pleaded. "Please believe me. Two men *did* try to kill me."

Osmund took a deep breath and exhaled slowly, his inner turmoil etched clearly on his face. He wanted to believe me, but I had lied to him once already. Suddenly he clapped his hands together. "If Leofric tells the truth," he said to the men around him, "the bodies of those two men will be found in the forest. Let us find them and we shall find the truth."

Duh, I should have thought of that one.

"Follow me!" I said as I rushed to the forest's edge, a jolt of excitement surging through me. With a crowd of people following, I retraced my steps to the tree where everything had started. Once I got there I halted and turned around a few times, trying to recover my bearings. Unfortunately, I had no clue where to head from here. During my mad dash for survival I had been scared and confused, and it had been dark. All the trees had looked the same at night, but now they looked completely different in the daylight.

Osmund dropped to one knee and held a broken fern frond in his fingertips. "Someone passed this way," he confirmed.

"And I see a boot print here in the earth," said another man, a few steps farther into the forest.

Deeper into the woods we went, following the smallest of clues. A broken twig. A scuff in the earth. Some kicked-up leaves.

"Here!" yelled one of the trackers over to the side. "Two men lie dead from arrows. And one holds a bloodied dagger. The boy is telling the truth."

A murmur of surprise spread among the men as relief washed over me. No longer was I Leofric, the Lying and Cowardly Peasant Boy. Now I was Leofric, the Mildly Interesting Peasant Boy.

A peasant turned over the body of the man who had taken an arrow in his throat. "Eadric of Clifton," he sneered. "A foul creature."

"And the other is Hengist of Acum," another said. "A lazy oaf who liked his drink, and liked the goods of others even more."

"We must inform the king of their treachery!" someone called out.

"Aye! To the king!"

Suddenly, we became a mob rushing back to camp, with the two dead peasants hauled along. Our numbers grew as word spread of what had happened to me, and by the time we reached the king's tent, we were a few hundred strong—with Osmund leading the pack. He strode along purposefully, his face set in a stone-like mask.

Housecarls met us just outside the entrance to the king's tent. "We must see King Harold," Osmund declared. "This boy was attacked in the woods and two men lie dead." He pointed to the two bodies now dumped unceremoniously on the ground.

A housecarl ducked inside the tent, and seconds later Harold himself pulled the tent flap aside and stepped out, looking every inch the king in his dark red tunic and blue cloak with gold trim. His lip curled in distaste as he nudged the bodies of my two attackers with the toe of his boot. "What happened to these men?"

King Harold listened intently to my story, his nostrils flaring slightly when I told him about how Sam had saved me. "And where is this hunter?" he asked.

"Gone. He didn't want any trouble."

"To what end would these two cowards have had you slain?"

This was the moment I'd been waiting for. I needed to lay it on thick this time. "Great king," I began, "these men tried to kill me to keep me quiet. They overheard me yesterday when I suggested that you attack to the east. They are in league with Tostig and Hardrada, and the two have set a trap for you at Riccall. If you go south, you are doomed. If you go east, you will have victory."

The king's face went pale, but he said nothing. Some of his housecarls swore or muttered angrily, while the men who had escorted me from the forest shifted uneasily.

A sense of smug satisfaction spread through me. I had him now.

A huge gray-bearded warrior with a scar across one eye stepped out from the ranks of the housecarls and squinted at me with his good eye. "And how does a boy from the fields know where to find Tostig and Hardrada?"

Oh ... crap.

The king stared at me, and his eyes narrowed. "Well, boy? What is your answer?"

The course of history depended on my next words. I stood there open-mouthed, sweat beading on my forehead, trying to think of an answer. What would the king believe? I couldn't pretend I had stumbled upon Tostig and Hardrada plotting in the forest. Even if that had been the slightest bit possible, Osmund could prove I was lying. In fact, he'd be able to disprove pretty much anything I said.

King Harold grabbed me by my collar, nearly lifting me off my feet. "Answer me, boy!" he commanded, his face just inches from mine. "Tell me how you came to know of this, or I swear, by the grace of God, I will have you beaten!"

Grace of God? That's it!

In medieval England, religion was the one thing that could always be counted on to sway the opinions of kings or commoners. I bowed my head in humility until I found myself staring at King Harold's belt buckle. "M-m-my lord," I stammered, "I stayed two nights ago in the church at Torp. As I lay awake and prayed for guidance, a divine voice spoke to me. She told me that I must join your army and guide you to victory against Tostig and Hardrada. It is because of her words that I know Riccall is the wrong spot. You must go east. God wills it."

King Harold's mouth opened in astonishment, and he let go of my collar. "Can anyone support your tale?" he asked, his tone softer now.

One particular redhead could completely corroborate my story, but telling them about her would only raise more questions. I pointed to Osmund, standing in the crowd of onlookers. "Osmund of Torp, a good and honest man and headman of his village, knows that I slept in his village church that night."

The king's brow creased, and he stroked his beard with one hand. I could almost see the thoughts going through his head. I was just a teenage peasant. Should he change his mind and follow my "divine" advice, or stick with his original plan?

The same scarred housecarl strode toward me and stopped just inches in front of me, staring into my face. I suppressed a shiver as his one good eye bored first into my left eye, and then my right, as if searching for answers. I managed to return his gaze, not pulling away. He wanted me to show signs of fear, to indicate that I was lying. But I stood there and stared back at his worn and wrinkled features, unflinching. After all, I had told them the truth. Maybe "divine voice" was a bit of an exaggeration, but a voice *had* spoken to me out of the darkness in the church. Who cared if it had been Sam's voice? The important part was that I had hooked the king and the rest of the crowd. Now I just needed to pass this last test, and then I could reel them in.

I don't know how long we locked eyes. I trembled as I stood, imagining what might happen if he decided I was a liar. No one in the crowd spoke as the king and his men watched our confrontation.

Finally, the scarred warrior stepped back. "He tells the truth."

The look on King Harold's face was hard to read. He paced in a small circle, clearly undecided on which way to proceed.

Another warrior stepped forward. "My lord, we know for sure that some of Tostig's and Hardrada's men will be in the east. So, even if the boy lies, we shall still have a battle."

King Harold raised his hands for silence. "We will go east," he decided, and his men began to cheer. The king turned and leaned toward me so that his mouth was right next to my ear. "Pray for victory, boy," he whispered, "for you shall not live long past our defeat."

Despite this threat, I felt triumphant. The rod, which had previously radiated cold, now felt warm against my lower back. With King Harold changing his plans, that could only mean one thing: I had succeeded in fixing history—and it was time to go home and save Dad. I just needed to find Sam so she could tell me how to leave this place. Did I just repeat the same words that had brought me here? Did I have to twist the sections of the rod to a different setting and say some new rhyme? She'd know.

I turned to leave the king's presence, but a firm hand clamped down on my shoulder, stopping me. "You will stay with us," King

Harold declared. "If you have weapons or armor, tell us where they are, and we will send a boy to fetch them." His voice lowered menacingly as he continued. "You will not leave our sight until the battle is over."

I gulped. The threat in his tone was unmistakable—I'd better be right.

CHAPTER 13

As the sun reached its highest point in the sky, a scout on horseback came racing down the road toward us. King Harold reined in his own horse at the sight of him, and with a clatter of hooves the army came to a stop. For the entire morning, we'd pushed hard along the old Roman highway that led from Tada, passed through Eoforwic, and headed for Stamford Bridge. And now, as the road climbed up a slight hill, it looked like our dash through the English countryside would come to an end.

The scout halted directly in front of King Harold. "Lord, just over this hill lies the ford across the Derwent," he said. "On both sides, the clearings are packed with men, maybe an army as large as yours. But they have not yet heard us. They talk and drink and boast of the treasure that shall be theirs." The scout's eyes shone with excitement. "Some carry axes, others spears and shields, but they have no armor! Some are even shirtless in the sun or swimming in the river."

A broad grin appeared on King Harold's face. He reached over and clapped me on my good shoulder. "You spoke the truth. We shall find great victory here today."

Harold climbed down from his horse, then turned to the rest of his men. "Dismount! We will take them by surprise."

On this command, the housecarls left their horses and then began to spread out along the road. With grim looks, the warriors tightened armor straps, gripped shields to forearms, and hefted spears and axes, ready to surge ahead.

"Are you fit enough to hold your shield?" King Harold asked me. "If so, I offer you the honor of fighting beside us, so you can win your share of glory."

Fight? Against Vikings? Was he insane?

This was one *honor* I could definitely pass on. I just wanted to get the hell out of here and get back home to see if Dad was okay. I raised my crappy shield slowly with my left arm, making sure to wince at every movement. It really did hurt to hold the shield, but I laid it on extra thick so King Harold would get the hint.

The king shook his head grimly. "Your wound is clearly too fresh for you to fight with us. Get yourself safely to the rear when you can."

"All right," I said in mock disappointment as I slung the shield across my back and began leading my horse toward the safety of the forest and out of the way of the housecarls. There I dismounted and picked my way through the underbrush to the top of the hill. Goose bumps ran along both my arms. I was about to have a front-row seat to the actual Battle of Stamford Bridge. I'd watched tons of battles in movies, but this was the real thing! Nothing I'd ever seen would compare with it.

Reaching the top of the hill, I peered down toward the river. Willow and oak trees crowded near the water but gave way to large clearings on both banks. On the side closest to us, a few hundred Vikings relaxed in the sun while thousands of their fellow warriors gathered on the other side.

Down the roadway, King Harold's men had assembled just beneath the crest of the hill. "They sit there like sheep in the fields waiting for slaughter," an older housecarl said, laughing as he poked his head up to look at the Vikings below.

King Harold nodded. "Aye, they do." Then he raised his spear high. "Onward! To victory!" he shouted.

Howling like a pack of wolves, King Harold and his men rushed down the road. At the sight of the charging Anglo-Saxons, the Vikings leaped to their feet with their weapons and shields. Some yelled to form a shield wall, while others jumped into the river to swim across or raced for the narrow wooden bridge spanning the water. The bridge was only wide enough to allow a few men to cross at a time, so a panicked mob massed at one end, pushing and shoving each other in their race to be the first across to safety.

With a thunderous clatter of shields, the lead housecarls plowed into the small shield wall that blocked their way. A warrior knocked aside a Viking's spear and swung at him with his ax. The shirtless Viking raised his shield to block the strike, but a second housecarl rammed a spear into the Viking's unprotected belly. The Viking's shield tumbled from his hands as he crumpled to the ground, and the two Anglo-Saxons leaped over his body to attack the rest of the shield wall.

My stomach roiled, and bile rose to my throat as men fell like cut grass. This real-life butchery was more horrific than any movie I'd ever seen. That guy screaming because his arm had just been hacked off wasn't acting. The man trying to hold in his intestines with his hands because his stomach had been sliced open wasn't a stunt double. All the blood staining the ground wasn't fake. The glassy stares of the dead met my eyes no matter which way I looked, accusing me of just standing there and watching it all.

Like a volcano, my stomach erupted, and I spewed my breakfast beside a tree. The housecarls and warriors streaming past my spot probably thought I was the biggest wimp alive, while the peasants following along behind to support them were no doubt having a good laugh at me. At some other time, I might've cared what they thought, but right now I just wanted to forget all the screams and death.

At a rustle of feet behind me, I whirled around, spear held weakly in one hand. My eyes felt gritty from vomiting, and my throat was scratched and raw.

Osmund stood a few paces away, his brow creased with worry. "It is only I, Leofric. Do not fear. Are you well?" Behind him, on the road, the press of men continued as they headed into battle.

I wiped my mouth with my sleeve and gestured to the hacked and bleeding corpses littering the ground. Not a single Viking remained alive on the near shore. "How can that not bother you?"

"Death is never easy." Osmund rested his hand on my shoulder. "Take small comfort in knowing that those men died as they would have wished—in battle." Lips drawn tight, he turned to the river. "This shore has been won. So King Harold and his warriors now cross over to take the fight to the rest of the Northmen. Will you have the strength to accompany us?"

His eyes and tone showed only concern for me, but I still couldn't help feeling ashamed. Dad had trained me since birth to be a warrior, and at the first sight of battle I had puked. Is this why he'd never told me about time-jumping—because he knew I'd suck at it?

I looked over to the east bank, where the larger group of Vikings now scrambled to arrange themselves for battle. Two distinct groups had formed: one rallying around a tan banner with a wolf's head displayed on it, and the larger group under a huge red pennant emblazoned with a black raven. "Yeah, I'll come with you," I replied. "What are we up against?"

Osmund pointed to the red raven banner, under which stood hundreds of the fiercest men I'd ever seen. They had long hair, bushy beards, and an untamed vibe. "Even in my quiet village, tales have been told of the battlefields where that foul raven has won victory. For that is Land Ravager, King Hardrada's personal banner. The men who fight under it will not die as easily as those encountered on this shore." He pointed to the emblem of the wolf. "As for Tostig's men, who knows how hard traitors will fight?" He spat on the ground. "May they all die the death they deserve. But first King Harold's men must take the bridge."

A lone Viking now stood in the middle of the bridge, gripping an ax in one hand, a large round shield in the other. Shirtless in the autumn sun, he beat at his shield with the flat of his ax and taunted King Harold's troops. "Saxon dogs! You face Gunnar, son of Leif. While you sat in filth with your pigs, I was raiding the cities of the Bulgars and drinking wine with the lords of Miklagard. Come. Fight me and meet your doom."

Thanks to the jump device, I understood what he said, though I don't know if anyone else did. Even without words, his message couldn't have been clearer. Warriors began pushing each other aside, eager to be the man who won the glory of defeating Gunnar. The first Anglo-Saxon rushed across the narrow planks and stabbed with his spear. Gunnar easily knocked the blade aside and sank his ax into the housecarl's shoulder. The wounded man staggered for a moment, then Gunnar kicked him off the bridge into the water, where the weight of his own armor dragged him to the bottom. A second Anglo-Saxon advanced along the bridge and Gunnar kicked the man's shield aside before driving his ax deep into the man's chest, splitting both armor and ribs.

I stood almost hypnotized as I watched the Viking fight. More than forty men set foot on the bridge's wooden slats, and he defeated each of them in turn, killing them on the bridge or wounding them so severely that they fell into the river and disappeared beneath the surface. Gunnar by now bled from numerous cuts, but he still stood strong, challenging others to attack him. He became so focused on the shore in front of him that he didn't notice a lone housecarl pushing a half-barrel out into the water and using it as a makeshift boat to float under the bridge. As the Vikings on the far bank shouted warnings, the Anglo-Saxon drifted directly underneath Gunnar and then thrust his spear up between the bridge's planks, stabbing it hard into Gunnar's thigh.

As a cheer went up from my side of the bank, more of our warriors rushed the bridge, determined to defeat the lone Viking. He tried to fight them off as he had done before, but his wounded leg robbed him of his balance. He shifted position to duck under a high blow, but his leg buckled beneath him and he tumbled into the river, just like the many men who had faced him.

With Gunnar finally out of the way, the Anglo-Saxons began streaming across the narrow bridge to the east shore, the housecarls leading the way. Archers from our side fired volley after volley into the waiting enemy, forcing them back so they couldn't attack King Harold's men as they crossed.

The Vikings retreated in the face of this advance and began forming defensive lines along a tall and wide hill that lay some distance from the bridge. Their retreat gave King Harold time to finish bringing across all his housecarls, and now the army of warriors supplied by the local lords was making its way to the other shore.

Osmund turned to me, a questioning look on his face. "Battle will start again soon, and I plan to stand at the ready for my lord. Will you join me?" he asked.

"Don't go, Osmund. You're a farmer. Let the king and the warriors handle everything. Stay at the back with me."

He looked at the strong shield wall the Vikings had formed, and his brow grew heavy. "Many men will die here today, and no one can say with certainty who will win the day. What type of man will I be if I let others fight for my home and land when my spear might make a difference?"

"You'll be a live man. Isn't that what your wife and kids would want?"

"I would be alive, yes, but what of my honor? How could I tell my wife and children that I stood back while others gave their lives for us?" He shook his head. "No. I will support my king and his men. And I ask you again, will you come with me?"

Damn it. I wasn't going to win this argument. "I can't," I said. And then, just to make sure he didn't think I was a complete coward, I added: "My shoulder isn't strong enough to support my shield."

Nodding, he clasped my forearm. "I must leave you then, but I hope to see you again after the battle. If not, tell my wife I died bravely."

"Good luck, Osmund," I said anxiously. "Be safe."

"I will." He gave me a reassuring smile, then turned away to join the rest of the peasants crossing to the eastern bank to support the fighters in front of them in any way they could. I watched him as I waited for the last group to cross—the old men and the boys. These were the ones who had been sent by their villages strictly to haul water and chop firewood and not get anywhere close to combat. I hung my head in shame as I walked across the bridge with these men—I wasn't used to being thought of as a weakling. But at least I didn't have to worry about any of those guys attacking me when my back was turned—they didn't look capable of attacking anything.

My shoes thumped over the narrow planks of the bridge, and I found myself a spot far to the back of the shield wall. In front of me stretched row upon row of actual fighters: King Harold and his housecarls holding the center of the line, with the local lords and their warriors on the left and right of them.

The Viking and Anglo-Saxon armies stood staring at each other, neither moving. Only about fifty paces separated the two hosts while flags stirred listlessly in the breeze and a silence fell.

Suddenly, Harold and twenty of his housecarls broke free of our ranks and strode toward the Viking army, their weapons sheathed and Harold's banners fluttering above them. Eyes watched them carefully as they neared, and the Vikings held their spears at the ready. Harold halted his men about twenty paces from the enemy shield wall.

"Brother," he yelled. "I would have words."

A ripple of motion stirred within the Viking lines, and then two men stepped out of the ranks. One was a near giant of a man with a two-handed sword resting on his shoulder, while the other was shorter and wore a gold-chased helmet.

"Just with you, Tostig," King Harold called. "Leave that oaf Hardrada."

The two men spoke for a few seconds and then the taller one returned to the Viking lines while the shorter one stopped a few paces in front of Harold. Removing his helmet, he revealed blond hair and a face similar to the king's. "What do you wish to say to me, brother?"

"Lay down your weapons, Tostig," Harold demanded loudly for everyone to hear. "You are my brother, and I have no wish to shed the blood of my kin. If you give up this fool's quest, I will give you Northumbria to rule as your own. The two of us can share this land."

Tostig threw his hands in the air. "Why did you not give me these words last winter?" he fumed. "That would have saved the lives of many men and would have been better for England."

"Let us not talk of what has passed, but of now. I would avoid battle with you, Tostig."

"As would I, brother. I lack numbers and armor, but my men are brave. And King Hardrada has already sent to Riccall for the rest of his men. The battle will be bloody, and victory awaits for the strongest to seize. Either way, many men will die, and the kingdom will be weakened for whoever survives to rule it. Tell me, brother, if I accept your offer, what will you give to King Hardrada?"

"You ask too much," Harold sneered. "He is not my kin—he is an invader. I will give him seven feet of English ground—or maybe a bit more, as he is taller than most men."

Tostig shook his head in resignation. "Then battle is our only course. The Northmen will never be allowed to say that I turned against them. I would rather win England by force of arms, or die with honor." He turned and walked away, retreating into the shield wall.

King Harold cursed and stomped back to our lines. He stopped in front of our massed ranks and pulled off his helmet. "Today is the day we rid our lands of these foul invaders," he shouted. "Never will we have a better chance. Their men are divided. They wear no armor. We have a larger force." He pointed his ax at the enemy while still locking eyes with his own troops. "What say you, men?" he yelled. "Are you ready to forever rid yourselves of this foe?"

"Yes!" the army roared back.

Harold turned toward the Viking shield wall and raised his ax skyward. "For England!"

A thunderous battle cry shook our ranks as the entire army lurched forward at a jog. Feet pounded the earth; chain mail rustled; shields and spears clattered together. I jogged along far behind the wall of men, my spear in one hand and my shield slung across my back. I was petrified of getting killed in the coming battle, but at the same time felt an incredible rush of excitement—a strange mix of panic and adrenaline.

Ahead of us, the Viking wall held firm. Men banged axes and spears against their shields, psyching themselves up. Arrows began to fly back and forth between the opposing groups, thudding into shields or finding flesh.

At just twenty paces from the Viking line, the Anglo-Saxons picked up speed and began to rush up the hill toward the enemy. A slow roar rose from the housecarls, building steadily in volume.

Ten paces.

Five paces.

With a deafening crash, our men slammed into the Viking shield wall. As axes and spears swung through the air, men yelled their ferocious battle cries while others screamed their last breaths. Like two glaciers colliding, the shield walls struggled for victory. Our initial onslaught hammered the Vikings back, but King Hardrada roared in defiance and led a ferocious counterattack. Swinging his two-handed sword, he hacked through shields and armor, slaying everyone he faced. Slowly our attack faltered, and we were being pushed back downhill.

"Hold the line!" Harold yelled, and somehow, those three little words worked. Men dug in their heels, gripping their shields close, and withstood the Viking counterattack.

For what seemed like hours, we struggled back and forth this way, with the Anglo-Saxons gaining the advantage inch by inch. I stayed in the back row of the Anglo-Saxon shield wall with the other weaklings and cowards, fetching water for thirsty warriors, gathering spent arrows to pass to our archers for them to use again, and bringing extra spears to replace any that had broken. But I was fine with all the menial work. My game plan for this battle had been to get through it without dying or killing someone, and so far it was working.

Over the general din, a horrible gurgling cry came from Hardrada—one of our archers had nailed him in the throat with an arrow. As blood spewed from his neck and down his chest, he dropped his sword and clawed at the arrow, trying to pull it out. But his hands slipped on the blood-slicked shaft, and he collapsed amid the heap of bodies at his feet.

A wave of fear coursed through the Viking ranks. As their leader's raven banner dipped in the air, the Viking lines began to retreat quickly up the hill.

"Attack!" Harold yelled, sniffing victory.

The warriors in front of me pushed harder, battering at the enemy. Tostig waved the dead king's raven banner above his head. "For Hardrada!" he cried. "For victory!"

The Vikings tried to hold off our renewed attack, but without armor they couldn't keep up with the onslaught. One by one they were cut down. Tostig took a spear to the chest and the raven banner fell from his grasp and fluttered to the ground. With his death, both men who had wanted to conquer England were dead.

The wave of fear among the Vikings grew into a tsunami. They knew the battle was lost—now they were fighting for their lives. Some tossed aside their shields and ran into the woods, abandoning their friends. Others attacked with the fury of men who knew they were doomed, trying to kill as many Anglo-Saxons as possible before they died.

I felt myself holding each breath, praying for this living nightmare to end. I wanted the screams, the dying, and the blood all to fade from my sight.

Just when I thought the horror might finally be over, a horn sounded, and hundreds of armor-clad fighters streamed out of the woods and charged into the clearing.

"Help comes!" a Viking yelled, trying to rally the men around him.

Others picked up the cry, and the weakened Vikings attacked with renewed spirit. The reinforcements from Riccall crashed into the right flank of Harold's troops.

I swung my head frantically around, trying to assess the situation. The Anglo-Saxon right flank was getting hammered. Our front lines were buckling. My fingers tightened on my spear shaft. Any minute now, the Vikings would break through, and I'd be standing face to face with someone trying to kill me.

As panic built up inside me, the assault on the right flank began to falter. Vikings collapsed in the clearing, exhausted after running all the way from Riccall in full armor. Those who managed to join the shield wall were panting heavily, with only enough strength for a brief flurry of fighting. Then their swings slowed and their shields hung limply in their arms. King Harold's forces rallied back from the initial attack and quickly overwhelmed the Viking reinforcements. With their deaths, the remaining Vikings fled, leaving the Anglo-Saxon army alone in the field.

I threw my head back and exhaled loudly. I had survived my first—and hopefully last—battle. The men in the front ranks, the ones who had fought the hardest, dropped their shields and leaned heavily on their spears for support.

King Harold removed his helmet and tossed it to the ground. His hair lay slick with sweat against his scalp. "Men of England," he began, and a hush descended over the battlefield. "On this day, you fought well to protect your lands. Let people forever know of your courage as you faced the invaders, and of the bloody victory you have won!"

A booming din erupted through the clearing as men battered their shields with their spears.

I didn't cheer. I didn't raise my spear. Thousands of men lay dead or dying in front of me. There was nothing to cheer about. I just wanted to find Sam, learn how to use the stupid rod, and go home. Against the small of my back, the jump device still pulsed warmly, signaling that home and Dad were both within reach. I just had to wait for the right moment to sneak away from the army and find my guide.

Unfortunately, that time wasn't right now. I assumed that with the battle over, we would all start heading home. Instead, while warriors stripped rings, armbands, mail shirts, and coin pouches from the Viking dead, all of us peasants were stuck gathering wounded Anglo-Saxons and placing them on litters to be carried back to camp. The Viking wounded received different treatment. Bile rose to my throat as warriors ranged the battlefield, mercilessly silencing with a spear thrust the groans of pain and the cries for mercy from any Northman.

When only the dead remained on the battlefield, the army began recrossing the bridge to get back to the other side of the river. King Harold and his housecarls led the way, with the rest of us trailing along behind in no particular order. Around me, men sang songs or boasted of their exploits in battle, but I stayed quiet. I hadn't fought. I hadn't done anything.

Looking over my shoulder, I tried to spot Osmund in the long line of men snaking behind me but couldn't see him. In the fading light, everyone looked similar, and with thousands of men crammed onto the same narrow road, he could be anywhere. I had wanted to say goodbye to him before I left, to thank him for all he'd done for me, but now I guessed it just wasn't going to happen. Instead, I walked miserably along, my thoughts returning to my own home. What would happen when I got there? Was Dad still alive? What about Victor? How would—?

A sudden chill touched my lower back, interrupting my thoughts. For a second I couldn't figure out what had happened. Then, like a punch to the face, the realization hit me—the rod was cold again.

"No ..." I said under my breath. "No!"

I clenched my fists to stop myself from screaming. This wasn't fair. I'd done everything I was supposed to do. I'd found the time glitch, fixed it, and even got stabbed in the process. For what? The rod was cold again—the way home was now shut.

CHAPTER 14

I took a few deep breaths, trying to calm my racing heart. I needed to find Sam—fast.

Ahead of me, King Harold called a halt on the hill overlooking the river. "We camp here tonight," he called.

As others began setting up their blankets and starting fires for warmth and cooking, I ditched my spear and shield next to a tree and headed for the woods. The hairs on the back of my neck rose as I ran through the darkening forest; the last time I'd done this, two guys had tried to kill me. Every few steps I glanced over my shoulder to make sure no one was following me.

"Sam!" I yelled once the clamor of the Anglo-Saxon camp was so far behind me that I knew none of them would hear me. "Are you out here?"

No answer.

I ran deeper into the woods, my ears alert for the slightest footstep. Leaves rustled in the breeze, and birds chattered in the treetops. The forest stretched in front of me, huge and mysterious. Where was Sam? Had she gone back home already? Was I stuck here without her?

"Sam!" I yelled again, panic creeping into my voice.

Again, no answer.

I began sprinting through the forest, calling her name at the top of my lungs. Shouting like a fool had brought her to me once—I prayed desperately that it would happen again.

For what seemed like an eternity I ran, until my legs felt like lead and my throat was raw from shouting. The last bits of sunlight had almost completely disappeared—if I ever wanted to find my way back to the camp, I had to turn back now. "Sam!" I cried out one last time.

"Over here!" came a shout.

For the first time since the rod had gone cold again I felt hope. "Where are you?"

About a hundred steps away, a dark shape moved from behind a tree. I couldn't see her features well in the gray light, but there was no mistaking that flash of red hair.

I raced through the trees and skidded to a stop in front of her, nearly breathless. "Is your rod cold again?"

Sam nodded. "They all change at the same time."

"But how could another glitch happen? Did we miss something?"

"I don't know," Sam said, her voice quiet. She twisted the end of a long strand of hair around her fingers and chewed at the end of it.

Sam seemed scared. That wasn't good. I'd already come to rely on her to save me whenever I messed up; she was my safety net. If something was serious enough to scare her, what did that mean for me? "How can you not know? I'm supposed to be the clueless one. You're the one with all the answers."

Sam looked over my shoulder toward the distant camp and stood staring at it, as if searching for something. "Something's not right. In all my other jumps, I just fixed the problem, then left. I think someone might be intentionally sabotaging things to try to keep us here."

My chest tightened. "How? You said these glitch things are completely random. How can someone *create* one?"

"Damaging history is a lot easier than fixing it," Sam said matter-of-factly. "I could take my bow and shoot King Harold right now, and that would definitely create one hell of a time glitch."

"Any chance this new glitch might have been random?"

Sam shrugged. "There's always a chance. But I still think there's another time jumper hiding somewhere in the army. Too many weird things have been happening for this to be just random."

"Awesome ..." I muttered. Endless days ahead of watching out for unknown attackers, sleeping in cold forests with one eye open, and traveling from one battle to the next flashed before my eyes. I held my jump device out in front of me. "Can you at least show me how to get out of here, so if we do fix the next glitch, we won't have to stick around for number three?"

Sam raised an eyebrow. "You don't know how to leave?"

"No. I don't know anything, remember?" I said. "I felt the rod kind of telling me it was okay to go home this morning, but I didn't know what to do."

"You just hold the rod and say the same words that got you here."

"That's it?" I asked incredulously. "So both of us could have been home safe and sound hours ago?"

"Safe?" Sam snorted. "You think that going home will make you safe? Think of your dad. They attacked him in *your own home*. Do you really think they're going to leave you alone?" She shook her head grimly. "I wake up most nights in a panic, expecting to be attacked by the same guys who killed my dad and brother." She shut her eyes for a moment as she clenched and unclenched her fist. "The only time I feel safe is when I'm alone somewhere in the woods. So, yeah, we could have gone home, but once the rogue jumpers know who you are, your home is anything but safe."

I shuddered. Sam was right—there was no such thing as *safe* any-more. Even if Dad was still alive, Victor knew I had the jump device, and he didn't seem like the type of guy to let me keep it. He would be after me for sure.

Sam turned her head away from me. "Sometimes I really hate stupid time-jumping," she said, her voice cracking.

I hated to see her hurting. I put a tentative hand on her shoulder and tried to think of the perfect thing to say. Something that would show her I was there for her if she needed a hug or a shoulder to cry on. Unfortunately, I drew a huge blank. "It sucks," was all I managed.

"It is what it is," she sniffed as she shrugged away from me and wiped her eyes with her sleeve. "If there is another time jumper trapping us here, we need to find him."

"And how do we do that? You just said it could be anybody."

"I don't know … but I do know this: if you find him—kill him."

"Kill him? Me? I've never killed anybody. I've been in two fights all my life, and one of them was this week."

"Well, you're going to need to toughen up if you want to survive this war," she said. "These animals stop at nothing. They've killed my family, and probably yours too." She jabbed a finger at my chest. "Don't ever show them mercy, because they sure as hell won't show you any."

I winced in pain as the memories of Dad flitted through my mind. Him lying propped up against the wall, blood seeping from the wound in his chest. Had Victor shown him mercy? Had the guys in the forest shown me mercy? Sam was right: this was war. "All right, I'm in. What's the plan?"

She motioned in the direction of the camp. "You stick with King Harold so you can fix this second glitch. I'll keep shadowing the army, and I'll watch out for anyone who looks out of place. As soon as our jump devices go warm, we just get out of here as quickly as possible."

"All right. Can I ask you something?"

Sam nodded.

"Why didn't you leave this afternoon when you had the chance?"

A faint smile flashed across her face. "I had a hunch you didn't know how to get home. And the idea of you lost in these woods for the rest of history kind of made me feel bad." She raised her hand to cut off any response I might have made. "Not for you, of course, Newbie. I just didn't think it would be fair to punish the Anglo-Saxons."

I couldn't help but smile back at her.

She slung her bow over her shoulder and began to walk into the forest. After a few steps, she glanced back at me. "What are you waiting for?"

"What do you mean?"

She turned to face me, her head tilted to one side. "You have three places to sleep tonight: right there where you're standing, back at Harold's camp where people might want to kill you, or with me at my camp." She put her hands on her hips. "Which one is it going to be?"

No need for a second invitation—I sprinted after her in the darkness. Tomorrow I'd return to King Harold's camp and start seeking out the newest time glitch. One of Victor's men might have trapped us here for now, but it was time for me to stop being the prey and start being the hunter.

CHAPTER 15

Sunlight filtering through the trees woke me.

"I was wondering when you were going to get up." Sam sat cross-legged with her back against a tree, using her fingers to brush the knots out of her wild mane.

I propped myself up on one elbow. "Good morning," I said, wondering how long I could watch her hair shimmer like copper in the sunlight before she caught me staring.

"Morning." She tossed me a heel of bread and a water skin. "How's the shoulder?"

I rotated my arm in a slow, tight circle. "Still bad, but getting better."

She nodded. "Good. So, do you have a plan for today?"

"Not really," I muttered. "I figured I'd go back to camp, find Osmund, then make it up as I go." I sat up and took a bite of the bread. It was dry and stale, but a swig of warm, leathery-tasting water made it edible. I chewed slowly, my eyes fixed on Sam as she drew her hair back and tied it into a ponytail.

"Um. Instead of creepily watching me do my hair, shouldn't you be getting a move on?"

"Oh, right. Sorry." I sprang to my feet and, for the second morning in a row, stood there awkwardly, trying to think of the best way to say bye to her.

She glanced up from her spot at the base of the tree. "See ya." She gave me a small wave.

"See ya," I replied half-heartedly, kind of disappointed at her casual response. Glumly I began the trek through the forest back to King Harold's camp. The first thing I needed to do was find Osmund, but where? Hundreds of peasants and thousands of unarmored warriors were milling around the camp, all now dressed similarly in brown or gray tunics and leggings.

As I walked back and forth through the camp, searching for Osmund, I finally managed to spot his friend Caedmon sitting with two others, eating breakfast beside a fire. "Good morning," I said, nodding hello to everyone. "I'm Leofric. I came here with Osmund. Have you seen him?"

"Nay, Leofric," Caedmon said. "I have not seen him since before the battle."

The other two men shook their heads and stared grimly at the fire.

I fought back a feeling of dread. Osmund had to be okay—I owed him so much. He'd taken me in at the village, trusted me even when he knew I was lying, and guided me through my first battle. When I'd thrown up at the sight of all the death, he'd been the one who helped me settle myself down.

No. He was fine. He had to be. He was probably just wounded and resting someplace with the other wounded men while he regained his strength. I'd see him again and he'd smile at me and tell me everything was all right.

But with or without him, I was still on a mission.

"Maybe you guys can help me," I said. "I'm trying to figure out why those men attacked me the night before the battle. Do you have any idea how I can get more information about them?"

"Find out if they came here with anyone else," one of the peasants replied. "Many villages sent two or even three men when their lords called for aid."

"Aye," said the other man. "The priest should be able to help you. He would have ensured that those two received their last rites and will know who from their villages arranged for them to be returned for burial at their village church."

"Why do you seek to know more of these men?" Caedmon asked. "They are dead. They will have few answers for you now."

"I think they were hired to kill me. I want to know who paid them."

Caedmon's brow furrowed. "A serious charge. Your advice to the king changed our course and brought us success in battle. How would someone gain by silencing you?"

"That's what I want to find out." I thanked the men for their help and set off in search of the priest. It took a while but, by questioning some boys running errands, I finally found him sitting beside a fire, eating a breakfast of roasted sausages and bread. I had expected some kindly looking old man wearing holy robes and maybe clutching a Bible. Far from it. This guy looked too young to be a priest, with greasy brown hair and a dirty tunic. Only the large golden cross around his neck gave me the confidence to push ahead.

"Good morning, uh, Father?" I said. He looked up, still chewing. "Sorry for interrupting your breakfast. I can return later."

"No need," the priest replied, a welcoming smile on his face. "The Lord has time for all men. Come share the warmth of my fire and tell me how I may serve."

I sat down across from him and spread my hands toward the fire. "Do you know what happened to those men who were slain in the forest two nights ago?"

The priest wiped the grease from his mouth with a sleeve. "I presided over their burial yesterday, before we left for the battle."

"They were buried? Didn't anyone from their village claim their bodies?"

"No man mourned them when they took their last rest."

Either these two guys had come alone, or they were such bastards in life that no one cared they'd died. "Did anyone claim their belongings?" I asked.

The smile vanished from the priest's face and his eyes narrowed.

"I don't want their stuff," I said quickly, holding up my hands. "I only want to know what they carried with them, so I can try to figure out why they attacked me."

The priest nodded and took another bite of his sausage. "No one claimed their goods, so I took custody of them in the name of the Church. Each man carried ten silver pennies, but nothing else of worth."

I wasn't a genius when it came to medieval money, but ten silver pennies sounded like a lot of cash for a peasant, so they weren't trying to rob me. And it seemed mighty coincidental that both carried the exact same amount of money. Sam was right: someone had hired them. "Do you know who might have given them that much money?"

"I know not the ways of the Lord." Spreading his arms wide, the priest looked to the sky. "I know only that He brought this wealth to my coffers. How it came to be in those men's purses, I cannot say."

This line of questioning was going nowhere. I thanked the priest for his time and wandered on through the camp, lost in thought. How could I find out who had hired those men? And what had caused the second glitch?

At the sudden thunder of hooves, I looked up to see King Harold and most of his housecarls riding down the road, a huge cloud of dust trailing after them.

What the … ? No!

I had one simple job—follow the king—and I'd let him get away from me.

I needed a horse—fast. But how? I was a peasant. Taking a horse would probably get me whipped for theft. Nope—cancel the horse idea. I needed to figure out where Harold was going and follow on foot.

I dashed around in a panic, trying to find someone who could tell me about King Harold's plans. After a bunch of nonhelpful answers from the first few people I asked, I finally found Caedmon heading toward yesterday's battlefield with a large group of peasants.

"Caedmon," I panted. "Do you know where the king went?"

"He has gone south to Riccall to offer terms to those few remaining Northmen who survived the battle."

I felt like a kid who suddenly realized he'd lost his parents. "Is he coming back?"

Caedmon laughed. "Not to here. After Riccall, he will most likely ride to Eoforwic to let his men rest from their long ride and to heal their wounds."

Good. Eoforwic was only a few hours' walk away; I could reach the city by the time the king returned from Riccall. "And where are you guys going?" I asked Caedmon.

"The king bade for all able men to clean the battlefield," he replied. "You should come with us. Many hands make a large task smaller."

Clean the battlefield? As in, touching dead bodies?

That sounded like the grossest thing ever. I thought about pulling the old "my shoulder hurts" excuse, but sitting in camp alone wouldn't get me any answers. So I grudgingly fell into step with Caedmon and the rest of the peasants and headed for the site of yesterday's carnage.

As we trudged up the hill that overlooked the site of the battle, massive flocks of black-winged ravens and crows circled in the sky, filling the air with their raucous cawing. A sense of unease rippled through me as I glanced up at the flock.

When I crested the rise and the battlefield came into view, it became obvious what had attracted all those birds—breakfast. My stomach instantly did back flips, and once again my barely digested food spewed out across the road.

Movies never show the aftermath of fighting, only the cheering and celebration after victory. I guess that's because only a horror movie could truly depict what a battlefield looks like the next day. Bodies littered the field—pale, lifeless forms lying there as if sleeping. Dew covered them, and missing ears and fingers showed where foxes, wolves, and other animals had come during the night to feast. Each body had at least two or three ravens perched on it, pecking at glassy eyes and cold lips. The birds seemed completely unconcerned about the peasants who ranged through the gore, busy moving bodies and looting corpses under the direction of the various lords and warriors who had remained.

"You there, boy," said a man in a bright blue tunic trimmed in gold. "Start acting like a man and get to work. Pile all the weapons you can find over there." He pointed to a spot on the east side of the river, near the bridge. Other peasants had already started the same job, so a small heap of axes, daggers, swords, and spears lay off to the side.

I wiped my mouth with the back of my hand, and then meekly nodded. "Yes, sir." Gingerly I proceeded down the hill and examined the first corpse I found. Long hair in braids? Check. No armor? Check. Clearly one of the Vikings we had surprised on the west bank. At least ten wounds perforated his body, and the earth around him was dark where his blood had seeped into the ground. His sightless eyes staring at the sky sent goose bumps along my arms. All I could think of was this guy suddenly rising from the dead, seeking revenge for me robbing him.

Come on, Dan, suck it up.

I took a deep breath, yanked his knife from his belt, and then leaped back. The Viking lay there unmoving, like corpses are supposed to do.

I shook my head. *You're an idiot, Dan.*

His spear lay beside him, so I grabbed that too.

One Viking down, only thousands more to go.

I continued gathering weapons from the battlefield, trying hard not to puke again whenever I saw a particularly gruesome wound.

With slow, methodical work, we began stripping the Viking corpses of anything that the king's housecarls and the local warriors hadn't already looted: broken armor, weapons, boots, stray coins—it didn't matter. We even took their clothes, which seemed totally disgusting at first. But I remembered Dad telling me that in medieval times all cloth was handmade, and a simple shirt took hours or sometimes days of work. So even a bloodstained tunic had significant value. Most of the peasants around me wore at least one or two extra pieces of clothing that they clearly hadn't come with and carried a few extra daggers in their belts.

We left the naked Viking corpses where they had fallen. There were just too many of them to bury. Our own dead we pulled aside, with their weapons and armor resting next to them, and arranged them into groups according to which lord had brought them. Those who had fought under the banner of a local lord would be carted off to be buried in the soil of their home churchyard, while any housecarls who had come with the king would be buried here, far from home.

As I went from body to body collecting weapons, I asked everyone I met if they had any information about the two men who had attacked me. Most knew nothing about them, and the rest could only tell me that the men had been rude drunkards who cheated at dice. Whoever sent them after me had chosen wisely: the guys came alone, had poor reputations, and kept to themselves.

I flipped over Viking corpse number sixty-two to get the ax that lay under him, and froze. Osmund lay beside him, his bloodless lips frozen open in a never-ending scream.

I sank to my knees beside his body, my chest feeling hollow. *Why,*

Osmund? Why had this kind, generous old farmer rushed into battle? He could have played it safe and held back. If he had, he'd be alive right now and going home to join his wife and children.

But I already knew why. He was just like my dad—he did what he felt was right, even if it meant meeting his death.

As tears welled up in the corners of my eyes, I wiped my sleeve across my face. I couldn't break down—not now.

I let out a slow breath and moved my hand over Osmund's eyes to shut them. I couldn't bear to have his lifeless eyes staring at me, as if accusing me of living while he died. Then, with my hands under his arms, I dragged his body across the field. My wounded shoulder spasmed with pain, but I didn't stop until I had Osmund off the battlefield with the rest of our dead. As a final touch, I laid the two spears and shields we had brought with us from Torp by his side. His village would know that he died as a warrior, with his spear in hand.

"Thank you, Osmund," I said quietly. "For everything." There was so much more to say, but the words caught in my throat.

I quickly turned and walked away before the pain inside me could come pouring out. I felt like a coward for not bringing his body back to his village and his wife. I had to keep telling myself I was doing the right thing. No matter how much I liked Osmund, I couldn't spend days on a side trip to Torp—my priority was to fix time. Osmund was all about duty and doing the right thing—he would've understood.

I took one last look at him and began heading back to the battlefield. As much as I hated abandoning my friend, I couldn't help him. Hell, I could barely help myself.

CHAPTER 16

The morning sun was just cresting the distant treetops when I headed down to the river to scrub my hands again. No matter how many times I'd washed them after handling all those bodies yesterday, I still felt as if the stench of death clung to them. As I bent over the water, a kid a few years younger than me came up to me, holding a wooden bucket.

"Are you the one who seeks word of the thieves in the forest?" he asked.

"Yeah," I muttered dismissively. After the day I had yesterday, I didn't feel like talking to some nosy kid.

"I saw the men you speak of, three nights past," he said, leaning closer and dropping his voice to a whisper. "I thought nothing of it at the time, but they were digging near our old camp. I think they hid something."

I startled back. "What did you see?"

The boy looked over both shoulders to make sure no one was watching, then leaned even closer. "I woke late at night after hearing a noise from the forest. I feared a bear and sought out the cause, as

I did not wish to raise a false alarm and have my master beat me for cowardice. But no bear was lurking in the woods. Instead, I saw two men digging near a large standing stone. I crept back to the camp, lest they see me, so I know not what they placed into the ground."

"Would you be able to find this place again?" I asked, my excitement level rising.

"My master demands I stay with him, but the stone lies one hundred paces north of the road marker to the east of the old camp. The men were digging on the far side of the rock, and you should be able to see the turned earth where they worked."

"Do you know anything else?"

"No time! I must return with water for my lord, lest he grow angry with me."

The youth then turned away, filled his bucket, and hurried back to camp, his legs moving in an odd, twitchy fashion as he ran up the hill.

"Thank you," I called after him, but he did not turn back.

I rushed back to camp to collect my bag of food. It was a long walk back to our old camp outside the village of Tada, and I wasn't doing that on an empty stomach.

As I gathered my food, I spotted Caedmon again. Like most of the other peasants, he was busy packing his meagre gear, while most of the lords and their followers had already gone. "Are you going home?" I asked.

"Aye. The fight is done, and the lords have no more need of us. I must return to my village so I can harvest the crops. Torp will no doubt need you as well." He cinched his food bundle closed. "I must go now, Leofric, as my wife will be anxious of my return."

I thought of Osmund's poor wife waiting at home for his return, each passing hour an agony. "I found Osmund yesterday," I said, casting my eyes to the ground. "I pulled him away from where he fell and laid him with our dead, but I have to follow the king, so I can't bring his body back to Torp. Can you please do this for me?"

"I shall," Caedmon said sadly. "Osmund was a good man and a good friend. He will be well missed." He clasped my forearm. "Farewell. May good fortune ever guide you on your path."

I gripped his forearm in return. "And good luck to you as well."

Caedmon picked up his food bundle and began heading for the battlefield, shouting for the two other peasants who'd been sitting with him by the fire yesterday to come help him.

I rummaged through my own food bundle and found half a loaf of bread and one leek. Not much of a breakfast, but better than nothing. I wolfed it down and then began jogging along the road to Tada. I passed countless peasants shuffling along under the weight of whatever they managed to loot from the battlefield. Most of them walked in groups, talking and laughing as they went.

My mind drifted to Sam, and for a second I thought of going back to find her so we could walk together. But knowing how much she preferred to stay in the shadows, I guessed walking along a road jam-packed with peasants would be totally out of the question.

By keeping at a steady pace, I dashed through Eoforwic and reached the site of the old camp outside Tada by around noon. King Harold's army had left behind a scar across the earth; the forest would take years to heal from the damage done by the thousands who had camped here. Trees had been hacked down and burned for firewood, plants trampled, and pits dug into the soil for latrines. The old camp had a ghostly quality to it. Only the skittering of squirrels and the calls of birds showed that anything lived here now.

I found the stone road marker and began counting off one hundred paces. What would I find? Had my attackers buried more coins? The body of a third accomplice?

The rock stood exactly where the boy had said it was. I circled it, trying to find a patch of soil that was a different color or looser than the rest. I even swept away leaves and scoured the musty earth underneath. But it looked the same all around.

With a sigh, I dropped my food bag and leaned my back against the stone. I was standing there trying to figure out what to do next when something whistled past my ribs and slammed into the rock behind me.

What the … ?

Next to me on the ground lay the broken pieces of an arrow.

Someone's shooting at me!

I dove to the ground, jarring my wounded shoulder, and rolled away until I was on the other side of the rock. Blood pounded in my veins as I poked my head up, eyes alert for any movement. I tried listening for my attacker, but all I heard was the thunder of my own heartbeat. When would I ever learn? There was no buried mystery here. It was a trap, and I'd been stupid enough to walk right into it. I didn't know what had saved me—dumb luck? Bad aim? A sudden breeze causing the arrow to drift? Didn't matter. That arrow had been meant for my chest and it had missed. And the person who'd shot it was still out there.

Think, Dan! Think!

But there was only one possible course of action.

I sprang to my feet and took off. With great noisy strides I crashed through the brush, trying to put as much distance as possible between me and my unseen attacker. Branches whipped across my face and tore at my arms. Every few paces I dodged to the side, avoiding imaginary arrows whistling through the air. My legs ached with each step, as I'd already jogged for hours to get here. After a few hundred paces, I couldn't push myself to run any farther. I caught a glimpse of a depression next to the roots of a large maple tree, so I fell to the ground and tucked myself in the hole, pulling fallen leaves and branches over me. I kept my head low, with only my eyes peering over the lip of the depression. My hand wrapped itself around the only weapon I could find, a rock about the size of an orange.

The forest seemed deathly silent once my heaving breath finally calmed and my pulse stopped pounding in my ears. A light breeze rattled the branches and stirred the leaves, but nothing else moved.

I lay there frozen with fear. The chill of the ground seeped into my body, magnifying every ache in my muscles and wounded shoulder, but I stayed still. Movement meant death. Only darkness could save me now—but night was still hours away.

A flicker of brown between the trees caught my attention. A figure with a bow in hand flitted silently from tree to tree. I almost leaped up, thinking that somehow Sam had followed me all the way here, but this person was bulkier and shorter. My attacker was hunting me.

I forced myself to slow my breathing even further. The archer stood only fifty paces away. The hood of his riding cloak hid his face in shadow, and thin black gloves covered his hands. This was no simple peasant, and his services could not have been cheap.

The archer crept forward, following my trail of broken branches and scuffed earth. I wasn't much of a tracker, but even I could've followed the trail I'd left in my mad flight. My fingers curled around the rock. The archer would find me, but I wasn't going down without a fight.

With slow steps, he moved along my trail, eyes alert to every sign my passage had left. He came within twenty paces, then stopped, his eyes lifting in my direction. My muscles tensed as I prepared to leap from my hiding spot, but he looked past me and into the forest.

An audible sigh escaped him as he turned away from my hiding spot. "Stupid kid," he muttered to himself. "Probably long gone."

Something about his voice sent a chill through me: definitely male, and definitely not someone I'd spoken to here in medieval England. But why did his voice bother me? I replayed his words in my head, and then it hit me. He'd spoken modern English and his words had come to me without translation from the jump device. This guy wasn't another hired goon—he was a time jumper!

I relaxed my grip on the rock as he walked away, all his attempts at stealth abandoned. I stared at his retreating figure, memorizing everything I could about him. Shorter than me, average weight, male; hooded cloak, gloves, and bow. Not much to go on, but more than I had known this morning.

The afternoon sun slowly crossed the sky as I lay there on the cold forest ground. The old Dan would have jumped up five minutes after the coast seemed clear. But the old Dan had almost died twice because of his stupidity. If I wanted to live to see seventeen, I'd better start showing some caution. For all I knew, the jumper was lying in wait. So I waited right back … and waited … and waited.

As the sun sank below the trees and the shadows lengthened, I finally stirred from my leafy hideout. With every crackle of dried leaves, I expected an arrow to fly at me from out of nowhere, but nothing happened. Grunting, I stretched all the aches from my body, then headed back to the old camp, furtively keeping to the shadows and watching for any sign of attack.

I passed the same standing rock where I had so foolishly stood waiting to be killed. Dad had warned me to trust no one, but I'd gone right ahead and believed every lie that kid had told me. I'd done some pretty dumb things in my life, but walking into that ambush was probably the dumbest. "You've got to be smarter, Dan," I muttered.

Next to the rock lay the arrow that had just missed me. Nothing special, just a hammered steel point with three goose feathers for fletching. Similar to all the other arrows used in battle against the Vikings. So trying to track down my attacker by the type of arrow he used was not going to get me anywhere. Why couldn't I find one decent clue to help me identify this guy?

My stomach growled, reminding me I hadn't eaten since the

morning. I looked around for my food bag, but it was gone, probably taken by the archer.

Damn it.

I had to find Sam. Lifting one tired foot after the other, I began plodding back to last night's camp, avoiding the road and keeping to the trees. This route was slower, but I wouldn't have to worry so much about being ambushed.

The moon was high in the sky and my legs felt as heavy as tree trunks when I finally reached the camp. Not that it felt like camp anymore. No campfires burned. No men laughed or sang. It was completely deserted. I opened my mouth to call Sam's name but stopped myself—the archer who'd shot at me was still out there. Sam might not be the only one who heard my cries.

A hollow ache settled in my chest. Everyone I trusted was gone—I was on my own now. Wearily, I crept along to the section of camp where the peasants had slept last night. I slunk around in the darkness, hoping to find a forgotten loaf of bread or maybe a half-rotten onion. Anything to fill the cavernous hole in my stomach.

Nothing.

Tired, dejected, and hungry, I walked into the forest, found a shallow depression, and buried myself in a bed of leaves. I lay in the dark, surrounded by rotting foliage, my shoulder throbbing and my stomach aching from hunger. I'd always heard the term *rock bottom* but could never really picture it. Now I'd received a crash course. The only good thing was that, now that I'd gotten here, the only way to go was up.

CHAPTER 17

Like a zombie crawling from its grave, I pulled myself out of my cold, leafy bed the next morning. Even though I'd had a miserable sleep, I was now awake enough to know my next step—I had to go to Eoforwic—even without Sam. I couldn't stay alone in the forest anymore; that was just asking to be shot.

I scanned the deserted camp, making sure the coast was clear before I started on my way. Suddenly, a twig snapped behind me.

I rolled sideways, my entire body tensing as I prepared to feel an arrow or a dagger plunged into me.

"Wow, you're jumpy in the morning." Sam stood off to one side, leaning against a tree, a broken twig in her hands and a mischievous smile on her face. Her cloak and tunic blended perfectly with the tree trunks, making her seem like part of the forest.

"Y-y-you're here!" I stammered as I picked myself off the ground and brushed the leaves off my tunic and pants. "How did you find me?"

"Dumb luck." Sam's smile faded. "I expected you to try to find me yesterday. When that didn't happen, I didn't know if I should follow the king or wait here. I decided to give it one more night." She shrugged. "I was just heading to the river when I saw you in the leaves." She tossed the sticks aside. "I thought you could use a wake-up call."

"That was a jerk move, you know, sneaking up on me."

"So was ditching me without telling me where you were going." She gestured toward the empty Anglo-Saxon camp. "So? What happened to you yesterday? How you'd end up lurking here alone?"

I ran through the nightmare list of terrifying and humiliating events from the day before. The more I spoke, the more my voice cracked and my hands shook as I relived each horrible experience. When I was done, I just stood there with my head bowed, feeling completely drained.

For a few seconds we both stood there, not saying a thing, then Sam placed her hands on my shoulders, sending a shiver up the back of my neck at her touch. "Are you going to be all right?" she asked, genuine concern in her green eyes.

I exhaled loudly, trying to focus. Was I going to be okay? Every day here brought another problem beyond my control. My mind and body were reaching the breaking point, and I felt like I might snap at the slightest little thing. But I wasn't about to admit any of that to her.

"I'll survive," I finally answered.

"Good. Then come with me." With barely a sound, she crept off into the brush.

I plunged into the forest after her, thrashing through the bushes and undergrowth as I followed her to her latest camp. Like the previous one, this camp lay hidden from sight, a smokeless fire burning next to a gray wool blanket.

"You can stay here for now," Sam said. "Do you want something to eat?"

I sat down next to the fire and gratefully accepted a leg of roast rabbit while Sam sat cross-legged on the other side of the flames, her bow resting across her lap.

"What do we do now?" I asked between ravenous bites.

"The plan hasn't changed. You still need to shadow King Harold. We have to figure out what the time glitch is, and fix it."

"He should be easy to find. The day after the battle he went to Riccall, so he should be heading for Eoforwic soon. According to history, he stays there a few days."

She shrugged. "I guess that's where you're going, then."

"Didn't you hear what I said happened yesterday? There's an actual time jumper out there who's trying to kill me!"

"I know you're scared," Sam said. "I would be too. But we have to find King Harold if we want to get out of England."

"I have a better idea," I said. "Why don't we just hide out in the woods and let the bastard who tried to kill me fix the time glitch? After all, he's the one who probably messed things up in the first place."

"Is that really what you want to do?" Sam made no attempt to hide her disappointment. "Some guy attacks you twice and you just want to run away and hide? Don't you want revenge—to stand up for yourself?"

Not a single part of me cared about revenge. All I wanted to do was go home and forget everything about Anglo-Saxon England. But I couldn't admit that to her. She was so strong and determined and I'd end up sounding so … weak. "Well, uh, yeah … I guess I want revenge," I lied.

"And what about your dad?" Sam pressed, sensing my hesitation. "Don't you want to fix this time glitch as soon as possible so you can get back and see how he's doing?"

"Yes, of course," I said. "But I also don't want to die."

"I know what it's like to feel scared and powerless," Sam said, an intense sadness in her eyes. "I also know the regret you'll feel if you don't do something about it. Maybe not today, or tomorrow, or even next week. But at some point, you'll wish that you had ignored your fear and fought back." She swallowed hard and her fists clenched. "Trust me."

My shoulders slumped—I already felt that regret every day. How many times had I replayed the moment I'd tossed the statue at Victor's head? If I could just have those few seconds back, I'd do so many things differently.

"All right," I said quietly. "But what do I do about the guy who's trying to kill me?"

"From what you've told me, he only tries stuff when you're alone. So don't be alone, and you'll be all right."

"What about you? What are you going to do?"

"I'll follow behind you and camp in the woods, like I always do. Don't worry; I won't be far off if you need me."

"Uh-uh! No way!" I raised my hands in protest. "You're the one who just told me *not* to be alone! I need you with me to watch my back. And you can't do that while you're hiding in a forest."

Her lips tightened, as did her grip on her bow. "I can't go with you—not to a city." A hunted look appeared in her eyes. "There are too many people there, too few places to hide when things go wrong. All my worst experiences have been in cities."

"But it sounds like a great idea for me to go there by myself? Thanks a lot."

Sam shook her head. "You don't understand. You're a guy. You won't get grabbed or assaulted in the streets by some creep."

"No, just ambushed by archers and hired assassins."

"Fair point," she admitted.

To me, the solution was obvious. "If *you* don't want to go alone, and *I* don't want to go alone, then how about we *both* go to Eoforwic and watch each other's backs?"

She pursed her lips, her eyes revealing a flurry of conflicted thoughts and emotions. Finally she stuck out her gloved hand. "I guess there's no other way," she grumbled. "We're partners."

I knew there was a stupid grin on my face, but I didn't care. I shook her hand. "Deal. Partners."

We began to walk along the road to Eoforwic. It was empty right now, but Sam still kept her bow at the ready, her eyes alert for danger.

"So why do you do all this?" I asked.

"All what?"

"The time-jumping. I mean, if it's so dangerous, why do you keep doing it?"

"Revenge," she said without hesitation. "My mom bailed on our family six years ago, when I was ten, so my dad was stuck looking after me and my brother." A wistful smile played across her lips. "Things weren't easy, money was tight, but Dad always let us know he loved us." Her smile faded and her lips drew taut. "But about three years ago, Dad was murdered, and things started going downhill. My brother, Steven—he was a couple of years older than me—sold the few things Dad owned that were worth anything, and he managed to rent a small place for us. I went to school and worked part-time to help pay the bills, and Steven found a job in a factory." Sam idly plucked at the string of her bow. "It was tough, but Steven kept saying things were going to get better, and it felt like they were. Then he was killed, and my life pretty much ended."

Sam's eyes narrowed and her voice turned bitter. "The day after Steven died, my mother appeared like a vulture. I hadn't seen her in years and suddenly there she was, clearing out Steven's stuff and dragging me off to some hick town in the middle of Virginia. And that's where I've been the past two years, living with my drunk mom and my disgusting pig of a stepdad who can't seem to keep his gross hands away from me." Sam slashed angrily with her bow at a sapling growing near the road. "That's my pathetic story. Everyone and everything I loved is gone, so the only thing driving me now is the dream of revenge against the people who took my happiness away from me."

"I'm sorry." There wasn't much else I could say.

"Don't be sorry—you didn't do it. Besides, you should feel sorry for yourself. You're most likely in the same crap situation now. I know this sounds harsh, but from what you've told me, your dad probably didn't survive."

That stopped me in my tracks. The thought had always been lurking in the back of my mind, but I'd never had the courage to confront it. What *would* happen to me if Dad was dead? There were a few distant relatives on Mom's side whom I'd never met. Would I be stuck with those strangers? Or would I be sent to live in a foster home until I turned eighteen and then dumped out on my own? A lump formed in my throat. Without Dad, I was lost.

"Do you need a minute?" Sam asked.

"No." I began walking again. "Let's go fix history. I need to go home."

CHAPTER 18

After a few hours of walking, the forest and scrub gave way to fields and pastures, and in the distance the defenses of Eoforwic came into view. An old Roman stone wall surrounded the city, with a medieval palisade of sharpened logs filling the gaps where the ancient stonework had crumbled away.

"So, what's our story?" Sam asked.

"Story?"

She looked at me incredulously. "There's no way I'm going into a city full of people without having a full backstory. I don't even have a name right now. People are going to get mighty suspicious when I can't even tell them my name or where I'm from."

"Well … King Harold and his men know me as Leofric, from the village of Torp. You could be my sister … um … Ealdgyth? It's the Anglo-Saxon version of Edith and it's the queen's name, so it's probably pretty popular."

"Edith?" Sam gaped at me in disbelief. "I get the chance to pick my own name, and you think I'd go for Edith? What else do you have?"

I racked my memory for names I knew from movies or video games.

"How about Aelfwyn?" I suggested. "It means joy of the elves. And you like forests, so that's pretty elvish."

"Aelfwyn," Sam said, as if testing the name out. "Beats Edith. Now let me just get dressed for the part." She stopped by the side of the road and smeared a handful of dirt over her face. Then she removed the blanket from her backpack and wrapped it around her torso under her baggy tunic. Finally, she pulled a piece of bark from a tree and chewed it for a few seconds before spitting it out. "So, what do you think?"

"Uh … what the hell?"

Sam's face grew serious. "Camouflage. I'm trying to make myself look as scummy as possible so no one gets any ideas."

Her face was now covered with a thin layer of grime. The blanket made her look significantly heavier, and she had bits of bark stuck to her gums, giving them a diseased look. But she still looked pretty hot to me. "Maybe do something with your hair?" I suggested.

"Right!" Sam's fingers flew through her hair, mussing it up so that it stuck out wildly from her head. "Better?"

"Much better. Adds that touch of crazy you were missing."

"You really know how to flatter a girl, don't you?" She chuckled.

We resumed our walk and joined the large stream of people heading into Eoforwic. A guard in leather armor stood outside the eastern gate—a high stone arch with two massive wooden doors currently open for traffic. He leaned on his spear, waving people through, a bored expression on his face.

"Welcome to Eoforwic, jewel of the north," I said sarcastically as we stepped through the gateway and into the city.

I'd been through the city three times in the last few days, once when riding with King Harold to battle the Vikings, and twice yesterday when I was rushing to Tada and back. In all cases, I'd been too hurried to pay any attention to anything except the animal crap on the streets. Now, with Sam, I could walk at a more leisurely pace and actually take stock of my surroundings. A few stone buildings and towers remained, the legacy of the earlier Roman settlement, but most of the houses were thatch-roofed and timber-framed, like the huts in Torp. People jammed the streets, where farmers tried to sell their harvests while beggars, maimed in Eoforwic's failed defense against Hardrada and Tostig's forces, thrust pleading hands and bowls forward, hoping for coins or food.

As we walked the muddy streets, Sam clung to my side, one hand never leaving the hilt of her sheathed dagger. Her eyes constantly darted around, taking stock of everyone near us, as if expecting an attack at any moment. She wasn't kidding when she said she didn't like cities. She reminded me of a rabbit in a cage, backed into a corner and baring its teeth.

"Everything's going to be okay," I said, happy to be the calm one for once. "We'll just go find King Harold, fix the glitch, and then we can get out of this dump."

"How are you going to find him in all this?" Sam's voice had a touch of panic in it.

"Simple. We ask." I walked over to a beggar sitting in the shadow of a low building and tossed into his bowl one of the few silver coins I might have "accidentally" liberated from a dead Viking when I'd been on battlefield cleanup duty. "Do you know where King Harold is?" I asked.

The beggar's eyes gleamed at the coin. "Thank you, good lord. But I cannot help you. Our noble king is yet to come to Eoforwic. Some of his men came through the gates yesterday, but they were the ones wounded in battle seeking a place to rest."

"Looks like we're stuck waiting for a bit," I muttered to Sam.

She glanced over her shoulders and visibly shuddered. "Well, I'm not hanging out here in the street. I say we just leave this craphole and wait in the woods."

"That's not going to help us keep track of Harold," I said. "We need to be in the city." I turned to the beggar. "Is there anywhere people can find a room for the night?"

The beggar pointed down the street. "There are many new widows in the city after the slaughter at Fulford. A few coins will open any of their doors."

"So, Sam. How about it? Shall we actually sleep under a roof for once?" I jingled the small pouch of coins I'd acquired.

"Fine," Sam muttered. "But I get first choice of bed, or pile of straw, or whatever it is we're going to end up sleeping on."

I thanked the beggar, and then Sam and I spent the next twenty minutes knocking on doors until we found a place to stay. The room was tiny, bare, and reeked of animals, but the straw covering the floor was dry, and the roof didn't look leaky. "You have to admit," I said to Sam. "It's better than sleeping under the stars."

"Not by much." Sam sniffed. "I'll probably end up covered in fleas and rat bites."

"Come on. It's not—"

A long echoing trumpet blast cut off the rest of my response. It was soon followed by another, and then another. Sam and I rushed back into the street, where a horde of people were flowing east toward the city gate.

She chewed her lower lip as her gaze drifted over the mass of townspeople streaming along the narrow streets. "What are the odds this isn't important?" she asked half-heartedly.

"Fat chance," I snorted. "You know it is. Now let's go check it out." I held out my hand to her, fully expecting her to ignore it, but she actually slid her gloved hand into mine, sending a little chill through me.

We followed the throng, keeping well behind them for Sam's sake. They stopped just inside the east gate, peering expectantly through the opening and down the road. Hundreds of armored horsemen approached, two banners—the Fighting Man and the gold dragon of Wessex—flying high above them.

"King Harold's back." I sighed in relief.

Cheers erupted as King Harold rode into Eoforwic. Even though his cloak was dusty from a long ride, he still looked every inch the king. He rode with his back straight and his head held high as he smiled and waved to the townspeople. As soon as he passed our spot, I made a move to follow him.

"Wait!" Sam gripped my arm.

"But he's getting away," I said.

"But he's going to stay in town for a few days, right?"

"Yeah. So?"

"So we can find him again anytime. But right now the entire army is going to march through this gate. We're going to have a chance to look at every *single* person who goes past. What if we can spot the kid who set you up or the guy who attacked you?"

Damn it. I should have thought of that. "We need to move higher up to get a better view," I suggested quickly, to show Sam that she wasn't the only one with good ideas.

She nodded and we went looking for a vantage point. The city wall was already jam-packed with people, so that was out, but another one of my coins bought us a spot on a turnip seller's wagon as well as a few turnips. From this elevation we had a great view of the riders as they entered the city.

"All I can remember about the brat we're looking for is that he's about ten, kind of grubby-looking, and has this weird twitchy way of walking," I told Sam. "And the jumper who tried to kill me is short and about average weight."

"That's all you got?" Sam asked.

"Well, if we're really lucky," I added, "he'll also carry a bow and be dressed in a hooded cloak and wearing gloves."

Sam faked excitement. "Do you think he'll also be carrying a sign that says 'bad guy'?"

I shrugged. "It would help."

The housecarls began riding past our spot, still wearing armor and with their shields strapped to their backs. Many were injured, and almost all of them led extra horses, signifying a housecarl who had fallen in battle. If the archer was in this group, I couldn't spot him. The armor and shields made everyone look bigger and stronger than the little snake who had ambushed me.

A smaller band of mounted warriors followed the housecarls. I'd seen this group in camp before. They were armed like housecarls and fought in the shield wall like housecarls, but they always kept themselves separate. I didn't know what their deal was. Many of them didn't have any visible wounds, and there were very few empty saddles. The crowd began to disperse now that King Harold had passed, no longer interested in the parade of secondary troops, but Sam and I stayed put, studying each of these men carefully. I'd seen so little of the archer that any one of these guys could have been him.

Lastly came the train of wagons carrying everything needed to support an army: extra armor, weapons, food, and tents. Servants rode on the baggage carts or ran alongside on foot, depending on their status within the pecking order. I scanned each cook, armorer, huntsman, royal page, cart driver, and serving boy who passed. "Come on," I muttered. "Where are—"

A twitchy walk caught my eye.

"There!" I said to Sam. "That's the kid!"

She laid her cheek against my shoulder to sight along my outstretched arm. Her face was so close to mine that I found myself completely ignoring the kid and focusing solely on her. The subtle aroma of wood smoke wafting off her hair. The deep green of her eyes. Her full soft lips—so close I could just turn my head and—

"I see him!" Sam yelled, jarring me out of my fantasy. She jumped off the turnip wagon. "What are you still doing up there? Let's follow him!"

I leaped off my perch and together we trailed the baggage wagons as they meandered through the city. Minutes later they crossed the west bridge over the Ouse River and were back outside the city, where they began to make camp.

"All right," Sam said. "The kid's there and the king's in the city. Who do we go for first?"

From a distance I watched the kid begin to unload cargo, surrounded by a bunch of other men. "Let's leave the kid for now," I said. "The last thing I want to do is start questioning him, have him yell 'stranger danger,' and then have a hundred of his buddies in camp start beating on me." I motioned toward Eoforwic. "King Harold should be our main focus. We need to find out what the new glitch is so we can leave."

For the next few days, Sam and I followed King Harold everywhere he went, but we never got anywhere close to him. He was always the guest of some lord, or performing kingly business, or praying at the huge church that towered over the city—basically doing stuff where two peasants would *not* be welcome. As for the kid, I'd spot him occasionally, rushing off with buckets of water in his hands or hay for the horses, and then just as quickly lose him. The streets were so narrow, and so filled with people, that it was easy to lose someone so plain-looking. Both Sam and I were starting to get frustrated at our lack of progress. All we'd managed to do so far was pretty much memorize every street, lane, and alley in Eoforwic—which wasn't really saying much.

We started our fourth day in Eoforwic the same as every other day. Wake up. Find the king. Stalk him like paparazzi waiting for the perfect shot. In the afternoon we ended up across the street from the church, twiddling our thumbs while King Harold and his entourage disappeared inside.

"This is soooooo freakin' boring," I muttered. "I wish you hadn't burned my phone. I had a few decent games on it we could be playing right now."

Sam laughed. "I'm sure you pulling out a phone in the middle of Eoforwic would definitely end any boredom. You'd probably even get an instant meeting with the king ... and the executioner."

"How about thumb-wrestling then?" I suggested. "I spy? Twenty questions? Truth or dare?"

"Yeah right," Sam scoffed. "Truth or dare is one hundred percent *not* happening."

"Come on. I've known you for a week and I can honestly say that I've learned pretty much nothing about you. What part of Virginia are you from? What's your favorite subject in school? What movies do you like? Anything?"

Sam chewed her bottom lip as if struggling whether or not to answer.

"Fine. I'll start," I said. "I live about half an hour outside New York City. I'm homeschooled and have learned so much history and Latin I could probably sue for child abuse. I'll watch pretty much anything except sappy English period dramas. Way too many frilly dresses and stuffy dialogue for my taste." I waved an encouraging hand toward her. "See? That's how easy it is. Your turn."

"You're like an annoying puppy, you know that?" She tried to sound irritated, but I noticed a slight smile on her lips. "Fine. I'll play your game—but only to shut you up. I'm from—" Her head snapped up as the doors to the church opened. King Harold emerged, followed by—if the fur-trimmed cloaks and gold jewelry were any indication—the lords and merchants of the town.

"Sorry," Sam said, without the tiniest hint of sincerity. "Back to work."

The crowd parted for the king as he and his followers descended the church's stone steps and made their way over to a long wooden building directly opposite the church. At one end of this building, two men in chain mail stood guard in front of a pair of ornately carved wooden doors. All afternoon, we'd seen housecarls entering, and loud shouts and laughter rang out every time the doors opened. As the king approached, the guards swung the doors open for him and he strode into the hall, the nobility of Eoforwic trailing behind him.

"And of course, King Harold is off to another dinner with the rich people," I grumbled.

"No. This isn't a normal dinner," Sam said. "Look at the size of this place. It's huge. I think something bigger is going on. You should try to get in there."

She said it like it was the easiest thing in the world, like I could just walk up, flash the guards a smile, and crash whatever private event was going on inside. "You're not serious, are you? I can't just walk in there. Look at me! I'm covered in more dirt than the beggars at the gate."

"Of course I'm serious. We're not going to fix this new glitch by standing outside like a bunch of tourists. You need to be near the king. And what better way to get close to him than a loud party?"

As much as I hated it, she was right. But I wasn't deluding myself about my chances either. I'd already been yelled at, shot at, pushed around, stabbed, and abused by the majority of Anglo-Saxons, so I didn't expect anything different from the two guards at the door. I took a few deep breaths to psych myself up, brushed the road dust off my pants to make myself more presentable, and then strode confidently toward them. *They're just like mall cops*, I kept telling myself. Nothing to be afraid of.

I stopped in front of the guards and pulled myself up to my full height so I could look slightly down at them. The key to dealing with mall cops was to always make them feel unsure of themselves. "I need to talk to King Harold," I said with authority.

"Leave this place," said the guard on the right. "King Harold and his men feast tonight. They must not be bothered by the likes of you."

"You need to let me in," I said. "This is a matter of—"

"Leave, boy!" snarled the guard on the left.

I raised my hands defensively. "All right, all right. I'm going."

I retreated and ducked into the narrow lane nearby where Sam was waiting. "Surprise, surprise," I said. "I failed. I guess we're stuck for now."

"Stuck?" Sam shook her head. "We're not stuck. You only tried the front door. A place this big has to have more than one entrance. We just need to find it."

"Uh-uh. No way. Even if we do find a back door, I can't just walk in and crash the king's feast."

"Of course you can. It'll be loud, dark, and crowded. You'll never get another chance like this." She jabbed her finger toward the hall. "No excuses now. Find a way in there."

It was really difficult arguing with Sam when she always ended up being right. "All right," I grumbled. "I'm going in."

"Be careful," Sam warned. "The rogue jumper is probably in there too."

"Trust me. I haven't forgotten." I scanned the outside of the dining hall. No windows. Guards at the front. My only hope was a back door.

CHAPTER 19

My shoes squished through the mud as I headed to the rear of the building, the smell of roasting meat getting stronger as I went. I counted off eighty paces before I rounded the corner and ran smack into the world's largest barbecue. The people of Eoforwic had set up ten huge fire pits, each with an ox or chickens or a pig roasting on a spit above it. Carts filled with loaves of bread and kegs of ale sat parked near the fire pits. Amid this, servants scurried back and forth, carrying platters of meat and pitchers of ale into the great hall through the rear doors. The area was way too busy; there was no hope of me sneaking in.

Unless …

A serving boy ran to the ale carts with two empty pitchers in each hand and a frazzled look on his face. I stepped out of my hiding spot. "Hey! Do you want some help?"

He barely slowed down. "Yes, fill these pitchers and pour drinks for the tables. I must fetch more bread." He slammed the pitchers on the ale cart and hurried off.

I filled the tin pitchers with ale from large casks on one of the wagons, then strode into the feast hall through the back door. The huge room, packed with long wooden benches and tables, was dimly lit by torches fixed along the walls and a huge central fire pit. In the corner, a pair of musicians strummed lutes, but their efforts were drowned out by the hundreds of men singing and laughing, feasting and drinking. Dogs roamed between the tables, looking for scraps, while servants ran back and forth over the rush-strewn floor, trying desperately to keep plates stocked and ale cups full.

At one end of the room, seated in the middle of a long table facing the rest of the hall, sat King Harold. He had changed from his fighting garb and now wore a burgundy tunic with a collar shot with gold, and over his shoulders was a fur-lined cloak. On both sides of Harold sat the elite of Eoforwic, their proximity to him identifying how much power they had in the city.

I kept my gaze fixed on the floor, not daring to make eye contact with anyone, and hoping to blend into the background. No one seemed to notice me, or if they did, they didn't care as long I kept topping up ale horns and mugs. At each table I quickly scanned everyone's face, searching for the rogue jumper, and I'd listen in on the conversations in the hopes of hearing clues about the new time glitch.

I don't know how long I spent running around tables, but serving those ungrateful, boorish oafs made the battle seem tame by comparison. They yelled at me if I was too slow or didn't pour them enough or spilled any drink. Shouts and the pounding of ale horns filled my ears, and drunken bearded faces were all I saw. No wonder the other servants looked so frazzled. And the worst part was that I still hadn't discovered anything useful.

I had turned to fill another empty cup when a hand snaked out and caught my wrist. "What are you doing, boy?" a gruff voice asked.

Ale sloshed onto the table as I tried to wrench my hand away. But that grip was like a vise. The thick fingers dug into my wrist and wouldn't let go, no matter how hard I tugged.

With my heart pounding, I turned and looked at the man who held me. It was the same one-eyed warrior who had challenged my story to King Harold. His grizzled beard was drenched with ale, but his one blue eye seemed clear as ever. "I—I—I'm serving ale," I stammered.

The warrior gripped even harder, and a whimper escaped my lips. My wrist felt like it was going to snap.

"You speak false," he said. "You pour drinks like a servant, but your eyes and body speak otherwise. You watch. You listen. For what?"

I was one lie away from a broken bone or worse. Not a good time for making up a story on the spot. "I'm trying to find the man who wanted me killed."

The grip on my wrist relaxed slightly. "And you think he is here?"

"I don't know," I said, not hiding my frustration. "My search is going nowhere. I have such a poor description of him that he could be anyone. All I know is that he had lots of money to pass around, that he would've been a fairly new arrival to the army, and that he probably has a mark on his forearm that looks like mine." I pulled back my sleeve to show him.

One-eye grunted as he peered at my tattoo. "How are you called, boy?"

"Leofric."

"I am called Ceolwulf. I have survived great battles, hunted countless foes, and learned a few things in my many winters. The key to defeating an enemy is to truly see him. See his strengths, his weaknesses, and where he is hiding. Look at these men at the tables. What do you see?"

A bunch of drunken, ungrateful slobs who need a bath and a crash course in manners. "I see warriors feasting."

A jolt of pain coursed through my wrist as Ceolwulf squeezed tighter. "Do not tell me what is there. Tell me what you see. Who laughs? Who sings? Who talks with friends, and who drinks alone?"

I turned around and tried to look beyond the frat-boy behavior of King Harold's finest warriors to see something else.

Nothing.

No great insight. No one who stood out. I gritted my teeth in preparation for more pain. "Please don't hurt me, but I don't see anything. Everyone is drinking, talking, and laughing."

"Exactly!" Ceolwulf slammed his hand flat on the table, rattling the cups. "You will not find your quarry here. These men are housecarls. We have fought together for years, and I know each one of them. There are no lone men here, and none who bears the mark you wear."

Ceolwulf was right. The only loner at this feast was me. The stories and boasts these men shared hinted at deep and long friendships. An outsider wouldn't be able to join this group or pretend to be one of them.

My shoulders slumped. I was getting nowhere. "Can I go now?" I asked.

"No," Ceolwulf said. "The king would have words with you."

This could not be good.

"Please," I said. "I didn't mean to sneak into the feast. If you just let me go, I won't bother anyone." What would they do to me? Beatings? Imprisonment?

Still grasping my arm, Ceolwulf stood up and banged his fist repeatedly on the table, bringing a moment of silence to the feast. "My lord!" he shouted. "I have the boy you seek!"

King Harold turned his head my way. He studied me for a moment through bleary eyes, then the light of recognition shone on his face.

"Boy, come here," he commanded as he waved me over.

Ceolwulf released his grip, and for one glorious moment I felt free. But with all eyes on me, I had nowhere to run. King Harold didn't seem angry, so I hoped to escape with only a stern lecture.

Rubbing my wrist, I ran to the head table and knelt on one knee beside the king's chair, bowing my head before him. I didn't know if that was the proper protocol in Anglo-Saxon times for greeting a king, but I figured it wouldn't hurt.

With a belch, King Harold staggered to his feet and clapped a hand on my shoulder. His fingers dug into me as he steadied himself. My body tensed as I waited for my punishment.

"Thanks to your well-timed words, we won a great victory," Harold said, raising his silver tankard toward the assembled warriors. "My worthless brother is dead, and so is that foul fiend Hardrada. My kingdom is now safe." He drained his tankard in one gulp and slammed it on the table to the cheers of those assembled. Letting go of the tankard, he pulled off one of his many gold rings. "I give to you this gift of gold, as my thanks." He placed the ring in my hands, then draped an arm around my shoulder and pulled me to my feet. "Come, you will feast with me and my men tonight." He motioned to the packed benches. "Find yourself a place at the tables and eat and drink to our victory!"

I stood there for a moment, too stunned to speak. I was being rewarded? When I finally got over the shock, I looked around the hall, trying to spot an empty seat. A scene of wild and drunken revelry appeared before me. Some men lay on the ground, sleeping where they had passed out. Others sprawled across tables. The heartier ones sang and drank even more. But only Ceolwulf met my gaze and pointed to the bench right beside him.

Why not? Sure, he had that creepy eye thing going on, and I always felt like he was judging me, but he seemed okay overall. And with him around, no one would mess with me—for tonight, at least.

"Hello again," I said, taking a seat on the hard wooden bench.

He grunted and pushed an ale horn toward me. "Drink, boy."

I took the horn and tipped it to my lips. This stuff smelled vile and tasted a hell of a lot stronger than the stuff I'd had in Torp.

"Bah! You drink like a woman." He grabbed his own ale horn and tilted it back, gulping noisily as he drained it. "That is how you drink!"

What now? Should I congratulate him on his fantastic capacity for crappy beer? He surprised me, though, by clapping me on the back. "I owe you a debt. Your counsel to the king has made me rich with plunder." He pulled a small leather pouch from under his tunic. Plunking it on the table, he counted out a small stack of silver coins. "I give these to you as my thanks."

The coins glittered in the torchlight—undoubtedly the biggest tip I was ever going to receive as a waiter.

"Aethelraed." Ceolwulf elbowed the man slumped face down next to him. "Wake up. This is the boy who brought us victory."

Aethelraed raised his head, blinked a few times, then peered at me through red-rimmed eyes. With a humongous belch, he staggered to his feet, slid a thick silver ring off his finger, and slammed it on the table in front of me, next to the pile of coins. "Come on, you drunken bastards!" he shouted to the rest of the hall. "Show the boy your thanks."

His words started a deluge of offerings. Men rose from their benches, staggered over, clapped me on the back, thanked me for victory, and then presented me with offerings of silver and bronze rings, coins, and armbands. I could only sit there dumbfounded as a small fortune built up in front of me. A few times I tried to mumble thanks, but for the most part the warriors just ignored me and went back to their feasting.

Ceolwulf lifted the cloak off a sleeping warrior and dumped my treasure into it. "Keep this safe. You are a wealthy man now." He tied the cloak into a bundle and tossed it at my feet. The clinking thud as it hit the floor was the most satisfying sound I'd ever heard. Instantly, thoughts of vacations, a motorcycle, a big house, and a huge TV flashed through my mind. With this fortune I could buy tons of stuff. The only tough part would be getting it all back home.

Dad must have seen countless treasures during his time jumps, so how did he get any of them back home? Did the jump device let him bring back things from the past, or did he bury the treasure near some long-standing landmark and then, when he got back to our time, dig them up?

Then it hit me. This was *Dad*—he would never have tried to profit from his time-jumping. Sure, we had the odd vase or tapestry hanging around the house, but he'd never sell those. Any money we had was earned from his book sales or university work. He did everything in his life with honor, and he'd be horrified to know that as soon as I got a few coins from history, my first thought was how to profit from it.

With my toe I nudged the bag and listened to the sound of coins clinking together. It sucked, but I knew I would have to give away the biggest fortune of my life. It was the right thing to do—the path Dad would want me to take—but that didn't make it easier. As I sat there brooding, another thought struck me. What if the rogue jumpers weren't so honorable? What if they were continually robbing history on their time jumps? That would make tons of sense, and it would explain why Dad was against them.

Ceolwulf emptied his ale horn and wiped the froth from his beard with the back of his hand. "So," he said, interrupting my train of thought. "What will you do with all your coin?"

I was about to answer when a flicker of movement caught my eye. A man dressed in a mud-stained riding cloak and gasping for breath pushed past the drunken men around the king's table and knelt in front of King Harold. "My lord," he announced, "I bring dire tidings from the south."

Men quieted as the messenger's words spread through the hall. King Harold stood up, his face pale and his eyes wide. "Out with it, man! What word do you bring?"

"What we have most feared has now happened. Duke William has brought his fleet across the South Sea from Normandy and has landed at Pevensey. He brings with him a great number of men to press his claim for the crown."

King Harold slammed his tankard on the table. "Will I never know peace? First my brother, now this?" He pounded his tankard on the table until every man in the feast hall was wide awake and staring at him. "Men!" he shouted. "Our time of celebration is at an end. I need your arms once more. You fought well against Tostig and his vile Northmen allies, but the war is not over. We must make haste to Pevensey and fight Duke William and his foul army of Norman invaders. Tomorrow, at dawn, we leave."

A few groans rose from the ranks, but for the most part the men remained quiet, many staring glumly into their mugs and ale horns. They had raced hundreds of miles north to defeat the Vikings; now they had to run back south to fight again.

I jerked upright, nearly knocking over my ale horn. King Harold was leaving tomorrow. How could Sam and I fix the time glitch when he was riding halfway across the country and we were stuck in Eoforwic? I swung my head around frantically, trying to get some spark of genius.

Come on … Come on … Think of something.

Ceolwulf said something, but I didn't catch it. "What?" I asked.

"Will you come south with us?" he repeated.

"I can't. I don't have a horse, or food, or weapons, or … or … anything!" I tossed my hands up into the air in frustration.

Underneath Ceolwulf's grizzled beard I could have sworn a smile peeked out. "Have you forgotten already? You have wealth now. That buys what you need."

A spark of hope ignited within my chest. "I have a sister also— Aelfwyn. Do I have enough to buy her a horse too?"

"You would bring your sister with us? Is that wise?" Ceolwulf practically recoiled in his seat. "No harm would come to her from a housecarl, but there are many other men who ride with us, and they might view her with less than honorable thoughts."

"I know," I said. "But I can't leave her here—she needs to come with me. So do I have enough coin for two horses?"

Ceolwulf eyed my bag full of coins. "Aye, you have enough."

"And armor?"

"Would you fight?" A smirk creased his lips. "Did the slaughter at the ford not sate your appetite for death?"

"Fight? Hell no! I just want protection. I've already been attacked twice."

"If it is protection that you wish, perhaps I can be of help. My son was ill with fever and could not ride with me when King Harold summoned us. I am an old man. I grow weary of setting up my own tent, fetching water, and chopping wood. Those are tasks for younger hands. You and your sister can be those hands. In return, I will do my best to keep you safe. What say you?"

This was a no-brainer. I thrust out my hand. "Deal."

Ceolwulf clasped my outstretched forearm. "Welcome to my service. May you not rue your decision."

I wasn't the slightest bit worried about fetching water or setting up a tent for Ceolwulf every night. What really had me stressing out was the coming clash between Duke William and King Harold—it was long and bloody, and it had to be the source of the next time glitch. And even though I'd signed on as a servant, I had this deep, nagging feeling that I wouldn't be able to avoid battle twice in a row. But if I ever wanted to see my home and Dad again, I'd have to follow King Harold, no matter where the path led.

CHAPTER 20

"Leofric!" A foot nudged me in the ribs. "Wake up!"

I opened my eyes to see Ceolwulf standing over me, looking none the worse for his night of drinking. In the feast hall, servants were rushing about while housecarls dragged themselves off the floors and tables.

"The army leaves soon," Ceolwulf urged. "And we still must buy horses if you and your sister are to ride with us."

I sprang to my feet and followed Ceolwulf outside, where the sun was just beginning to rise. Despite the early hour, the streets were busy. Men and boys packed up gear and saddled horses, while carters stocked their wagons full of goods for the journey south. "Where are the stables?" I asked.

"Stables?" Ceolwulf snorted. "We have no need for the plow beasts and cart horses that you will find in Eoforwic. We will find you a mount suitable for the long ride ahead." With purposeful strides, he led me along the twisting city streets, across the bridge over the Ouse, and through the western gate of the city. We ended up in the wide plain outside Eoforwic where the supply carts had camped for the last few days and the army was now gathering. Ignoring the tumult all around us, Ceolwulf stopped at a cart filled with weapons leftover from the Viking slaughter. He picked up and tossed aside a few different blades, then chose a seax—an Anglo-Saxon war knife—and a long-handled ax.

"Take these." He passed me the two weapons.

From the long line of tethered horses, he used my stash of coins to purchase two strong mounts whose owners hadn't made it back from the Battle of Stamford Bridge

"Do you need to find a boy to saddle the horses for you?" Ceolwulf asked.

"No. I got it," I said. "I've been riding since I was old enough to not fall off."

"Good. Then make haste. We leave soon," Ceolwulf called over his shoulder as he strode toward the rest of the housecarls. "If we leave without you and your sister, follow when you can."

"I will."

I quickly saddled both horses and then rode frantically along the muddy lanes of Eoforwic, back to the little hut where Sam and I had rented a room. Breathlessly, I tethered the horses out front and then rushed toward the rear of the place. Sam was sitting just outside the door of our room, bow in hand, looking despondent. She leaped up as soon as she saw me. "What happened to you?" It was more accusation than question.

"So much has happened since last night," I panted. "I'll fill you in later. The important thing is that the army is leaving right now. I got us both horses and jobs as servants."

I had expected a thank-you, or maybe a *Wow, Dan, you're so smart.* I got neither.

"Jobs with the army? Are you kidding?" Sam exclaimed, her eyes wide. "Armies are even worse than cities. Nothing but bloodthirsty, drunken, armed men."

"So what? You want to stay here? King Harold and his entire army are heading south—now! If we want to fix this time glitch, we need to go with them."

Sam crossed her arms over her chest. "You said you got me a horse. So *you* can join the army and play at being a servant. I can ride my own horse and follow you at a distance and camp in the woods at night. Just like I've been doing."

"But how are we going to watch each other's backs that way? I need you with me."

Sam rolled her eyes and shook her head. "Do you *ever* think? The rogue jumper already knows who you are. If I start hanging out with you, he'll be after me too." She jabbed at herself with her thumb. "We'll both become targets."

"Oh …" Why was she always right? I had to think of a way to keep her out of danger but still have her around to back me up. I remembered Ceolwulf's words from last night. "I got an idea that should work for both of us!"

Sam's eyes narrowed as she waited for me to spill it.

"As servants, we're supposed to ride way in the back of the army with the rest of the nonfighters. But the guy we'll be serving, Ceolwulf, didn't like the idea of you being with them. He'll probably let you ride up ahead with him for protection. Think about it. We'd be close enough to watch out for each other, but far enough away so no one knows we're together."

Sam's back stiffened. "Nope. Not happening."

"I get it—it's tough to trust anyone around here. But Ceolwulf is one of the king's most honorable warriors. He'll keep you safe."

"You met this guy yesterday," Sam scoffed. "How can you be sure he's so *honorable*? Deep down, all men are the same."

"*Please*, Sam," I begged. "I wouldn't ask you to do this if I hadn't almost died twice already. Trust me on this one. Ceolwulf *will* protect you."

Sam's lips pressed together, and for a few seconds she didn't say anything. "All right," she finally sighed, though she didn't sound one bit pleased. "But I'm warning you now"—she jabbed a finger at me—"if I get even the slightest bit creeped out by this guy or anyone else, I'm going back to my first plan of hiding in the forest."

"No problem." I motioned toward the street, where our horses waited. "Can we get going now?"

Sam took one last look at the quiet little yard and then exhaled loudly. "Fine."

We collected our gear from our room and retraced my meandering route through the streets of Eoforwic until we passed through the west gate. King Harold's army had already broken camp and was now a dust cloud in the distance. "So how do I find this Ceolwulf guy?" Sam asked.

"Look for an older guy with a long gray beard and a huge scar across his left eye. He'll be riding near the front. Tell him that you're Leofric's sister."

"I guess I'll see you tonight when the army stops to camp." She gathered the reins in her hands, ready to ride off.

"Wait. The kid who set me up will be traveling with the rest of the servants. When do you think I should confront him?"

"Tonight. Watch where he sleeps. If he's alone, grab him—but make sure he doesn't yell."

She explained it so simply, like I'd be ordering sandwiches at a deli. "And if he does?"

She didn't answer; she just nudged her horse forward, leaving me in her wake as she rode off to find Ceolwulf. I watched her leave, annoyed that she hadn't answered my question. We were talking kidnapping here, something completely out of my league. Although, to be fair, why would Sam know any more about it than I would?

I gave her a good head start before I set off, knowing that we couldn't show up together. When I eventually caught up with the army, I found myself a place among the rest of the servants, just ahead of the baggage wagons. For the rest of the day, I mostly stared at the back of the guy riding in front of me. There wasn't much else to do. On one occasion, when my horse crested a rise, I caught sight of Sam in the distance, riding between Ceolwulf and Aethelraed. I could tell by the way she tossed her head back that she was laughing. I smiled. She was safe.

After the sun had set and the road became too dark to see where we were heading, we made camp by torchlight. In my new role of servant, I had to unpack Ceolwulf's gear, unsaddle and feed all our horses, get firewood and water, and set up his tent. Sam had it easy; all she had to do was throw a slab of salted pork over the fire and let it roast for a bit.

I ate in silence, too tired after the long ride to talk. Even if I felt like talking, Ceolwulf and Sam never shut up long enough for me to get a word in. Those two seemed to be having a great time together.

After I finished my meal, I lay down to get some rest. Anticipation of the task that lay ahead of me made it impossible to sleep, but with my blanket pulled over my head I was at least able to block out some of the laughter coming from my dinner companions.

I lay there for hours, listening to the activity in the camp wind down. When I finally sat up, everyone was asleep, and the only light came from the red coals of waning fires. I tiptoed past the sleeping men, heading for the eastern end of camp, where I'd seen the kid lay his blanket down after setting up his master's tent.

Slowly I crept past all the sleeping men, my head turning from side to side constantly to see if I was being watched. My nerves were so tense that I nearly leaped into a tree when a coal popped in one of the dying fires.

After a seeming eternity, I found the kid, curled up in a blanket and fast asleep. In the dim moonlight he looked quiet and peaceful. Was he really a bad kid? I was about to find out. With one last look around, I drew my knife, crouched, and clapped a hand over his mouth.

"Don't say a word," I hissed, my voice sounding loud in the stillness of the night.

The kid's eyes popped open, and he struggled against my hand. But a wave of my blade in front of his face quieted him down.

"We're going for a walk," I said. "If you make any noise, I'll kill you." I hoped he believed it because I sure didn't. I needed to act tough, though, if I wanted answers.

The boy nodded and I motioned for him to get up. We crept through the camp until we were a few hundred steps along the road. There, I pushed him against a tree and waved the blade again in his face. Time for years of watching police shows to come into action.

"Do you know who I am?" I asked.

The boy nodded.

"Do you know why I have my knife at your throat?"

The boy shook his head, and in the moonlight, the glint of tears shone in his eyes. That wasn't fair. In cop shows, the suspect always buckles under pressure and confesses. This kid obviously had no idea what was going on. I needed to change tactics. Time for the good-cop routine.

"Look, I don't want to hurt you. I just want answers. Was that story of yours about seeing those two men back at the old camp true?"

"N-no, my lord," the boy stammered.

"Then who told you that story?"

"The warrior I serve sent me."

"And how do I find him? What does he look like?"

The boy's lip quivered, and a tear tracked down his dirty cheek. "My master sleeps in a tent near the edge of camp. He has black hair and is very tall. He carries a sword instead of an ax or spear. Some call him the Ox."

I nodded. I knew the guy he meant. Not many people had black hair in Anglo-Saxon times. And the sword was a huge giveaway. Almost every warrior in Harold's army preferred long-handled axes or spears.

Only problem was that this guy was way too big to be my attacker. "Are you telling me the truth?"

The kid dropped to his knees and bowed his head. "Please, my lord, I tell the truth. My master told me the tale I should tell you. He said I would be beaten if I did not do as he commanded."

Either this kid was the world's best liar or there were two guys involved: one to set it up and one to take shots at me. Great, *another* guy who wanted to kill me. Maybe it would be easier if I just tried to figure out who *didn't* want me dead.

The kid had given me the information I needed; I had just one more thing to check.

"Take off your tunic and show me your arm," I said.

With unsteady hands the boy pulled his tunic over his head, revealing a scrawny white chest that heaved in fear. No tattoo on his arm, and no jump device tucked into the waist of his pants. He was just a kid from this time period who had gotten dragged into a bad situation.

"Put your tunic on and go back to camp," I instructed. "Never tell your master what happened here. Can I trust you?"

The relief on his face gave me my answer, but he still added, "Yes, my lord, I will tell no one."

I took a few silver coins from my pouch and placed them in his hand. He closed his fist and ran, not once turning back.

To my surprise, Sam emerged from behind a tree and came toward me, seeming to almost glide out of the night. "He told you what you wanted to know?"

"I thought you'd be sleeping," I said. "After all, it must have tired you out, laughing and chatting with Ceolwulf all day long."

"Don't be like that." She leveled a flat stare at me. "I still have your back. We just need to be careful. Did the kid tell you anything useful?"

"Yeah, he told me who paid him to lead me into the trap. It's the huge guy with the black hair. Getting to him will be tough, though; he's always surrounded by other warriors. And there's something else—he's too big to be the guy who attacked me with the bow. So we're probably dealing with another rogue jumper."

"Damn it!" Sam kicked at a rock lying in the road and sent it skittering into the forest. "Bad news just follows you everywhere, doesn't it?"

"Any ideas?"

Sam sighed and looked back to the camp. "We'll need to set a trap."

I snorted. "I'm pretty good at walking into traps, but I have no clue how to set one."

"We'll think of something. We just need to watch and wait for our opportunity."

Sam went back to camp first, leaving me alone in the darkness. My thoughts kept drifting back to what Ceolwulf had told me on the night of the feast: that he knew all the housecarls, and that none of them would try to attack me. But, if that was true, why had one of them set a trap for me? Was Ceolwulf wrong? Or was he in on it too?

CHAPTER 21

After a fitful sleep haunted by dreams of rogue jumpers and a treacherous Ceolwulf, I woke to see Ceolwulf standing next to the fire, eating a bowl of porridge. He must have stoked the fire himself, since I'd shirked my servant duties by sleeping through them. Sam was nowhere to be seen, probably cleaning out the porridge pot.

"Good morning, Leofric," Ceolwulf said. "You slept poorly last night—constantly turning."

I tossed aside my blanket, got up, and stretched the kinks out. "That's because I found out who tried to kill me," I replied nonchalantly while watching for his reaction. "He's a housecarl."

Ceolwulf snorted and waved his spoon at me. "Which man do you name a traitor?"

"The tall one with the black hair and the sword. His serving boy said he's called the Ox."

"This is what I have to say about your Ox." A long stream of spit left Ceolwulf's lips and hissed into the flames. "He is no housecarl. He is a sell-sword who joined our army as we hurried north. There are many others of his ilk riding with us—foul dogs with no honor who fight only for coin."

Yes!

A wave of relief flooded over me. Ceolwulf wasn't in league with the jumper. But that still left me the problem of a giant warrior who clearly wanted me dead—not to mention his partner. "So what should I do?"

"Kill him," Ceolwulf said matter-of-factly.

"What? I can't just go up and kill a guy. I'm not a murderer."

Ceolwulf shrugged. "That is the only way to end his threat."

"But ... but ... isn't that against the law? Wouldn't I be in trouble with the king or the housecarls?"

"Challenge him to fair combat. Then no man can fault you if he dies."

"Uh-uh. No way. He's like three times my size. And my shoulder isn't fully healed yet. I can't beat him in a fair fight."

"Not all fights need to be fair. If he has dealt with you treacherously, then perhaps you can return his ill favor." Ceolwulf raised an eyebrow. "Would that fiery maiden whom you long for be willing to fight with you?"

"I don't *long* for her. She's my sis—"

Ceolwulf's backhand caught me across the face. My cheek burned as I blinked in shock.

"Do not tell me lies!" His nostrils flared with rage. "No man looks at his sister like that." He raised his hand to his shoulder. "Do you still claim she is of your blood?"

"No," I mumbled.

"And you are no peasant. Your hands have never worked in the fields." Before I could react, he grabbed my wrist and turned my hand over to examine the palm. "In truth, it looks like you have never done any hard work. No, you are no peasant, and she is not your sister. And if you lie to me again, you will taste more than the back of my hand.

So I ask you again, would the flame-haired wench fight with you?"

"Yes." I didn't dare lie to him.

"She is the mysterious hunter who killed those two men outside Tada?" He stated this more than asked it.

"Yes."

"Good." A broad grin spread across his face. "Then I think I have a plan for you."

The sun was a few hours past its highest point when Ceolwulf came riding along the side of the road, heading in the opposite direction from the huge convoy of riders and wagons streaming south. He slowed his horse as he neared the servant section where I was riding. We were near the tail end of the column of troops, just after the mercenaries and in front of all the wagons. With a stormy look on his face, he scanned each of my fellow riders until his eye lit on me "Boy!" he yelled. "Where is my spear?"

I hung my head as I reined in my horse next to his. "I left it at the last camp."

"What?" Ceolwulf yelled, even louder than before. "Your job was to sharpen it, not leave it behind! What sort of fool do I have in my service? Go back and fetch it!"

"But that's half a day's ride," I whined. "We took lots of other spears from the Northmen. Can't you just use one of those?"

Ceolwulf leaned forward in his saddle and for the second time today backhanded me. "Do not dare talk back to me," he snarled. "The issue is not the spear. The issue is your lack of memory. Now go fetch my spear so that next time maybe you will not forget it!"

Without another word, I turned my horse around and began to head back the way we had come, the laughs and jeers of the other servants ringing in my ears as I rode past.

I traveled for about five minutes until the path swerved and disappeared behind some trees ahead of me. About a hundred paces after this curve, Sam stepped out of the forest and motioned me over. I reined in next to her and leaped off my horse.

"One end of the rope is already tied to a tree." She pointed to a coil of thick hemp rope lying on the road. "I'm going to take my position over there." She took the reins of my horse and led it off into the forest.

I nodded and dragged the rope across the road, then covered it with a thin layer of dirt and dust to hide it as much as possible. When I was satisfied that it wouldn't be instantly visible to anyone coming down the road, I found a tree with a branch hanging at about the height of a horse's ears, then tossed the end of the rope over the branch and pulled it behind the trunk.

With my heart pounding in my ears, I stood behind the tree trunk, watching and waiting. Would this plan work? It hinged entirely on the rogue jumper actually hearing my phony altercation with Ceolwulf and then choosing to follow me. But what if he somehow missed our little scene? Or what if he'd noticed Sam sneak away earlier and had us figured out?

The rhythmic thump of hooves on the road interrupted my panicked thoughts. Around the bend, and through the trees, the black-haired mercenary was riding hard.

He'd taken the bait! My hands grew slick with sweat as I held the loose end of the rope and prepared to spring the trap.

Closer.

The horse was almost around the corner when, with a grunt, I yanked hard on the rope. It sprang up from the road, leveling out at the height of the branch. Quickly I threw a loop of rope around the tree trunk as an anchor and held on to it with all my strength.

The Ox ducked to one side to avoid the rope, but a split second too late. The rope caught him high in the chest, almost at neck-height, and his body flew backward from the impact, sending him tumbling out of the saddle and crashing onto the road while his horse continued without him.

I rushed forward, my ax raised high.

Before I could cover the space between us, the fake mercenary jumped to his feet, pulled the shield off his back, and whipped out his sword, each movement punctuated by the rustling of the chain mail under his riding cloak.

"Pretty smart, boy," he growled in English. "Not good enough, though." He grinned as he raised his sword into high guard.

The grin turned into a grimace as an arrow embedded itself in the back of his thigh, just below where the armor ended. He grunted and stumbled but recovered quickly. "Two of you?" He shifted position so the large shield would protect him from any more arrows from that direction, then advanced toward me.

"Surrender!" I yelled. "We got you outnumbered!"

He gritted his teeth in pain but kept his sword and shield ready. "Tell your archer friend to come out where I can see him, then I'll think about it."

Think about it? What the hell?

This wasn't going at all like planned. He was supposed to see he was outnumbered, surrender, give up his weapons and jump device, and then start answering a ton of questions. After that, the plan got a little hazy. Ceolwulf and Sam were both on the kill-him-and-dump-his-body-in-the-woods side of things, while I was open to pretty much anything else. One thing I hadn't prepared for was for him to *think about it*. "Sam," I called out. "Come out where he can see you."

Sam stepped out from the forest, her bowstring pulled back to her cheek, and an arrow nocked and trained on the mercenary.

His eyes narrowed to slits and he gave me and Sam each a cold, calculating look, as if weighing his options. "All right," he finally said, "you got me. I'll surrender. Now what?"

"Throw down your sword."

He flung his weapon aside so it clattered on the earth-covered cobbles.

"Where's your jump device?" Sam yelled.

The Ox whipped his head around and a smirk crossed his lips. "A girl? This is too funny. If you guys are resorting to using girls, then we've pretty much won."

"Pull out your jump rod and toss it in front of you," Sam ordered. "Dan, if he starts saying anything that doesn't sound like English, kill him. Got it?"

"Got it," I said, although my hands trembled at the thought.

The mercenary reached with his right hand into his left sleeve and fiddled around for a few seconds. He then pulled out a gleaming hexagonal rod, just like mine. "Here you go, cowboy," he said as he tossed it toward me.

My eyes followed the glittering arc of the rod as it traveled high through the air. It looked like it was going to fly over my head, so I reached up with my free hand to catch it.

At that instant, the rogue jumper leaped across the space between us. It took me a split second to figure out what he was doing—and another split second to react. Too late. The edge of his shield slammed into my face, knocking me off my feet.

Blood spewed from my nose, and I tried to blink away tears. A shock hit my ribs as he knelt over me, one knee planted on each side of my body. The edge of his shield slammed into my chest and the breath whooshed out of me. Through bleary eyes, I saw a knife glint in his right hand, plunging toward me. Without thinking, I raised my bad arm to block his strike, only succeeding because sheer terror gave me a momentary burst of strength. With my good hand, I tried to push his wrist aside.

His shield resounded with the thump of an arrow hitting it, but he ignored Sam's attack and leaned into the knife. My arms slowly buckled under the increasing strain, and the knife inched toward my face.

He was too strong. I was going to die.

With my weaker hand, I reached for his leg, trying to topple him before his knife plunged into me. My hand caught on something sticking out of his thigh. The arrow! I jammed the shaft deeper into his leg. He bellowed with pain and for a moment his knife faltered.

That was all I needed.

I wrenched the arrow out of his leg and, grasping it in the middle like a knife, stabbed at his chest. His chain links deflected the first blow, so I just kept jabbing away frantically. He gritted his teeth and pushed down again with the knife, putting all his strength into it. There was no way I could hold him back this time. I stabbed higher with the arrow, hoping to miss the chain mail. The steel point of the arrow slashed him sideways across the throat, slicing it open.

His eyes went frantic as his blood spewed over me, covering my face in a warm torrent of metallic-tasting death. For a second, his knife still hovered shakily over my face and then, without a sound, he tumbled sideways off me.

A patter of feet came rushing down the road and Sam knelt beside me. "How bad are you hurt?"

My shoulder ached, my face felt like it had been used for batting practice, and my ribs weren't much better. "I think most of this blood is his," I wheezed as I kicked my legs out from under the corpse and spat the foul taste of the mercenary's blood from my mouth.

"We need to get you cleaned up so we can see where you're bleeding." Her green eyes were filled with fear, and she chewed her lip in concern, showing her perfect teeth.

"You're beautiful," I mumbled.

Sam rolled her eyes. "You're delirious. Now shut up and sit still for a second." She pulled out her water skin and poured some over my face, wiping away the blood with her scarf. "Your lip is busted and your nose is probably broken. How's your chest?"

"Sore."

"Can you take a deep breath?"

Unsteadily, I pulled myself up and inhaled through my mouth like I was at the doctor's office. My ribs ached, but I didn't think they were broken. "I'll live."

With the toe of her boot she prodded the lifeless form of the rogue jumper. "I'm so sorry," she said. "My first shot missed and my second one hit his shield. I was so worried about hitting you that my aim was off. You could have died because of me."

I clasped her hand. "It's all right. He didn't get me." I don't know if I said that for her sake or for mine. The battle replayed itself vividly in my head. Another second and I would've been dead—and for what? Why was someone trying to kill me? What was the point of it all?

I glanced at the bloody arrow still in my other hand and threw it away in disgust.

Sam must have sensed the way my thoughts were going. "You had to kill him. You'd be dead otherwise."

Her words did little to comfort me. I wasn't a killer. I didn't even like violent video games, but I had just taken someone's life.

"I remember my first kill," she continued. "It's not a normal instinct to kill another person. I was lost in a haze for days, wondering if I did the right thing." She pulled her hand away from mine, gripped my shoulders, and looked me straight in the eye. "I'm telling you now: you did the right thing. He wouldn't have stopped until you were dead. Okay?"

"Okay," I said without much conviction.

"Good. Now help me move his body off the road." Without waiting for an answer, she began dragging the rogue jumper by his legs toward the ditch.

I watched her struggle with the corpse of the man I had just killed. Did he have a family? Would people back home wonder what happened to him? His blood still dripped off my hands onto the dirt, each droplet another reminder of the life I'd taken.

"Dan, snap out of it!"

With my body on autopilot, I helped her pull the body into the forest, where we stripped it of its armor and coins, and left it buried under a pile of leaves.

CHAPTER 22

B ack on the road, Sam handed me the sword and the bloodied armor. "Take these—they might keep you alive someday."

I looked at the bloodstained neck of the mail shirt. How could I ever wear that thing? It would be a constant reminder of the man I'd killed. I took them anyway, if only to keep Sam from pestering me. We cleaned up the rest of the crime scene, removing the rope, pocketing the jump rod, kicking dirt over the bloodstains, and recovering our horses. Then we began the ride back to catch up with Harold's army.

What would Harold and his warriors say when they found out I had lured a man into a trap, killed him, and then stolen his stuff? In the modern world, I'd get life in prison. Sweat slicked my palms and back, and my fear increased with every step our horses took. I couldn't go back; I had to run. But if I did run, I was stuck forever in this time period. Either way I was doomed. Why had I killed that guy?

"Time to stop, Dan," Sam said, interrupting my panic attack. Without waiting for me, she pulled her horse off the road and led it through the brush until she reached a clearing on the bank of a slow-moving river.

I followed in a daze while she tied her horse to a tree, then gathered up some dried pine needles and some strips of thin birch bark. A few sparks from her tinderbox coaxed out a small flame.

"Do we have time for this?" I asked.

"We do," she said as she added a handful of dry twigs to the tiny fire. The flames licked at the wood, and soon, with the addition of a few fallen branches, a decent fire blazed. She then strung the rope we had used to ambush the mercenary from tree to tree, at shoulder height, so it circled the fire.

I dismounted, tied my horse next to Sam's, and left her to whatever she was doing, choosing instead to sit on a log at the edge of the shore. My gaze drifted out across the water as the fight replayed over and over in my mind. Could I have done anything different? Did it have to end with his death? With blood-caked hands, I stirred the earth with my sword—the dead man's sword. If only I hadn't been so close to him, he wouldn't have tried to attack. And if I hadn't fallen for his diversion, I would've been better prepared for his charge. So many stupid mistakes.

Leaning forward, I looked at my reflection in the water. A vision of horror confronted me. Blood matted my hair, bruises surrounded my eyes, and my nose and cheeks were swollen.

Ripples ran through my mirror. I looked up to see Sam, still dressed in her tunic and pants, walking into the river. She stepped in until the water was waist-deep and then dove under, only to break the surface seconds later. She stood up, tilted her head back, and smoothed her soaking-wet hair.

"Um, what are you doing?" I asked.

With a smile, Sam crouched until only her head was above the dark surface. She reached underwater with both hands and pulled her tunic up over her head. I caught a glimpse of pale freckled shoulders before she ducked down to neck-depth again. "Laundry," she explained. "You might enjoy looking like a mugging victim and smelling like a bear, but I haven't had a bath in days, and my clothes stink."

With loud splashing noises, Sam kneaded and scrubbed at her tunic. After a minute or two, she wrung it dry and tossed it across to me. Her aim was good, of course, and the wad of laundry landed with a wet thud at my feet. "Can you hang that up by the fire?" she asked.

At least now I knew what the rope was for. I hung her tunic up. When I turned around, Sam still stood neck-deep, this time with her pants in hand, scrubbing them. I leaned against the tree, watching her hair billow out behind her in the water and the occasional flash of her pale shoulders and arms. Her pants landed on the shore, then she dunked herself again. When she surfaced, she stopped so the water came up to her chin. She wriggled around for a few seconds more and then tossed her underwear and sports bra onto the shore.

My pulse raced even faster, and a lump formed in my throat. *Why did the water have to be so dark and murky?*

Sam looked up at me, a devilish glint in her eyes. "Do you always find laundry so interesting?"

Underneath the bruising on my face, I could feel my cheeks flush.

"You know," she said, "instead of just staring at me, you might want to think about rinsing that blood off yourself." She waved an arm over the water. "This river is big enough for two."

I did stink—no denying it. I dumped my shoes on the ground, leaving both jump devices inside them. Then I waded into the river, watching a dirty, bloody scum spread out around me. Yeah, I really needed this bath.

I dove underwater and swam along the bottom for a few seconds. When I broke again for air, I began scrubbing at my scalp and face, my hands coming away red. I scrubbed and scrubbed, rinsing off the memories of the mercenary's face, the smell of his breath, and the blood of his life.

My tunic, pants, and underwear came off, too, leaving me naked except for the soggy bandage covering the wound in my shoulder. I thrashed at my blood-stained clothes, beating them in the water. I'd never scrubbed anything so thoroughly in my life, but I kept thinking that I saw another spot of blood that needed to be washed out. I finally tossed all my clothes onto the bank, next to the fire, and stood submerged with the water up to my chin, letting the coolness of the river soothe the pain in my ribs.

"Feeling better now?" Sam asked.

"Not really. I still can't get him out of my head. His eyes …" I stirred the water with my hands. "How did you handle it, your first … ?"

Sam looked past me to stare at the riverbank and the flames of the fire. "It happened almost a year and a half ago, during my second jump," she began, her voice low. "I heard a noise outside my camp one night just as I was coming back from hunting. I snuck up and saw a man rummaging around my things. I thought I had a clear shot at a rogue jumper, so I sank an arrow into his back." She slapped idly at the water. "It turned out he wasn't a jumper at all, just some poor peasant trying to find food. I cried for days after that. Even now, his dead face haunts me."

"Great … So this guy's face will be stuck with me forever?"

"Afraid so," Sam said. "But at least you nailed someone who deserved it. He could've been the guy who killed my dad or my brother. You should be happy he's dead, not moping about it."

"Do you feel less guilty when you kill these guys?"

Sam sighed. "I've never killed any of them. The one time I came close, he jumped out before I could do anything."

"What do you mean? I thought you can only jump out when the time stream is fixed."

"The rods can take a whole bunch of commands. By twisting the sections to new positions and saying different phrases, you can do all sorts of different things. I don't know them, though; my dad never trained me how to use the rod, and my brother only taught me the jump in and jump out commands because I kept bugging him to teach me something. We're lucky this guy didn't jump out as soon as we knocked him off his horse. He probably thought he could still finish you off."

I couldn't stop the shudder that ran through me. "He was almost right about that."

Sam tilted her head to look at me. "Are you coming back to the land of the living any time soon?"

The dead man's face would probably haunt me forever, but I was pretty sure my zombie state was over. "Yeah, I guess so."

"Good, then we should probably get out of the water and dry off. Ceolwulf is probably getting worried about us."

Keeping low, she walked past me through the water, until finally the river grew too shallow and she stood up to her full height. My jaw dropped as her water-darkened hair fell halfway to her waist and I got a full view of the back of her. The baggy tunic and pants she wore had been hiding a body even more incredible than the one I had imagined an embarrassing number of times. But my glimpse of heaven lasted only a second before she wrapped her riding cloak around herself.

Sam rearranged our clothes so they stretched along the line surrounding the fire, then turned to face me. "Planning to stay in the water forever?" The smile was back on her face and her eyes sparkled with amusement.

"Turn around," I said.

Sam laughed. "Not as much fun when you're the one being watched, huh?"

My ears burned with embarrassment as I covered my groin with my hands and ran out of the water to grab my cloak. I sat on the ground on the other side of the fire from Sam, rubbing my arms and legs to dry off.

My gaze drifted over Sam's exposed arms. They were pale, lightly freckled, and totally empty of any ink. "Where's your tattoo? I thought you said all time jumpers had them."

The smile on her face faded, and she drew her cloak tighter around herself so that her forearms were hidden in its folds. "Yeah, but I also told you these magical time thingies are passed from father to son—not daughters. My dad practically had a fit every time I asked him to train me. He'd always say time-jumping was too dangerous for girls—that I shouldn't even think about it." She exhaled slowly and clenched her fists. "Instead, he spent all his time with my brother," she continued, her voice sounding strained. "And I was left on the outside, looking in, just praying for some attention. One time, when I was about eight, I even drew a tattoo on my arm, hoping that maybe, if I was more like them, they'd let me join them." She shook her head sadly. "Fat lot of good that did me."

Sam got to her feet and piled more wood on the fire until the clearing blazed with heat. For a few minutes, neither of us said anything. We just sat and stared at the fire, listening to the crackle of wood and the hiss of steam from our clothes on the line.

"What's it like when you go back to the real world?" I finally asked, desperate to break the awkward silence. "Isn't it tough, knowing what you do?"

"The real world sucks. Do you know how hard it is to sit in a classroom, listening to some teacher droning on about studying hard and the importance of getting good grades, when I know that I'll never do anything more meaningful in life than what I'm doing now?"

I shrugged. "I've been homeschooled all my life. My only friends are the people I chat with online. I've never met any of them, and I don't even know if they really are who they say they are."

She wrung out the water in her hair. "Not going to school would be a blessing for me. My school is filled with the stupidest hicks you'll ever meet. Most of the girls ignore me because, even after two years there, I'm still 'the new girl.' And the guys just want to get into my pants. They seem to think that showing off their pickup trucks or bragging about how many beers they can drink will impress me so much that I'll just rip my clothes off. Morons." Sam jabbed at the fire with a stick, and sparks rose into the air. "All I want is for some guy to look me in the eye and ask me out to a movie or a dance. Having a few flowers in hand would be a nice touch, too. I'm not looking for a knight in shining armor to show up on horseback and sweep me off my feet—I'm not dumb enough to believe that's ever going to happen. But a little decency doesn't seem like too much to ask for."

"Those guys are idiots. You deserve so much better."

"Thanks," she muttered as a blush crept to her cheeks.

"Is there anything you *do* like about where you live now?"

"The forest behind my house," she said, her voice going soft. "It stretches on forever, and I can just lose myself in there." Sam stopped poking the fire and pulled her knees up to her chest. "Except for that, everything sucks. Ever since I moved in with my mom, she's acted like I'm the world's greatest inconvenience. Even though I'm in school, she charges me rent. So I have to bust my ass working at a part-time job just to pay her—and she just spends it all on booze and bingo. And her disgusting husband is a total pig. Every time he looks at me, I feel like vomiting. My mom blames me whenever anything happens."

Sam closed her eyes and clenched her fists, then swallowed hard before continuing. "I've already broken two of his fingers after his hands ended up in places where I didn't want them. He keeps claiming that his hands slipped 'by accident.' Yeah, I broke those fingers 'by accident' too, jackass." Sam lowered her head so that her hair fell forward over her face and knees. "If I don't leave that house soon, he's going to end up dead."

She came across as so strong and confident. I never would've imagined all she'd been through in her own home. Before I could say or do anything, Sam jumped to her feet, yanked her clothes off the line, and disappeared behind a stand of trees. She appeared moments later, fully dressed, her eyes puffy and red. "Ready to go?"

"Yeah. But hey, I just want to say I'm really sorry ... about—"

"Don't be." Sam shrugged. "Not your fault."

She was clearly done talking about it.

I ducked into the trees to change. I tucked the two jump devices into the back of my pants, and then headed to the riverbank with the bloody shirt of mail. I spent a few minutes scrubbing it with sand and rinsing it with water, then tossed the links into the fire for a minute to burn off any last traces of dirt and blood. With a branch, I dragged the armor out of the fire and dipped it in the river once more to cool it off. The mail fell heavily over my shoulders and back, but the weight was oddly comforting. I belted the mercenary's sword at my side and strapped his shield onto my back. No more ax or crappy peasant shield—now I was properly dressed for war.

Sam looked me up and down and gave me a mock wolf whistle. "You know, if you take away the broken nose, split lip, black eyes, and puffy face, you actually don't look too bad right now."

"You probably say that to all the guys," I joked.

We rode silently, each of us lost in our thoughts, and in about an hour, we saw the dust thrown up by the trailing wagons. I knew what that meant, so I reined in my horse and let her pass me. "Here's where we split up again." I sighed. "See you at dinner."

"We don't have to split up," Sam said, reining in her own horse. "You could join me up front with Ceolwulf."

"I can't. Servants have to ride in the back."

Sam laughed. "Look at yourself. I don't see a servant here, and neither will Ceolwulf. You belong up front."

"What about the other jumper? Aren't you afraid he'll figure out you're with me if we ride together?"

She smiled at me. "Dan, you've done something I haven't been able to do in almost a year of trying—you killed one of those bastards. If anyone should be afraid, it's him."

CHAPTER 23

We found Ceolwulf near the head of the army, riding as always with Aethelraed. I licked my split lip as I drew near. What would Ceolwulf say when he saw that I wore the arms and armor of a dead man? As my horse fell into step beside his, his one good eye took in my new gear, and I held my breath, waiting for his reaction.

"I see you have new armor," he said. "Where's the former owner?"

"Dead."

Ceolwulf nodded and turned to Aethelraed. "You owe me ten pennies. The boy killed the Ox, just like I said he would."

Aethelraed scowled as he reached into his belt pouch to take out a handful of silver coins, then slammed them into Ceolwulf's outstretched palm. "Bah! A weak serving boy like him could not have won without trickery. You have earned your coin in a foul manner."

Ceolwulf shrugged and slipped the coins into his own belt pouch. "Our wager was not about *how* he would kill that coward; it was *whether* he would kill him. It is clear that he bested the man."

"You may have won my coin," Aethelraed said, thumping his chest with one fist, "but by no means shall the boy wear the mail and carry the sword of a man slain through foul trickery. I must claim them instead, else we shall all have our servants attacking us while we sleep."

"Hey! I killed him in a fair fight," I said. "Look at my face. He attacked me first and he nearly killed me."

"Do not tell lies, boy. You are merely a servant. You fetch water and make fires. You have not the skill to defeat a warrior, let alone one as huge as the Ox. Now give me that armor and sword before I beat you."

"But he did kill him fairly," Sam interjected. "I saw the whole thing."

Ceolwulf raised his hand to stop the discussion. "Leofric, do you swear to me you won this armor through honorable contest and not through foul murder?"

"I do."

"Aethelraed, I believe the boy. And therefore I back his claim to the Ox's goods."

Aethelraed scowled. "Well, I challenge his tale. No one saw the fight other than a serving girl whose words hold no weight. I would test him myself by combat when we camp tonight. If he fights well, I will accept his story. But if he fights like a servant, as I expect he shall, then I demand his sword and mail, and that he be struck ten times across the back with an ash wand for lying."

"Done!" Ceolwulf spat in his palm and extended his hand. "Tonight at camp. And I will bet another ten pennies that the boy beats you." Aethelraed in turn spat in his palm and shook Ceolwulf's hand.

"What?" I shouted, drawing looks from other riders nearby. "I don't want to fight him."

"Ha! As I suspected," Aethelraed said to Ceolwulf before turning to me. "Give me that armor and sword and get back among the servants."

As much as I didn't want to fight Aethelraed, I wasn't about to just roll over and give away what I'd nearly died to win. "Fine," I muttered. "I'll fight you tonight. But doesn't anybody care that I killed a man? He fought alongside you only a few days ago, and now you're ready to argue over his possessions."

"He was only a hired warrior." Aethelraed snorted. "And a poor one at that."

"Aye," Ceolwulf said. "He was no friend of ours, and no use in battle. I will not mourn him. Why do you?"

Good question. "Well, I feel bad. I didn't want to kill him, but I knew that if I didn't, he'd kill me."

A smile peeked through Ceolwulf's gray beard. "That is how a true warrior should feel about killing. Look at the men around you. We ride now to battle, but all of us would prefer to remain on our lands, enjoying the hunt or seeing our sons and daughters grow old and strong. But we are here because our king calls us, and we must defend our country. None of us would ever kill for mere coin. You cannot eat silver. It will not bring you warmth on a cold winter's night, or joy in old age. Hired spears are not true warriors." His lips curled in distaste. "They have no honor. They fight for no cause—only for wealth. A true warrior will never mourn them. We rejoice instead that one less killer is in the land."

"So I'm not in trouble?"

"Only if you fight poorly tonight. Lose, and your claims shall be called false, and you shall be treated as a servant who murdered one of his betters. Fight well, and you shall thenceforth be treated as a warrior."

Just what I needed—another fight. My face and ribs still ached from the first one. I slowed my horse and let Aethelraed, Ceolwulf, and Sam pass me by. Sam cast me a concerned look, but I waved that everything was okay. I just needed to put some space between me and Aethelraed—I couldn't spend the day hanging around him.

I continued letting horses and warriors pass me by until the baggage wagons finally appeared and I rejoined the flow of traffic. I took off the armor and shield and dumped them next to Ceolwulf's provisions. If I had to fight tonight, I didn't want to tire myself out by wearing that much extra weight all day. With the battering my body had already received, I figured I had about one minute of fighting left in me, maybe two at the most. I had to make sure I won quickly.

Dusk came altogether too soon. As the army halted to make camp, a buzz of anticipation filled the air. Servant boys followed my every step, taunting me about how I was going to get my butt kicked. I barely had time to unsaddle all the horses before Ceolwulf approached.

"Aethelraed would fight now," he said.

"But I still have to fetch the firewood."

"There will be time for that later. Now is the time for you to defend your honor. Gird yourself for battle."

I gathered my gear from the wagon, pulled the shirt of mail over my head, and belted my sword around my waist. With shield in hand, I followed Ceolwulf to the middle of camp, where hundreds of housecarls already stood around a cleared circle about twenty paces in diameter. Serving boys sat in the trees or jostled each other at the back of the circle, craning their necks to see over the housecarls.

Ceolwulf escorted me through the crowd to the edge of the inner circle. "Watch out for his shield," he whispered. "He likes to strike with it so a foe is off balance, then he attacks." He clapped a reassuring hand on my shoulder then stepped back to join the eager spectators.

A rousing cheer greeted Aethelraed as he strode into the center of the circle. He was dressed like me, with mail and shield, but instead of a sword, he carried an ax. Although his hair was graying like Ceolwulf's, I didn't think for a moment that he was too old or slow to take me down. He probably knew more battle tricks than I could dream of.

"Brothers!" he yelled. "We all knew of the man we called the Ox—a coward at Stamford Bridge but still a warrior." Aethelraed gestured with his ax at me. "This peasant claims that the Ox was the one who tried to kill him in the forest, and that he himself slew the Ox in fair combat to avenge that insult." A chorus of jeers greeted his words. "A weak serving boy could never have defeated the Ox in fair combat, so I name his words false and say that he has no right to the man's sword and armor, which he now wears. I challenge him to a trial by blades, with you, my brothers, as judges. If he fights well, then let his claim stand and let him have ownership of the Ox's goods. However, if I defeat him, as I no doubt will, then let me claim ownership of these goods—and let this lying peasant be whipped for his falsehoods."

"Try not to hurt him too much, Aethelraed," one warrior shouted. "He still needs to carry firewood tonight." Laughter greeted the comment.

Aethelraed smiled at the crowd and then turned to me. "Do you still claim your lies as truth, boy?"

What had I gotten myself into? My stomach was in knots, I could barely breathe through my broken nose, my ribs throbbed, and my shoulder still ached from where I'd been stabbed a week before. But there was no backing down. I licked my split lip. "I do."

More jeers greeted my response, and then hands shoved me forward. I stumbled into the circle and tried unsuccessfully to spot a single friendly face.

Sam had remained at camp, choosing to avoid "all the testosterone" as she called it. As for the housecarls and servants, none of them cared about me; I was merely their amusement for the evening. Nothing like watching some peasant boy get beaten to add some excitement to a boring day. And the way things stood right now, Aethelraed would beat me easily. I could barely hold up my shield, and my armor felt like it was made of bricks. I'd be lucky if the fight lasted a few seconds. Unless …

I drew myself to my full height and glared at Aethelraed. "You call my claims false. Well, so be it." I tossed my shield at his feet with a loud clatter, then unbelted my sword and threw it on top of the shield. Finally, I unbuckled my chain mail, pulled it over my head, and let it drop to the ground. "I will not use any of the Ox's gear in our fight. I only ask for someone to lend me two light blades." This silenced the crowd. A few warriors even nodded their approval, and four blades quickly appeared in the circle.

My speciality had always been in two-handed fighting, not the ax-and-shield stuff the Anglo-Saxons favored. I bent down on one knee to pick up the two longest and lightest blades. Their leather-wrapped grips felt loose in my sweat-slicked hands, so I put them down again and ground a clod of dry earth between my hands. I concentrated on watching the dirt as it blotted the wetness from my palms. I needed to clear my mind, not look at the hostile faces, not think of losing. There was just me, the dirt, and my hands.

I gripped the swords again and stood up. The warriors in the circle around me faded from my view as I focused only on Aethelraed. He stood with a smug smile on his face, surely dreaming of victory.

Breathe.

Aethelraed was used to fighting an opponent equipped with an ax and shield, like him. My twin swords would confuse him.

Relax.

His armor would slow him down.

Focus.

I could beat him.

Without warning, Aethelraed lunged forward, trying to batter me down with his shield. I leaped to his ax side and swung with my left sword at his head. He knocked that sword aside with his ax, so I stabbed at his chest with the right sword. His shield swung in to protect his midsection, and my blade dug into the wood.

Aethelraed drew back his ax, ready to strike. My foot lashed out, kicking him in the side of one knee. He stumbled backward, giving me an opening. Both my blades swung down from opposite sides, each aimed at his neck. Aethelraed recovered from his stumble in time, and his shield and ax flew upward, blocking my blades just above his head. Before he could counter, my knee slammed into his stomach, his chain mail providing no protection from the blow. The wind whooshed out of his lungs, and he doubled over. Without hesitation, I reversed my grip on the swords and crossed them under his chin, each blade scraping his neck.

"Yield," I ordered, my breath coming out in ragged gasps.

The shock on his bearded face melted into a grin. "Aye, I yield, Ox-Slayer," he said before tossing his ax to the ground.

I exhaled slowly and let both swords fall from my fingers. *I won.*

Ceolwulf stepped out of the circle of watchers and raised his fist victoriously. "Well fought, Leofric—or should I say Ox-Slayer?"

Aethelraed pulled himself up. "Aye, a battle well fought, although I myself was on the wrong end of it. How does a peasant come by such skill with blades?"

"My father made sure no one could push me around," I replied, and I left it at that. I was so pumped with adrenaline I could barely stop shaking.

One of the warriors pushed an ale horn into my hand. "Ox-Slayer, we need good men in our fight against the Normans. Your skills are clearly wasted in hauling wood for that old goat Ceolwulf. Give up your servant's life and join us in the line. What say you?"

All eyes were on me. I glanced at Ceolwulf, and he nodded almost imperceptibly back at me. "I will join you," I shouted, then tilted back my ale horn and drank.

"Ox-Slayer!" yelled the housecarls, and they all drank.

A warrior with a flowing mustache patted Aethelraed's shoulder.

"So, my friend. My serving boy does everything too slowly. Should I tell him to work faster, or should I let it be, in case he decides to fight me as well?"

Aethelraed scowled as jeers and laughs rang out at his own expense this time. "Bah! Who could have known this boy would use blades so well?" He turned on his heel and stormed away.

Ceolwulf chuckled as he watched him leave. "Poor Aethelraed will have to live with such jests from these men for many long nights. And he will have to live with my jesting for the rest of his life." He snapped his fingers and his eyes sparkled. "That sheep-headed fool also owes me ten more pennies. Gather up your armor and then let us go claim my winnings."

I retrieved my discarded gear, and then we hurried after Aethelraed. The old warrior wheeled around at the crunch of our footsteps. "Just speak the words you burn to say, you old goat."

With a huge smirk spreading across his face, Ceolwulf raised his hands in mock defense. "What? I have no words. You fought extremely well against Leofric. I am sure that if I faced your serving boy, I would fare no better."

Aethelraed's face turned red. "I need to find some drink," he muttered. "Only a row of empty ale cups in my wake will take the sting from my shame."

"Allow me to help empty your purse as well. We had a bet."

"I am glad that I call you friend"—Aethelraed drew his lips tightly—"for I would hate to have you as an enemy." He dug into his pouch, counted out ten small silver coins, and slammed them into Ceolwulf's outstretched palm.

Ceolwulf laughed and threw an arm around his friend's shoulders. "Come, you swine herder, let us show young Leofric here how to celebrate like a housecarl."

CHAPTER 24

W e headed back to the campsite that Aethelraed and Ceolwulf shared, where Aethelraed's servant had already set up his master's tent. Sam hovered over the fire, cooking what smelled like stew. She looked up as we approached, taking in the sword belted at my hip and the armor and shield on my back. Our eyes locked for a moment and she nodded. Not much of a gesture but just enough to say *good job*.

That's it? I had fought and won two single combats in just one day. A feat like that deserved more than a nod. Maybe she was playing it cool with Aethelraed and Ceolwulf around. We were still supposed to be servants—and siblings—no matter our real motive for being here.

Despite her lukewarm reaction, I smiled back at her and then moved over to the large cloth bundle that lay near the fire. Even though I was bone tired, I started unraveling the hemp cords that held Ceolwulf's tent together.

"What are you doing?" Ceolwulf demanded.

"I'm putting your tent up."

"But you are no longer my servant. You have just proven yourself in battle—even though you only fought Aethelraed."

"When I had nowhere else to turn, you helped me and let me join you. I told you that I would work as a servant, and I will."

Aethelraed hoisted his ale cup and nodded at me. "You fight well and you have honor. That is quite the serving boy you have found, Ceolwulf."

I finished setting up the tent and then stockpiled some firewood for the night. Only then did I sit down for dinner with the two warriors and Sam. None of us spoke much during the meal—Aethelraed was probably still fuming, and Ceolwulf was more interested in wolfing down his food after a long day in the saddle.

After the meal, I stretched out on the ground and pulled my blanket over me. "Goodnight, everyone," I said.

"Why do you lie there on the ground?" Ceolwulf asked.

"Umm, because I'm tired."

He snorted. "Do not sleep under the sky like a common servant. You have been accepted into our brotherhood, so set your tent up with us."

"I don't have a tent."

"Do you forget that the Ox had a tent? You slew him in fair combat, to avenge a wrong he did you. Since no kin have stepped forward, all his other goods are yours now too—not just his weapons. Ask the boy who served him where these things are to be found."

Any fatigue I'd been feeling melted away instantly. We had the Ox's jump device already, but what other things had the rogue jumper possessed? What if he had an instruction manual for the rods? I took a few steps in the direction of the servants' section but stopped. Sam should share this with me. Without her help, I'd never have slain the Ox, so everything was half hers too. But how were we supposed to behave together in camp? She had barely acknowledged me earlier. Would she even want to come? Things were so much easier when we didn't need to worry about what others thought of us.

Ceolwulf must have sensed the reasons for my hesitation. "Take Aelfwyn with you," he barked. "I need to tease Aethelraed some more, and it is not fitting for a pretty maid like her to see a grown man weep."

With a look of relief, Sam sprang to her feet, and together we hurried away from the circle of firelight.

"How are we going to act in the camp now?" I asked as soon as we were out of earshot. "Do we still pretend we're brother and sister? Are we both servants? What are we exactly?"

She stopped walking and drew a hand through her hair. "I don't know. This entire partner thing is weird for me; I'm used to doing everything alone." She gestured at the fires all around us, where hundreds of men still ate or already slept. "And I'm definitely not used to being in the middle of this kind of scene. I'm so far out of my comfort zone right now it isn't funny." She tossed her hands upward. "I don't know how to act—I don't even know where to sleep tonight. Last night I slept outside Ceolwulf's tent, but I woke at every crackle of the fire, every snoring housecarl, and every guy taking a midnight trip to the bathroom."

"Uh, you *could* stay with me," I suggested.

She raised an eyebrow.

"You heard Ceolwulf," I continued. "I've got a tent now. It's half yours, because you helped me win it. And I have weapons and armor too. We'll have each other's backs, just like we did in Eoforwic—except the space will be a bit smaller."

For a few seconds she didn't respond—she only stood there, chewing on her bottom lip.

I put up my hands in a gesture of innocence. "We *are* supposed to be brother and sister, after all. It would look weird if I slept in the tent and you slept outside."

"Fine," Sam grunted. "We'll be camping buddies. Now let's go get our stuff."

"Ladies first," I said, giving a half bow.

We found the rogue jumper's serving boy sitting atop a mound of goods on a small wagon, looking around helplessly, with tear tracks on his dust-covered cheeks.

He jumped off the cart as we approached and tried to stand tall, as if hoping to give a good impression. "Are you my new master now?" he asked.

"Master? No. You're free, kid. You don't have to serve anybody."

His lips began to tremble, and his eyes started tearing up. "But … but … what shall I do?" he wailed. "My old master was cruel, but he paid. My family badly needs the coin my hard work brought us."

Sam dropped to one knee in front of the boy. "What is your name?"

"Sigebert." He sniffed.

She gently placed a hand on his shoulder. "And where are your parents?"

"They live in a village not far from here."

"And they're fine with you just wandering across half of England with some bloodthirsty killer?" I exclaimed.

Sigebert bowed his head and avoided looking at us. "My parents have no wealth, and I have far too many brothers and sisters. When the old master came to our village some days past, looking for someone to serve him, my father was happy to let me go. I have served my master faithfully, for the sake of my kin."

Sam pulled out her money pouch and pressed a handful of coins into Sigebert's palm. "Would you like to go home?"

The boy's head jerked up and his eyes shone. "Yes, please, my most generous lady. We should pass by my village on the morrow. King Harold's army passed it as they marched north to fight the Northmen at Eoforwic."

Sam stroked Sigebert's messy light-brown hair. "Tomorrow, I want you to go home. Tonight, though, can you show us your old master's belongings?"

Beaming, Sigebert showed us the gear he had been faithfully guarding.

Like a kid at Christmas, I rooted through the pile, only to find the equivalent of stockings full of coal. No instruction manual. No clues that would lead us to the other rogue jumper. Just a tent and some food.

Sigebert helped us set up our tent near Ceolwulf's and Aethelraed's. The boy insisted on sleeping outside under the stars while Sam and I shared the newly acquired tent, lying back-to-back.

I lay there in the dark, nearly asleep, comforted by the thought of the armor at my feet and the sword lying on the ground by my side. With Ceolwulf and Aethelraed nearby, I felt safer than I had in days. Despite this feeling of security, I couldn't sleep. Having Sam's warmth pressed against my back was intoxicating. She was everything I'd ever dreamed of in a girlfriend—smart, strong, pretty—but we were in Anglo-Saxon England. This was no time for me to be even thinking of anything except solving the time glitch.

Brother and sister, Dan. Brother and sister. I had a feeling this was going to be my new mantra.

I felt her stir behind me. "You still awake?" I asked.

"Yeah, I can't sleep."

"What are you thinking about?" I asked.

"This battle that we're all rushing off to, when is it going to happen?"

"About another ten days," I muttered. "Why?"

"Ten days? It's going to take that much riding to get to the battlefield?"

"No, we'll probably hit London in two or three days. According to history, King Harold stayed in London for a few days while his brothers and men from all over the south of England marched to join his army. Then, once he'd gathered sufficient men, he went to fight the battle."

"Damn it. We're running out of time to catch the other jumper."

"How do you figure?"

Sam turned toward me and propped herself up on one elbow. "You said we reach London in two or three days. Well, we haven't had any luck finding the jumper so far. Imagine how hard it's going to be when there are thousands more troops and an entire city for him to hide in. We need to find him before we get to London."

I let out a long sigh. She was right, as usual. "Any ideas?"

"We need to start asking the right people the right question."

"Which is?"

"Simple: Who's new? The housecarls all know each other, so we know he isn't to be found among them. And the servants and the mercenaries should all have worked or fought together as well. If we find a newcomer to either of these groups, we've got our man."

"That's it? That's the plan?" I couldn't help shaking my head. "Just because I carry a sword on my belt now doesn't mean people are going to be ready to talk to me."

"Then we need to persuade Aethelraed and Ceolwulf to help us."

"And if they won't?"

"Then we'll never find the guy who's keeping us here, and we'll be stuck with him calling all the shots." Sam pounded her fist on the earth floor of the tent. "It's time we take the fight to him. You in or not, Dan?"

Question every last person in King Harold's army during the next few days, and hope that we found the guy who'd tried to kill me? Seemed pretty hopeless to me, but I didn't have a better plan.

"Yeah, I'm in."

CHAPTER 25

I woke the next morning riddled with aches but still feeling a bit better. The swelling in my face had gone down to the point that I could actually take a few whistling breaths through my nose. Unfortunately, that was the only good news. Sam and I now had only two, maybe three days until we reached London, and finding the rogue jumper in that short time seemed like a hopeless task. There were so many men to question, and so many places for him to hide.

Despite my hesitations, I figured I'd do my best to get some help from Ceolwulf and Aethelraed. Maybe it wouldn't feel so hopeless with all of us working together. The universe owed me at least one small stroke of luck. I stepped out of our tent and took a seat by the fire next to Ceolwulf, Aethelraed, and Sam, who were already wolfing down a breakfast of boiled barley sprinkled with a few beans.

"Guys, we need your help," I began.

"What troubles you, Leofric?" Ceolwulf asked.

"I need to find the man who tried to kill me."

"What of the man you killed yesterday? You said he was the one."

"Well ... he wasn't the only one." I filled a bowl and then proceeded to tell them everything that had happened to me since I'd joined King Harold's army—leaving out the time-jumping bits, of course. Some of it Ceolwulf already knew, or might have guessed at, but to Aethelraed, it was all new. I told them about the two peasants attacking me in the forest and how Sam had killed them both. This earned her nods of respect from both housecarls. I followed up that story with the tale of Sigebert sending me off to be ambushed at the Ox's orders and how a man who was not the Ox had taken a shot at me and tracked me into the forest. Lastly, and this one took a lot of verbal gymnastics to explain while avoiding all mention of jump rods and time travel, I told them how this same archer was likely giving the king bad advice that would lead us to ruin when we encountered Duke William's forces.

When my story ended, Aethelraed pulled out his dagger and rasped it across a whetstone. "So he is a traitor as well. How do we find this man?" His voice was low and full of menace.

"Here's what we need to do," Sam said. And she proceeded to tell the two housecarls her plan.

Aethelraed listened without saying anything, but the scowl growing on his face showed his opinion of her idea. "I like it not," he said once she'd finished. "It lacks bravery."

"The girl has a fine plan," Ceolwulf argued. "When hunting deer, you do not go stomping noisily through the woods; you go slowly and sneak up on your quarry. The traitor they seek will not be found by any brash actions. We must stalk our prey. Do you have a better way?"

Aethelraed glanced away from Ceolwulf and instead stared at his food. "Bah! I have no better plan, but I still do not like this one. I like to have my foes in front of me where I can see them. Makes them easier to stab."

"But we must find these foes first," Ceolwulf said. "Then you can stab them."

"So be it." A glint came into Aethelraed's eyes. "I will try the girl's plan. Let our foe at least be worthy of the chase."

"So when do we start?" Sam asked.

"*We?*" said Ceolwulf. "You shall not be coming with us."

"But it's my plan!"

"And a fine plan it is. However, if we do find this traitor, we may need to take up arms against him. It is not fitting for us to put a fair maiden in harm's path."

"Men!" she spat. "You think you're the only ones who can fight?"

"You have a warrior's spirit," Aethelraed said, not unkindly. "But a warrior also needs to know when to back away from a fight. This is your time to do so."

Sam slammed her bowl onto the ground. "Seriously? I'm stuck sitting on my horse and doing nothing all day?" Sam glared defiantly at both men, her face flushed and her arms crossed. When neither looked like they would reconsider, she settled for scowling at me. Like a coward, I said nothing, just withered under her burning glare and hunched over my breakfast, not lifting my head until she gave up glowering and stormed away. If there was one thing I was learning from this time jump, it was that I had to pick my battles carefully. And arguing with Sam when she was in a bad mood was not a fight I wanted to chance. Hopefully she'd calm down by the time we got back.

As soon as the army began moving again, Ceolwulf, Aethelraed, and I rode ahead to find the priest. As the man who was supposed to look after the spiritual well-being of the army, he'd know who attended church regularly and who didn't. He should be able to give us names of any men he felt suspicious about.

We found the priest riding in a small wagon that looked like a medieval version of a stagecoach. It had four walls, a roof, and cutouts on the sides that acted as windows, but curtains hid the interior of the wagon from view. Two draft horses pulled this wooden contraption along, and it shook and rattled with each bump in the road.

I knocked on the side of the wagon and a curtain slid aside, revealing the familiar round face of the priest.

"Good health to you," Ceolwulf began. "We wish to speak with you on a matter that demands few ears overhear us."

The priest leaned out the window. "Speak, my son. God and no one else will hear what words pass between us."

"We seek a traitor and have little with which to find him. We believe that he is newly come, though, and that is why we seek your aid. Who among the king's household has not attended church or confession?"

The priest rubbed a jewel-studded hand along his jowly chin. "It is not as simple as asking me who is not present in church. There are many men in the king's household I have never met. I minister to the king himself and his most faithful retainers; I do not minister to every serving boy and horse wrangler. A better question is to ask who *has* actually been to church and to confession. I can give you a list of men I can vouch for. The priest began rattling off a slew of them. "Cuthebert, Sigemund's son, the cook. Wiglaf, Aelfgar's son, the smith …" The list went on and on until Ceolwulf, Aethelraed, and I each had committed to memory six or seven names along with everyone's occupations. These were the leaders of King Harold's household and therefore men we could trust. Now we just had to find them and hear from each one who he trusted and who was new. Eventually, we'd find the rogue jumper.

We started off by heading for the cook wagons, since they would be a great place for a time jumper to hang out. No risk of battle but always in sight of the king and able to talk to him. We ignored all the serving boys and went straight to the head cook himself.

"Good morning, friend," Ceolwulf greeted. "If you please, we would have knowledge of the men under your stewardship."

"To what end?" the cook asked.

"We seek out a traitor and wish to know who among your staff has not been with you for more than two months."

The cook crossed his meaty arms across his chest and tilted his head. "There are over twenty men and boys under my charge and I know them all. Most served with me during the reign of the old king, and some joined me when King Harold took the crown. None of them are newly come. And though some are lazy, that is no crime. I would vouch for all of them."

I hadn't realistically thought we would find the jumper on our first try, but I still couldn't help feeling disappointed.

We thanked the cook and proceeded to ride up and down the ranks of King Harold's household, talking to all of those on our list and asking them about the men in their charge. It was a tedious process; the king's household was huge. He had brought with him cooks, servants, advisers, horse wranglers, hunters, wagon drivers, armorers, smiths. Even so, by noon we had cleared a large part of the list—but without a single lead.

"Bah! All this talking is women's work and leads to naught," Aethelraed grumbled. "Is there no manly way to find this traitor?"

"Shall we go now among the hired fighters?" Ceolwulf suggested. "Putting them to question might be more to your liking."

"More talking, no doubt," Aethelraed sneered. "But fine, let us hear what those spears-for-hire have to say."

The mercenaries traveled in their own group, separate from the housecarls. There were about two hundred of them riding in no particular order. I rode among the men and their servants, trying to envision any one of them in a brown cloak, gloves, and armed with a bow. Most of them were too tall or too broad in the shoulders.

Ceolwulf rode up beside an older mercenary. "Good day, friend. I would speak to you," he began.

"Aye, what would you know?"

"Who ministers to the men?"

"We have our own priest who travels with us. A fat, useless fellow he is, but he knows the words, so we keep him." The mercenary pointed to a heavy man near the rear of their group. He wore a threadbare cloak over a dirty tunic that strained against his girth. The poor donkey plodding underneath him was wheezing as it struggled to keep up with the horses of the mercenaries.

"Bah! More priests and more talking," Aethelraed spat as we rode over.

Ceolwulf ignored him and pulled his horse up next to the donkey. "Greetings. We seek a traitor and wish to know who is new to the band or who is unknown to you."

The priest coughed into one fleshy palm and then held it out. "A donation to the poor might speed my thinking," he began.

Ceolwulf's eyes narrowed in distaste, but he tossed him a silver coin, which the priest quickly hid in the folds of his tunic. "There are seven men I do not know," the priest said. "One was slain by the lad you ride with, and the other six ride over there." He pointed to a group of tall blond men traveling together. All of them had bushy beards and long hair, reminding me of the Vikings we had fought at Stamford Bridge. One of them turned around at that moment and caught us looking at him. He scowled and leaned forward to whisper to his companions. All six swiveled in their saddles and scowled at us too.

Six time jumpers?

"We'll need help!" I cried out to Aethelraed and Ceolwulf, fear making my voice crack.

"Bah!" Aethelraed said. "These are merely sell-swords, not housecarls. They are no match for our skill."

"But they're not regular men," I pleaded. "They know ways to fight that you don't."

Ceolwulf shrugged off my warnings. "Skilled or not, if they are traitors, they must die. I will not run from this fight."

This was crazy. Ceolwulf was going to die if he fought them.

Screw that—*I* was going to die if he fought them.

With my hand resting on my sword hilt, I guided my horse into position beside Ceolwulf's. My eyes darted around to each of the six men, looking for any sign that they were about to attack.

Ceolwulf slowed his horse to ride alongside their small group. "I bid you good day," he said, his voice lacking any warmth. "I would have words with you, if you please."

The tallest of the group, a man with shoulder-length hair tied in two braids, squinted at Ceolwulf. "What do you want?" he asked, his voice a hoarse rasp, as if he struggled to speak. Across his throat, a long white scar showed where a blade had once nearly ended his life.

"Your name first, as I would know who I speak with. I am called Ceolwulf."

"Njal, son of Eirik."

Ceolwulf nodded and continued. "The priest who rides with your group says that none of you attend his church. Is that true?"

Njal spat on the ground. "Aye, it is true. We worship the gods of our ancestors, not this man-god the Saxons pray to. Tyr and Thor give us strength in battle. But the Saxon god demands I be meek and love my enemy. He is not a fitting god for one who rides to the slaughter fields, and so I will not pray to him."

With his one good eye, Ceolwulf sized up Njal. "And how long have you been in King Harold's service?"

Njal slapped the shoulder of the warrior next to him. "How long have we been fighting for this king?"

"Too long, Njal. The pay is good, but your smell gets worse every day."

"And you still fight like a woman, Rolfe."

A faint smile appeared on Ceolwulf's face, and even I started to relax. It didn't seem like these jokers were traitors or time jumpers, just a bunch of Viking mercenaries.

"Have you six fought together for the same length of time?"

"Aye," Njal said.

"And can any outside your group vouch for that claim?"

Njal reached into his saddlebag and pulled out a half-eaten heel of bread. With uncanny accuracy, he pitched it at the rider in front of him, smacking him in the back of the head. "You, sheep head! How long have I ridden with you?"

"Go to hell, you blasted Dane!" the man yelled as he rubbed the spot where the bread had hit him.

"Answer me," Njal yelled, "or the next thing to hit the back of your head will be my ax."

The man scowled back at him. "For eight sorry months, I have had the misfortune of riding with you, and you still haven't died, you fool."

I breathed a long sigh of relief. These guys weren't the traitors, and I wouldn't have to fight them. Even better, all the mercenaries were vouched for, meaning our traitor was definitely somewhere else. I mentally ran over the list of names we'd been given. We'd already talked to three-quarters of them; just a few more and we'd have our traitor.

"Shall we continue with the next person on our list?" I asked.

The two Anglo-Saxon warriors nodded, although Aethelraed seemed less than excited about doing so, and we kicked our horses to gallop ahead. We had just passed the tail end of the housecarl section of the moving army when I saw a group of eight horsemen riding toward us against the main stream of traffic. These men didn't look like regular housecarls. They wore fine cloaks and carried themselves with a superior air. As soon as they caught sight of us, they fanned out and blocked our path. They shifted uneasily in their saddles, as if expecting a fight, while their hands gripped spears and axes.

This wasn't good. Who were these guys, and why were they stopping us?

"Eadward," Ceolwulf said, pushing his horse ahead of mine and Aethelraed's. "What do you seek by blocking our path?"

A man in a blue riding cloak trimmed with gold rode forward. "We have no quarrel with you, Ceolwulf. King Harold wants to question the boy who rides with you."

"You need eight men to bring a boy to speak with the king?" Ceolwulf asked, his tone icy.

"Do not worry yourself about my men or what the king wants," Eadward said. "Just ride away and let us do as we have been bidden."

Aethelraed cleared his throat noisily and discharged a long stream of spit. It landed in the dirt of the road with an audible plop. "This boy was a servant merely days ago, and beneath the notice of the king. Why is he of interest now?"

Eadward reached for the ax handle sticking out above his shoulder. "Do you block my way?"

Ceolwulf raised his hands. "Peace, Eadward. The boy travels with us and has been a good companion. We just would know why the king wishes to question our servant."

Eadward's eyes narrowed and bored into me. "He has been accused of treason against the king."

"Treason!" I yelled. "I've done nothing but help King Harold. How can someone accuse me of treason?"

"Do not speak again, traitor, or I will cut out your tongue!" Eadward snapped with such ferocity that I shut my mouth instantly. He turned to face Ceolwulf. "Now I ask you again, do you intend to block my way?"

Ceolwulf guided his horse aside. "Nay, Eadward. I will not block your way. But I will not let you take the boy alone. I will come with you."

"As you wish," replied Eadward.

"I will come as well," said Aethelraed. "I know not who accused this boy, but I know that it is a false charge."

Eadward nudged his horse beside mine. "Give me your weapons and shield, traitor," he said. "Be warned that any ill-thought move will be your last."

My entire body went numb with fear. Somewhere the rogue jumper must have been laughing his head off. No one else could have set me up like this. With slow, careful movements, I passed my sword, seax, and shield to Eadward.

He motioned to his men, and they formed a circle around me, penning me in between their horses. Ceolwulf and Aethelraed stayed outside the circle, and as a group we rode toward the head of the army. Housecarls shouted out as we passed, wondering what was happening. Eadward told the first few warriors that I was a traitor, and soon the entire column knew of the accusation. Men glared at me as I passed, judging me guilty already.

My hands trembled so badly that I could barely grip the reins of my horse. The penalty for traitors was death. I had to prove my innocence. But how? I didn't even know what I was accused of. This meeting with King Harold would be my one and only chance to plead my case. I needed to be ready to argue every lie and accusation thrown at me. If the king didn't believe me, I wouldn't live past tonight.

CHAPTER 26

I spent the rest of the day with two guards watching over my every move. When I stopped to let my horse drink from a stream, they were there. When the army paused for a rest, they stayed glued to my side. Even when I went to take a leak, they followed me into the forest and hovered a few steps behind me, not giving me two seconds away from them. For the entire ride, they were my shadows, never leaving me an inch of space in case I decided to bolt.

At dusk, when the army halted, Eadward quickly dismounted and yanked me off my horse. "Come with me, traitor," he spat as his guards surrounded us.

He shoved me into the center of a large clearing, where housecarls gathered in a circle around us, shouting back and forth over what should be done with me.

"Gouge his eyes out!" yelled one man.

"That's too good for him!" yelled another warrior. "Kill him!"

I stood shaking with fear as rivers of sweat ran down my back. Except for Ceolwulf and Aethelraed, no one in the surrounding crowd looked the slightest bit sympathetic toward me. They wanted blood—my blood.

The noise died down as King Harold strode into the circle, his brow creased with unease. "Men," he announced, his voice ringing out for all to hear. "It grieves me that in this desperate hour, while we rush to defend our land against foreign invaders, I must call you together when you would rather rest and eat after a long day of riding. But word has come to me that this boy has committed foul acts of treason against both my person and our great country—and these accusations must be dealt with, here and now."

An angry murmur rumbled through the crowd, and Harold raised his hands for silence before turning to me, his face grim. "You have been accused of slaying three men in my service, cowardice in battle, and spying for Duke William. How do you respond to these charges, boy?"

"I'm innocent," I stammered, my voice catching in my throat. "I've been loyal to you. Don't you remember the battle against Tostig and Hardrada? I was the one who advised you to head east!" My chest rose and fell rapidly, and I could feel myself hyperventilating.

The king hesitated before responding. "I am well aware of the service you have done—"

"And who accused me?" I challenged. "Don't I have the right to face my accuser directly?"

King Harold's lips drew thin. At first I thought it was because I had dared to interrupt him, but then I noticed the look of hesitation on his face. And, around the circle, men began shouting that they, too, wanted to know who had accused me. If I could just keep up the pressure on him, I might beat this charge.

"I know not," answered the king. "A letter of warning was left outside my tent. A letter that lists your crimes."

"Which coward accuses this boy but will not show his face?" someone in the crowd yelled. A chorus of shouts followed, each supporting my right to confront my accuser.

When nobody stepped forward, King Harold raised his hands for silence. "We must try this boy, even though his accuser will not step forward. His crimes, if the accusations are true, are too weighty to leave unjudged." The king faced me directly. "Did you slay three men who were in my service?" he demanded.

Dang it! I knew killing the Ox would get me in trouble. "No, only one. And he was trying to kill me."

The king nodded. "And do you have proof of this plot?"

"His serving boy said so."

"And is this serving boy here to support your claim?"

Aggghhhh! Sigebert had left for his home village only a few hours before. And with the army rushing south, there was no way we'd head back now just to hear his tale. "I sent him home," I muttered.

"So no one else here can confirm this plot against you?" the king asked, his voicing rising to ensure everyone could hear him.

I hung my head. "No."

"And what of the two men who were killed in the forest outside Tada? You claim that a hunter killed them. Did anyone see this hunter— or even see the hunter's camp?"

My story was evaporating like water in a volcano. I could only shake my head.

"Hmm ... interesting." King Harold stroked his bearded chin. "So the only support you have for your stories are serving boys who have gone home and hunters no one has seen. Yet three men lie dead at your hands. And you are now richer, with armor, horses, and weapons. And yet you have not fought a single enemy of mine."

"But I proved myself in a trial by combat!"

King Harold jabbed a sharp finger into my chest. "That was incriminating in itself! No serving boy should be able to fight like you did. You are clearly no serving boy—you are a spy for Duke William! Do you know the penalty for spying? Death!" King Harold said with finality.

"But I'm not a spy! I was *looking* for spies! I've been out all day trying to find them."

"What better way to throw hunters off your trail than pretend to hunt the same quarry?"

"I'm innocent!" I yelled. "I'm not a spy!" I sank to my knees and clasped my hands in front of me. "Please believe me."

The king's face softened. "No one can claim your tales false. Yet no one can claim them true either. Are there any from your village who will speak in your favor?"

"No," I said.

"What?" the king exclaimed, a stunned look on his face. "How can you have no one who will vouch for you? Mother? Father? Village priest?"

"No one," I murmured, and from the muttering going on around me, I knew I'd just convinced everyone of my guilt.

"I will vouch for the boy," Ceolwulf said. "I have known him only since Tada, but during that time, he has behaved with honor and courage."

"Thank you, Ceolwulf," the king said. "But to fully judge him innocent of this serious a crime, we require many more men of good standing to support him. You are but one."

"What about trial by combat?" I pleaded. "Can I fight anyone to prove my innocence?"

King Harold's eyes narrowed and his lips drew thin. "Your accuser remains silent, leaving it to me to bring his claims to light. Would you fight me?"

"No!" I said. "But there must be some other way."

The priest stepped forward. "With a lack of witnesses, there is only one clear path. We must try him by ordeal. If what he says is true, the Lord will protect him."

My stomach lurched. Dad had told me about trials by ordeal. They usually involved some sort of painful task like holding a red-hot iron bar or plunging a hand into boiling water. Medieval people believed that God would protect an innocent person from harm. I didn't share their faith. All I saw coming out of this ordeal was excruciating pain followed by a quick execution. "Is there no other way?" I asked.

"Do you fear trial by ordeal?" the king asked in an accusatory tone. "You can proclaim your guilt now. I will show mercy if you do."

"But I'm innocent!"

"So be it," the king said. "I agree with my priest. You shall be tried by ordeal. Let God judge you."

The priest turned slowly around, making sure all eyes were on him. "We have not the time for an ordeal by fire. I say we try him by water. To the river!" he shouted.

"To the river!" the housecarls yelled back.

They rushed me to the river we had camped next to. Two men bound my hands and feet with rope and shoved me to the edge of the water while the rest waited at the shoreline, casting bets on the outcome of my ordeal.

The priest stood beside me and held up a small glass bottle for everyone to see. He unstopped it and poured a clear liquid into a tin cup. "I will now give him holy water to drink. If he is innocent, he will sink to the bottom of the river. If he speaks false, the river will try to expel him, and he will float to the surface."

What!?

If I floated, they'd kill me for being a traitor. And if I sank, I'd prove my innocence but die from drowning. I was dead either way.

"Are you ready, my son?" the priest asked.

"I'm innocent," I pleaded. "Please don't do this."

"Have faith in the Lord," the priest said soothingly. He tilted the cup and I swallowed a mouthful. Other than a slight metallic taste from the cup, it tasted like normal water.

"He drank of the holy water," the priest announced. "Now I shall place him under the water for all to witness his guilt or innocence."

The priest grabbed my bound wrists and dragged me deeper into the river until we were both waist-deep and the icy water lapped at my belly.

"I'm innocent!" I screamed as I struggled against my bonds, but they were too tight. How was I going to get out of this if I couldn't move my hands and feet? I tried to peer into the dark current to see if there was anything beneath me that I could use to cut the rope.

Without warning, the priest put a hand on my forehead and pushed me backward. A shock of cold washed over me as I sank below the surface. The din from the men on shore faded to a dull throbbing sound, and a world of murky darkness surrounded me. The only light came from above, where the dispersed rays of the setting sun glowed on the surface. My body bobbed in the slow current, neither rising nor sinking. Suddenly, the priest placed his foot on my chest and drove me to the bottom, the large rocks of the riverbed digging into my back.

The priest's trying to kill me!

I thrashed and wriggled under his foot, attempting to free myself. But with my hands and feet bound I had no leverage, no strength to force him away. Even worse, the struggle was using up precious air in my lungs.

I stopped thrashing and lay motionless on the bottom. The longest I had ever held my breath was about two minutes. After two minutes … then what? The answer was horribly clear—a cold, lonely death at the bottom of a stream, a thousand years in the past.

Why was the priest doing this to me? Was he trying to skip the trial and head straight for the execution? Had the rogue jumper bribed him? Not that it mattered—death was only seconds away. That painful realization hit me like a knee to the gut. I never thought my life would end like this. I let my thoughts drift to the people in my life. My dad, the mom who I never knew, the few friends I'd made on the internet—and Sam.

Other than my dad, how many people would mourn me?

My lungs ached for air, but only water surrounded me. The light above me grew dim. Despite the massive pain in my chest, I would not open my mouth. I wanted to cling to every second of life left.

Goodbye, Dad.

CHAPTER 27

As my last precious breath ran out, the priest's foot moved aside, and two hands took me by the shoulders and yanked me upward. Cheers and shouts assailed my ears the moment my head broke the surface. My aching lungs greedily gulped air while water trickled from my hair into my eyes. Through blurred vision, I saw men splashing into the water toward me.

"It is over, my son," the priest said, putting his hands on my shoulders. To the crowd of onlookers on the shore, he then announced, "Not once did this boy's body rise from the water. He has been judged by the Lord and found innocent. Let no man blaspheme by saying otherwise."

"Thank you," I sputtered, feeling muddled. "But why did you hold me underwater?" I asked quietly.

The priest pulled me in close to him. "You chose trial by ordeal rather than calling yourself guilty and thus accepting a lesser punishment," he whispered into my ear. "That convinced me of your innocence. My foot on your chest made sure everyone else became convinced as well."

He pushed away from me as Ceolwulf and Aethelraed approached.

"Fare thee well, my son."

"Are you well, Leofric?" Ceolwulf asked as he put an arm around me to support me.

"I'm alive," I coughed.

Aethelraed took out his knife and sliced the ropes that bound me. "A foul trick to accuse you of treachery. The man you seek clearly fears your approach. We shall find him soon, and then we shall see how he enjoys being put to trial."

I rubbed my wrists and let myself be led out of the water. The same housecarls who had been shouting for my death a few minutes before now clapped me on my back, congratulating me on my innocence. In a daze, I mumbled my thanks. The faces around me were just a blur, their voices just noise. I kept reliving that moment of lying on the riverbed and seeing the light fade away. Helpless. Feeling death approach and unable to do anything about it.

Somehow I made it back to the camp and put the tents up. At least I think it was me. Most of the time, it felt like I was viewing the world from inside someone else's body. I watched my hands put up tent poles and tie fabric to the posts, but my mind was elsewhere. At dinner, I only grunted to anything said to me, even from Sam, so everyone stopped talking to me after a while. This was the third time I'd almost died in less than two weeks, and for what? I was trying to find some guy who was clearly smarter than me—and if I kept going after him, he'd surely kill me. Maybe it was time to throw in the towel.

After dinner, I headed away from the fires and wandered into the woods. I didn't know what I was searching for, but I knew it wasn't there in the camp. I found myself a spot on the leaf-covered ground and lay down, staring up past the tall trunks at the darkening sky and the few stars that were already out.

After a few minutes, the faint crackle of dry leaves alerted me to someone's presence. Whoever it was moved cautiously, with little noise and no light. The rogue jumper? I really didn't care anymore. "Just let me go home," I yelled. "You win. I'm done."

"Giving up already, Newbie?"

Great. The one time I didn't want to see her and she'd sought me out. "Leave me alone, Sam."

The crackling grew louder and then she stood over me, blocking my view of the sky. "Are you seriously lying out here in the forest, waiting to be killed?"

"I'm done. I'm too tired to fight anymore. You go save history. I'm clearly incompetent."

Sam lay down next to me. She didn't say anything, and we remained silent, staring up at the sky. Bats fluttered between the trees in search of prey and insects hummed in the night.

"You're not going to try to talk me out of it?" I finally asked, my voice sounding unusually loud over the quiet of the forest.

"If I were you, I'd quit too," she said.

"Are you saying I suck at time-jumping?" I snapped, for some reason bristling at her words.

"No, you don't suck. You're stuck on the most challenging time jump I've ever seen. And since you've had no proper training, I wouldn't expect you to follow through."

I took a deep breath and blew out some of my anger with it. "You mean this isn't normal?"

"No," Sam scoffed. "This is anything but normal. On three of my jumps, another time jumper fixed the glitch because I felt the rod go warm without having to do anything. And on the one I did fix, all I had to do was pick up a dropped message and get it back to the messenger. But this? This is the toughest one I've ever experienced."

"Lucky me," I muttered.

I heard a rustle of movement and then felt Sam's hand on mine. "You can't quit, Dan," she said.

My pulse quickened, like it usually did at her touch, but I fought against the feeling. Following her was going to kill me. "Why not?"

"Because if you do, the bad guys win."

"So? I don't even know who I'm fighting—or what I'm fighting for. Why should I care if they win?"

"Do you trust your dad, Dan?"

"Yeah."

"Then you're fighting for whatever he believed was worth dying to save."

I'd never forget the pain and surprise on Dad's face when Victor stabbed him, or the way Dad used his last bit of strength to throw me the rod. There was no way I could let the bastards who stabbed Dad win.

I rolled onto my side to face Sam, who lay there staring at the sky. "You always know what to say to keep me going. But why do you put up with me and all my whining?" I asked. "This is, what, the fifth or sixth pep talk you've given me? Wouldn't it be easier for you if you didn't have me dragging you down all the time?"

She remained still and didn't answer.

I lay on my back beside her in silence. The night turned black, the sky filled up with stars, the moon rose, and the air cooled. The only sounds were the rustle of forest creatures and the wind sighing through the branches.

"When you're around, I don't feel alone anymore," she said softly. "That's why I don't want you to quit. I don't want to be alone again."

She squeezed my hand then let it go, then she jumped up and sprinted toward the camp. I stumbled after her, but by the time I ducked into our tent after her, her blanket was pulled tight around her, her eyes already shut. Message received: talk time was over.

I lay down beside her and pulled my own blanket around me. As I stared at the tent ceiling, I could feel my resolve strengthen. Tomorrow this nightmare would be over. I'd find the rogue jumper, force him to set history right again, and my stupid adventure could finally end.

CHAPTER 28

A hand clamped down over my mouth, waking me instantly. In the dim light of a covered lantern, a figure knelt beside me. His dagger rested on my neck, just above my Adam's apple. The archer had found me!

"So, you're awake," he whispered, his words coming out in modern English. "Good."

My entire body buzzed with fear, but I didn't dare move—the blade felt razor sharp against my throat.

The archer lifted his hand off my mouth. "Get up. But I'm warning you: if you try anything, you're dead."

I sat upright in the low confines of the tent, facing him. He had a nondescript face, a crude haircut, and wore a frayed tunic with leggings that had holes in the knees. He looked more like a simple Anglo-Saxon peasant than half of the nonfighters in Harold's army. I probably passed him twenty times and never noticed him. "What do you want?" I asked, my voice cracking.

His eyes narrowed. "It all depends on whose child you are."

I needed to keep him talking; it was my only hope of surviving.

"Why does that matter?" I asked while I reached my hand under the woolen blanket and nudged Sam.

She stirred and opened her eyes. "What's up, Dan?" she asked groggily.

"Danny's having a job interview," the archer said.

With a jolt, Sam sat up and pulled out her knife.

In a blur of motion, the archer's other hand whipped out and connected with her wrist, sending her blade tumbling into the far corner of the tent. "You'll have to be faster than that," he chortled.

"One scream from me and the entire camp will be at our tent. Are you faster than that?" Sam asked defiantly.

"Go ahead, scream," the man said. "Dan here will die before you finish, and you'll be dead before the echo of your scream fades." He gave a smug smile. "Now, if we're done with useless threats, answer my question. Who are your fathers?"

"James Renfrew," I said.

"Robert Cahill," Sam whispered.

The archer sucked in his breath. "You're Robert's brat?" An eerie chuckle escaped his lips. "Oh, if only he was alive to see this." His grip tightened on his knife and it pressed harder against my throat. "How many trips into history have you done?"

"This is my first," I squeaked out.

"Fifth," Sam said quietly, her head bowed.

"A first-timer and a female," the rogue jumper mused. "The universe never ceases to amaze me. And what did your dear old dads tell you about the schism among time travelers?"

"Nothing," Sam said, a tinge of sadness in her voice. "He told my brother everything, but he skipped me because I'm a girl."

"My dad didn't even tell me about time-jumping," I said. "I'm here by accident."

"Oh, this is too much." The archer chuckled, and I could tell he was truly laughing because the knife mercifully retreated a fraction from my throat. "New and clueless! Well, let me tell you what your dads didn't," he said, his tone losing its mockery. "Being a time traveler sucks. You save the world constantly, but it just keeps needing to be saved. And what thanks do you get? None. You risk your life to save history, and when you get back to your own time, all you have to show for it are some bruises, cuts, and maybe a few gold coins that the time stream won't miss. Not much of a thank-you," he scoffed. "So some of us decided it was time to change our role."

"You're robbing history, aren't you?" Sam said.

"Don't be so simple," the archer snickered. "People with no imagination dream of being rich. Wealth has destroyed our world. Poor people die of curable diseases while rich corporations spend their heaps of cash in the quest for even more money. Our world leaders lie and steal while the people they're supposed to serve live in poverty and hunger." He gestured with his free hand around the tent. "There's one thing I've learned from my trips into the past: the quest for wealth is the root of all suffering, and people need to be led by those who don't give a damn about wealth."

"Let me guess: people like you, right?" I sneered.

"Not just me," he said. "All the other time travelers who have realized that the world needs better leaders, those who can rule with vision. Look at what great thinkers did for the ancient world: the Great Wall, the pyramids, Stonehenge. The modern world has a million times the wealth of the past, and infinitely superior technology, but we will never build things like that again because our era is poisoned by greed and short-sightedness. Our world needs rulers who can look beyond their own simple needs and instead lead with visions of greatness. Cancer could be cured. Hunger could become a thing of the past."

"What's the catch?" I asked.

"Catch?"

"Yeah, the catch. Because everything you're saying sounds awesome. But my dad wouldn't have fought against you unless there was a catch."

The archer's eyes narrowed. "As much as I liked your father, he always failed to see the big picture. The change we're looking to bring about can't exist without some collateral damage."

Collateral damage?

My skin crawled at that phrase. The military always used it to describe civilian deaths. As if some fancy words could hide the horror of the truth. "How much *collateral damage* are you talking about? Hundreds of people? Thousands?"

His face took on a chilling calm. "Billions."

"You're insane!"

"Not insane. Visionary," the archer insisted, a wild fanaticism in his eye. "You cannot hope to rebuild if you don't destroy first. We are building a new society, free from corruption and greed. And I'm giving you the chance to be part of it."

Now I was completely confused. "But you tried to kill me—twice!"

"You can blame my now-dead partner for that. He viewed anyone not allied to the cause as a threat to be immediately eliminated. When you survived the first attempt, that only made him more focused on your death. He forced me to recklessly create another break in time, hoping that you, and whoever was helping you, would stay and we could eliminate you at our leisure." The rogue jumper pricked me under the chin with the point of his dagger so that a droplet of blood trickled down my neck. "But my partner underestimated you, didn't he? You proved to be much more capable than the bumbling fool you first appeared to be."

This guy was a real charmer. "Uh, thanks?"

"Unfortunately," the archer went on, "the struggle between the rival factions has resulted in the deaths of many skilled men. Once we've gained our final victory, we'll still need competent time travelers to repair anomalies while we rule. You could be one of those." He looked me straight in the eyes. "Your father fought against us, but I hold no grudge for that. Although he was misguided, he struck me as a good man, and he fought for what he thought was right. I just hope that you can show more wisdom than he did. I'm offering you a chance to *make* history, not just fix it, the chance to lead the world to greatness instead of letting it choke to death on its own greed." He shifted his knife so the blade was pressed across my throat again. "But this is a limited-time offer. You need to make your choice right now: either you join us or you die."

My mind scrambled for options, but I saw only one path that would get me out of this tent alive. "All right, I'll join you."

"Me too," Sam said.

The archer laughed at her. "I'm sorry," he said with no trace of sincerity. "This offer is open only to Dan." Without taking his knife away from my neck, he reached across and picked up Sam's fallen knife. "I have in mind something more fitting for the daughter of Robert Cahill—a sort of a thank-you for how that arrogant bastard treated me for so many years." He pressed Sam's knife into my hand. "Kill her."

"What?" I exclaimed. "Why? We said we'd join you."

"Consider this a test of your loyalty."

My fingers closed around the hilt of the knife. How could I stab the archer before he slit my throat?

I couldn't. But there was no way I would kill Sam. She'd saved my life so many times I'd lost count. We were a team. We were partners. And even though I'd known her for only a couple of weeks, she was my best friend.

"I can't."

"Sure you can. Why choose death here in some forgotten time when you can create the future you want?" The archer shifted position so he was now behind me. His knife was still at my neck and his lips hovered close to my ear. "You can do it. Kill her."

My hand trembled and the blade shook in my grasp.

"Please, Dan," Sam pleaded.

"Do it," the archer urged, his knife pressing so hard against my throat now that it split the skin.

Die here in this tent, or kill Sam and try to save the world?

A single tear tracked down Sam's cheek and I let the knife drop from my fingers. "No."

"You idiot," the archer said. "Now I'll—"

A meaty thud shook the tent and the rogue jumper slammed against me, his knife tumbling from his fingers. I picked it up off the ground and whirled around to stab him.

Too late.

A long-handled ax protruded from his back. Through the open tent flap I could see Ceolwulf looming toward us, a broad grin across his bearded face.

"One of my better throws, I think," he said as he ducked through the opening. He placed his boot on the archer's body and wrenched his ax out.

Sam closed her eyes and let out a long breath. "Thank you."

I leaped to my feet and clasped the old warrior by the forearm. "Thank you! You saved my life."

"Bah! I only quieted that prattling swineherd. Sleep would not come to me with all that whispering from your tent." He nudged the body with the toe of his boot. "Is this the last one?"

"I hope so."

"Good. Maybe now I can get some rest." Without another word, he headed back to his own tent.

I turned to Sam. "You okay?"

She slammed her foot into the lifeless form of the rogue jumper. "Better than I was two minutes ago," she said, and kicked at his body again. "Now let's see if this jackass had anything useful on him."

Unfortunately, just like the other rogue jumper we'd killed, this one also had nothing on him but his jump device—which Sam took— and a few coins. Once we finished our search, we raised our tent and moved it away from the body and the large pool of blood spreading around it. No doubt there'd be questions tomorrow, but right now we, too, needed sleep. Not that I could sleep. As I lay on my blanket, my mind kept going over everything the rogue jumper had told us. The plot sounded crazy, but it had been serious enough for Dad to fight against, and he wasn't the type to be scared over nothing.

"So what do you think about everything he told us?" I asked.

Sam turned to face me. "I don't know. Everything he described sounds impossible. How can just a few time jumpers cause that much destruction?"

"Only a week ago I thought time travel was impossible. Now *impossible* has pretty much ceased to have meaning."

"Stop all that blasted yammering!" yelled a voice from one of the nearby tents. "Men are trying to sleep."

I rolled back over and sighed. All the fights I'd had in this time period were only a warm-up. The biggest battle waited for me back in my own time—if I ever got home again.

CHAPTER 29

"Murderer!" a man howled, breaking the stillness of the morning and rousing me from my fitful sleep.

Someone had found the rogue jumper. I opened my eyes to see Eadward crouching inside our tent, sword drawn and leveled at me.

"No more will you get away with your foul deeds," he spat. "Killing one of the king's household is an attack on the king himself."

Normally, waking up to find a man waving a sword at me and accusing me of murder would be enough to get my adrenaline spiking. But having men wave weapons in my face was becoming a way of life. Plus, I was innocent this time, and I had Ceolwulf as a witness to prove it. "Good morning to you too, Eadward," I said, yawning.

He scowled. "You would not be so calm if you knew what lies outside. The ground itself speaks against you this time, so the priest will not be able to save you." He brandished his sword at me again and withdrew from the tent.

"Never a dull moment when you're around, is there?" Sam observed, propping herself up on one elbow.

"Nope," I said grimly.

We stumbled out of our tent and into the clearing to find ourselves surrounded by a large group of housecarls. They formed a wide circle around the archer's body and the spot where our tent used to stand. Men pointed out to each other the bloodstains on the sandy soil and the gouges in the ground from when Sam and I had dragged our tent to its current location. Angry mutters broke out as the crowd caught sight of us.

King Harold, accompanied by his closest retainers, pushed his way through the crowd. His cloak hung crooked on his shoulders, and like all of us, his face looked weary after so many days on the road. He glanced at the corpse lying sprawled on the ground, and his posture stiffened. "Who has dared kill one of my household?"

Angry eyes turned to me and Sam. "I can explain," I stammered. "He crept into my tent and—"

"I killed him," Ceolwulf declared as he strode confidently into the circle.

King Harold turned to Ceolwulf. "This man lies dead from a wound in the back. Yet I know you, Ceolwulf, son of Guthraed, and you are not one to slay a man in such a cowardly manner. Why do you protect this boy?"

"I tell you the truth," Ceolwulf said. "That treacherous snake had a knife at the throat of Leofric here. I saw he meant to murder the poor boy and also the girl who shares his tent. So I sank my ax into his back. Not a heroic deed but necessary to save them."

"You, boy," King Harold snapped at me. "What was this man's grievance against you?"

I gave a short bow to the king. "He's the traitor I've been looking for, my lord. He was worried I'd find him, so he tried to kill me before I did."

My announcement produced a remarkable change in the house-carls' collective demeanor. They turned their vicious glances from me to the corpse.

"What proof do you have of his traitorous intentions?" Harold asked.

"None. But look at the bloodstain. It lies where my tent was standing last night. He clearly came looking for me. I didn't go to find him."

One of the housecarls crouched next to the stain. He hovered with his fingers over the soil, as if reading a passage from a book. "The ground here is hard to read as men have already walked over it this morning." He moved in a wider circle around the stain. "But I see shoe prints leading to the old tent site. They are light and small-spaced, which means that whoever left them was trying to make little sound as he approached. The ground tells me he came stalking these two and was not forced into their tent."

The king closed his eyes and steepled his fingers, not yet saying anything. Here was the fourth man to die because of me. I was innocent, but would the king see it that way—or would he decide I was bad luck and get rid of me?

After a few agonizing seconds, he opened his eyes and addressed Ceolwulf. "The death was clearly deserved, and I am rid of a traitor. For this, I thank you." He pointed to the corpse. "Leave his body for the wolves. He does not deserve a proper burial." With that, the king turned to walk away.

I couldn't let the king leave, not without first getting some information. "My lord," I called out. "Did this man tell you anything about fighting Duke William?"

The king stopped and looked at me, his eyes flashing with annoyance. "I do not know this man. He has never spoken to me."

"Are you sure, my lord?" I pressed. "He would have spoken to you just after our victory over Tostig and Hardrada. He might have tried to give you bad advice that would let Duke William win."

I braced myself for the worst as King Harold inhaled deeply. But then he paused and glanced one more time at the face of the rogue jumper, studying it intently for a few seconds. "I do know him," he said, sounding surprised. "He brought me my horse after we crossed the bridge at Stamford."

"Did he tell you anything?"

"Yes. He advised me that in any future battle, I must ensure that the men stay together and we do not chase after retreating foes unless the day is won for certain. Strange words to come from a man who does not fight, but very sound ones."

"Is that all?"

"Aye. I have not seen him since."

"What about his tent?" I asked. "Could we have a look inside for any evidence that might explain his treachery?"

The king frowned at me. "My priest will read through all missives found in this man's tent and inform me of any foul purpose."

"But could I just—"

"You forget your place!" King Harold snarled. "You have done me a great service by finding this traitor, but I will not let a simple peasant boy root through his possessions. Men I know and trust shall do the search."

I put my hands up and stepped back. I knew they wouldn't find anything of use to them. The guy was a time jumper, not a traitor.

The crowd dispersed quickly to break camp, men pausing only to spit on the archer's corpse. Sam and I intentionally took our time packing up so that the army would depart before we finished and we could talk without being overheard. Aethelraed offered to leave his serving boy behind to help us, but we waved him off, assuring him and Ceolwulf that we'd catch up.

"What are we going to do about the time glitch?" I asked Sam as soon as the last stragglers of the army had passed us.

She finished tightening a strap on her horse's saddle. "We have to figure out how to undo the damage the rogue jumper has already caused. How much do you know about the Battle of Hastings?"

I thought back to my lessons at home: musty old books, tons of history websites, a few animated computer programs, and a lot of lectures from Dad with details drawn out on a whiteboard. "The Normans invaded England because their leader, William, thought he deserved to be the king of England—he was distantly related to the king before Harold, I think. But, as we have seen, Harold isn't the type of guy to hand over his crown to any dude with a few boats and an army. So Harold's going south to fight William's army. They'll meet up near the town of Hastings."

"That's great," Sam said, her voice dripping with sarcasm. "What do you know about the *actual* battle?"

"I know that the Anglo-Saxons lost," I said.

"That's it?"

I shrugged. "Sorry. My dad never actually explained to me why I had to study all this stuff. If I'd known that I was going to have to fight the battle myself, I would've paid a lot more attention."

"You know more than I do, at least. My dad never taught me anything about history." She tossed up her hands in exasperation. "And he sure as hell never warned me about any insane plot to take over the world."

"Yeah, my dad skipped that part too. But let's just concentrate on how to get out of here alive. Since the archer told Harold to keep his troops together, I'm guessing the Anglo-Saxons lost the battle because they broke formation."

"All right," Sam said. "So if we want to fix this glitch, you'll just need to get Harold to ignore the idiot's advice."

"You're kidding, right? What would I tell him? That staying in formation is a dumb idea, and that he *should* scatter his army around and chase after false retreats? No thanks. I've had one near-drowning; I don't want another one."

"There must be some way," she insisted. "The guy wouldn't have created a time glitch if he didn't know how to fix it."

"I wonder if he was planning to kill King Harold," I mused. "You know, let the battle rage on, then just kill Harold so the Saxons lose heart and run away?"

Sam snorted. "I wouldn't put it past him."

"But killing King Harold doesn't mean for sure that the Anglo-Saxons would lose," I said. "There has to be a better way to fix this."

After about an hour of completely useless brainstorming, Sam and I gave up. We hadn't figured out a single decent plan. As we rode along in the wake of the army, I kept imagining how much the world would change if the Anglo-Saxons did win. Without William as king, the next thousand years of English kings and queens would be totally screwed up—the entire history of Europe and potentially the world could change. But what else might get messed up? Would Sam and I suddenly fade away to nothing because we'd killed off our own histories? I didn't know what scared me more, the thought of being stuck forever in this time and spending the rest of my life as a medieval peasant or just … disappearing.

If I had the dates right, we had just over a week until the Battle of Hastings; that had to be long enough for us to figure out an answer.

CHAPTER 30

On the fifth day out of Eoforwic, it finally looked like our long ride south was coming to an end. Ahead of us, on the banks of a wide river, stretched a huge walled city that could only be London. All manner of ships sailed or rowed along the river, while endless cart and foot traffic went in and out of the city's gates.

"Aaah, home," Ceolwulf said. "It will be good to get some rest for a few days before we set out again."

Rest. What an awesome word. After all the beatings and wounds I'd suffered, I desperately needed time off. "Are you staying here?" I asked.

"No. I will go to my lands outside the city," Ceolwulf said firmly. "The fight against Duke William will not be an easy one. If it is to be my last battle, I would like to have time with my family." He turned his head to the west, staring out past the fields that surrounded the city. "I have not seen them in over a fortnight. My son will no doubt chafe at missing the slaughter of the Northmen and will beg me to tell him all about the battle. I will tell him tales of glory and of bloody combat. Some of those tales might even be true."

Ceolwulf bowed his head and his voice grew quieter. "I hope he is still ill, though, for I do not wish him to join me against the Normans. They ride their horses in battle and have many skilled warriors fighting under their banner. If I am to die, I would have it that my son remains safe to carry on my line." He turned toward me and Sam. "And what of you two? Will you join me at my hall, or will you stay here?"

Sam and I both gazed out over the wide expanse of the Thames River curling off into the distance before exchanging a quiet glance. "I think we'll stay here in the city for the next few days," Sam said. "I've never been here before."

Ceolwulf bowed his head to Sam then grasped my forearm. "We shall meet again soon, then. Once the king has gathered enough men to move against Duke William, I will return."

Aethelraed clapped me on my back. "I go to see my wife and children as well, and to make sure the harvest has been gathered from the fields. I look forward to putting aside my spear for a few days and instead holding a good honest rake."

The two of them turned their horses and headed off along a trail that branched from the main road. "Enjoy the city," Ceolwulf called back to us. "We shall see you again in a few days."

Many of the housecarls followed their example and departed for their homes, but there was no shortage of men still in the city. For the next few days, a steady stream of warriors poured into London, answering the king's call, just like the lords around Eoforwic had done previously.

Sam and I didn't see King Harold during these next few days, but from some of the housecarls we learned that he was constantly hurrying around the city, meeting with advisers, dispatching messengers, or praying for guidance as he planned for the coming conflict. With the army in a holding pattern, we had free rein to explore the city. There wasn't much to see, though. Big Ben, the British Museum, the Tower of London, and anything else touristy didn't exist yet. What we found instead were wood buildings crowded on top of each other, narrow muddy streets separating them, and raw sewage lying everywhere.

Despite the lack of tourist attractions, I tried to show Sam a good time without seeming too desperate or annoying. Barring an epic failure on my part, these would be our last days together, and I wanted to make the most of them. I told her jokes, took her on walks along the riverbank, inquired to find the best taverns and inns for meals, and talked about my life growing up. I was about as smooth as sandpaper, but I couldn't help wanting to impress her.

And Sam opened up to me, too, telling me about all her time jumps and quite a few things about her childhood—happy memories shared with her father and brother.

Our time together was ending, though. On October 10, Harold sent messengers throughout the city announcing that the army would be leaving the next morning. Sam and I spent our last few coins on a meal at a decent pub, listened to minstrels in the square, then headed toward the Thames to view the sunset.

We sat on the grass, watching vibrant reds and yellows light up the sky. A cool wind blew over the water, and Sam huddled against me for warmth. I put my arm around her, deliberately drawing her into me. She felt so good next to me, like she belonged there. I should have been happy, enjoying this moment while it lasted, but a question kept burning inside me. I tried not to speak and maybe ruin the moment, but ultimately I just couldn't stop myself.

"Sam," I began, my voice starting to crack. "We head south tomorrow. If a miracle happens and we somehow save the day, then we're done here. Assuming I live through it, what happens after that?"

"What do you mean?"

I fidgeted and tried to find the right words. What I really wanted to say was *You're incredible and I can't stand the thought of not being near you.* "Well, if everything goes right, we'll jump back to our own time.

What happens to us? Will we … see each other again … you know, in our time?"

She twisted her hands together nervously for a few seconds before responding. "Don't take this the wrong way," she began, and I could feel my heart crumble. "I think you're a great guy. I feel safe when I'm around you—just like when my brother was still alive."

My insides turned to jelly. *Brother.* Even though it had been my mantra for days, hearing her say it was brutal. She should've just stabbed me; it would've been less painful.

She rested her hand on my arm. "I really like you, Dan." Her voice sounded raw. "You're funny and brave. But we can't be together."

"Why not?" I asked, searching her face for an answer. "I know it won't be easy, but Virginia and New York aren't that far apart."

"No. It's not that." She avoided my gaze, casting her eyes to the ground. "I like it when you're around, and we work great together, but I can't let myself get close to you."

"What's wrong with me?"

"Nothing." Sam turned away from me. "Just let it go."

"I can't. Please, Sam. Just tell me what's wrong."

Sam leaped to her feet and turned to face me, her cheeks flushed and her eyes glassy. "You really want to know? It's because everyone I've ever loved has left me." She sniffed back a tear. "My mom, my dad, my brother—they all left. I will *not* let myself care about anyone again."

"I won't leave you," I protested, but she didn't stick around to hear me out. She had already raced off down the riverbank, a receding figure against the darkening sky.

I charged after her, trying to catch up, but after a few streets, I lost her in the maze of alleys. Heartbroken, I slunk back to the tent we shared next to the river and waited for her to return.

I should have kept my damn mouth shut. I just wanted to see her again, to tell her I was sorry. But I fell asleep without her warmth beside me, and she still wasn't there when I woke up the next morning.

The king's army assembled outside the city in preparation for the march south. Our numbers had swollen by thousands of men, hastily gathered from all over the countryside. Many were mounted, but even more traveled by foot. I easily found Ceolwulf and Aethelraed among the housecarls, and I breathed a sigh of relief when I saw Sam next to them. She was safe but doing her best not to look at me.

"Good morning," I muttered as I pulled my horse up beside them.

"There is very little good about this morning," Ceolwulf growled.

"What's wrong?" I asked.

He spat on the ground and grimaced. "King Harold orders us to move south today. We have not enough men, and few archers. It is foolish to march to the attack now."

Aethelraed nodded. "Aye, a fool's errand. But the king has heard of Duke William's ravaging of the southern lands, and Harold will not let his people suffer that blasted Norman's attacks any longer. Our king hopes to rush south and surprise the duke, like he did with Hardrada and Tostig in the north."

"So he is sending only half an army to fight William and his Normans?" Ceolwulf snorted. "Did his brothers provide him with this ill counsel?"

"Peace, Ceolwulf," Aethelraed chided. "Gyrth and Leofwine both advised Harold against this course. It was a decision of his own making."

Ceolwulf shook his head. "May we at least find good ground to fight on so that the Normans will not have too much of an advantage. With few archers and not a complete force of warriors, we will be hard-pressed to gain victory. My only joy is that my son has not fully recovered, so he will not be part of this slaughter." Ceolwulf turned to face me. "And you should leave too. Take Aelfwyn and head back to your homes. You have a full life left to live. Don't let your blood stain the ground because our king is not wise enough to wait a few more days."

I'd love to go home. I'd love to sleep in my warm bed, eat real food, not worry about people killing me, and find out how my dad was doing. But none of that could happen until I made sure that Ceolwulf, Aethelraed, and the rest of the Anglo-Saxons lost the battle. I lowered my eyes, feeling like a traitor. "I can't leave you guys," I said softly.

"Stubborn, like my own son," Ceolwulf remarked, but by the way he nodded, I could tell he meant it as a compliment.

We started the march out of London with no inspiring speech from King Harold. Just a single horn ringing out, then the horses and men began heading south. King Harold and his two brothers, Gyrth and Leofwine, took the lead, followed by his housecarls, then the rest of the mounted troops, and finally all the foot soldiers streaming behind us.

During the ride south, I kept trying to talk with Sam, but any time I pulled my horse next to hers, she galloped ahead or slowed down and put other riders between us. And when we camped at night, she busied herself with random chores or chatted with Ceolwulf and Aethelraed—anything to avoid me. The only time I got close to her was in our tent at night, but she would just quickly mutter goodnight, then close her eyes and turn away from me.

We managed only a few short conversations during the entire journey south, and these were always time-glitch related. And we always reached the same conclusion: we still didn't know how to solve it. So for most of the journey I traveled in silence, guiding my horse along the country roads and forest trails, my anxiety building with each step closer to Hastings.

In the late afternoon on the third day out of London, the army came to a halt in a forested area that the scouts said lay only a short distance away from the enemy's camp. This was it. Tomorrow morning I'd be facing the Normans. Thousands of men would come charging at me with the sole goal of seeing me dead. I'd have to worry about arrows, spears, swords, axes—and who knew what else—hurtling toward me. One wrong move and that'd be it—game over. And through all the chaos, I'd have to somehow fix history and make sure my side lost. The immensity of my situation felt like an elephant sitting on my chest. I was only sixteen years old. I shouldn't be here. And the one person I'd counted on to help me, who I'd poured my heart out to, wouldn't even talk to me. I cupped my face in my hands. My life utterly sucked, and I had no clue what to do about it.

Ceolwulf rested a hand on my shoulder. "Your brow looks heavy with thought. Do you fear tomorrow's clash?"

He probably expected some manly, chest-thumping answer, but I gave him the truth. "Yeah."

He nodded. "All men should feel some fear on the eve of battle. Many will die and never see their homes and loved ones again. But a man can choose two ways in which to spend what may be his last night. He can sit and pray like the Normans do, hoping to convince God that their side is right and that they should be victorious. Or they can do things my way." He reached into his cloak and pulled out an ale skin. "I choose to spend what may be my last night in the company of friends, having one last celebration of the life we all have lived." He held out his ale skin to me. "There is plenty of drink to go around. Will you join us now, or will you spend this night some other way?"

The girl of my dreams wasn't even talking to me, there was a good chance that I'd die tomorrow, and even if I did survive, time would probably be messed up beyond repair. Only one thing to do. I took the ale skin, swigged down the bitter, warm liquid, and then wiped my mouth with the back of my hand.

"If this is my last night alive," I muttered as I passed the ale skin back to him, "let's make sure it's unforgettable."

CHAPTER 31

October 14, 1066, was, without a doubt, the most important day in my measly sixteen years of existence. The next thousand years of history depended on me being able to step up and be at the top of my game, today. What a totally crap time to have a massive headache.

Actually, calling what I had a headache would be like calling the Battle of Stamford Bridge a minor disagreement between brothers. My head was pounding as if someone had hammered railway spikes into it and my mouth felt dry and puffy like it was full of cotton. I was in no shape to fight, never mind save history.

Ceolwulf peered into my tent. "Rise, Leofric! We march to battle!"

"Shh ... not so loud," I croaked as the full extent of my hangover hit me.

He threw back his head and laughed. "I see you are regretting now the large amount of ale you drank last night." He slapped the side of my foot. "Come, rouse yourself! Battle waits for no man."

"It's still dark outside. Too early for fighting," I mumbled, grasping my head in my hands as I staggered to my feet. A wave of vertigo almost sent me back to the ground, but I grabbed a tent post to support me.

"We must leave now if we are to take Duke William's men by surprise." He dumped a water skin and a heel of bread onto my blanket. "Eat while you dress yourself. We head for the field of slaughter soon. Meet me by the horses."

Ceolwulf exited the tent, leaving me alone. Sam's blanket lay empty next to mine. That figured. Ever since that awful night in London when I'd poured my heart out to her, she'd been making sure to get up before me. I knew she was scared that I'd want to talk more about that night, so I kind of understood her running away. But this was different. This was the day of battle. She could've at least had the decency to say goodbye. I shrugged, then guzzled the water and nibbled at the bread, my stomach churning at each mouthful. Why had I drunk so much?

Through the tent flap, I saw men scrambling out of their tents and donning their own armor. Judging by the lack of light and how tired I felt, I figured it was around five in the morning. I pulled the cold links of my chain mail over my tunic, then belted on my sword and seax, gripped my shield, and tucked my helmet under my arm. A shiver ran through me as I stepped out into the cool morning air before heading to the picket lines where the horses stood.

By the light of a blazing fire, men saddled their mounts, inspected their shields for cracks, and sharpened weapons one last time before battle. I found my horse standing near the end of the line of pickets and heaved the saddle across its back. I couldn't help muttering to myself as I worked. Sam's horse was already saddled. So she had woken up early, crept out of the tent, and was probably hoping to sneak away without even seeing me. Did I mean that little to her?

As if on cue, a figure stepped out from the trees. She wore her hood up, hiding her red hair, but there was no mistaking Sam.

"Hi," she said hesitantly.

I really didn't have time for her games. "You finally decided to talk to me? What's the big occasion?"

She reached out toward me, but I pulled away from her. She dropped her hand to her side and bowed her head. "I'm sorry, Dan. I shouldn't have ignored you. I just—"

"But you did! You're not the one going out there into danger. *I am.* I'm putting my life on the line to save us, and you wouldn't even talk to me."

"I'm talking to you now."

"Ooh, lucky me," I said. "I'll throw myself a party once the battle's over. If I survive."

"Please don't be like this," she pleaded.

"I'm tired, I've got a massive headache, and I've got an excellent chance today of either getting killed or being trapped here forever. How do you expect me to be?"

She drew her lips together tightly and shook her head. I turned away from her, tossing the bridle over my horse's nose and neck. As I moved around the animal's head, Sam appeared right beside me. She took my hand and placed two brown tablets in it.

"What's this?"

"Ibuprofen. No time jumper should be without it." She gave a half-hearted smile and gazed at me expectantly.

"Umm … thanks," I muttered as I gathered what little saliva I could from my cotton mouth and swallowed the chalky painkillers.

She rested her hand on my forearm. I didn't pull away this time. "I'm really sorry, Dan."

It was impossible to stay mad at her. Despite my constant efforts to fight it, I'd fallen for her—hard. I couldn't help it, though. She was the most incredible girl I'd ever met, and we'd been through so much together. Maybe she didn't feel the same way about me, but how long was I going to act like a jerk toward her? If this was our last moment together, I'd rather spend it as friends.

"I know. I'm sorry for snapping at you," I said, my tone softer. "You know, I actually had fun here."

"Me too." She smiled.

I nodded toward her horse. "Where are you going?"

"King Harold's wife and some other noble ladies are supposed to be coming to watch the battle. I'll hang with them. Maybe I'll get lucky and pick up some last-minute info that could change the outcome."

"What do you think our chances are?"

She twisted a strand of hair in her fingers and chewed on the end of it. "I don't know. It doesn't look good, though. The rogue jumper probably had some great plan to undo all the damage he'd caused, but we're stuck."

"You know, um, if we do make it out of this … can I call you? Or text you?"

"I really—" Sam began but I held up a hand to stop her.

"Look, I'm not trying to stalk you or anything. If you're right, and my dad's dead, I'll be completely alone when we get back. I just want someone to talk to."

Sam's eyes crinkled with amusement as she reached into her sleeve and pulled out a scrap of parchment about the size of a business card. "Actually, what I wanted to say, before you interrupted me, was that I really would like that. You're the only person I can talk to about all this." She put the fragment in my hands. "Here's my number. Don't lose it."

Our hands sat there, hers on mine. My skin tingled at her touch and I gazed for what could be the last time into her eyes that sparkled like emeralds.

"Time to move!" King Harold yelled, shattering our moment.

I tucked the piece of parchment into my belt pouch. "I guess I have to go now," I said as men began to mount their horses and lead them along the narrow trail heading south.

"Don't be a hero." She gripped my arm tightly. "As soon as that rod gets warm, get the hell out of there."

"You too, Sam. Take care of yourself."

She smiled sadly. "I always do."

Without warning, she put her arms around me and kissed me. Not just a sisterly peck on the cheek, but a full-fledged, lips-on-lips, open-mouthed kiss. In that instant, only Sam existed. The smoky smell of her hair, the feel of her cloak under my fingers, the curve of her in my arms. She pulled back from the kiss. "Don't die, Dan," she said breathlessly.

I stood there speechless as she hopped on her horse and snatched the reins into her hand, ready to ride off. Suddenly, she turned in the saddle and locked eyes with me. "Two hours due north of Roanoke. I get straight As in English and history. And I love rom-coms."

"What?" I asked, totally confused.

"Those are the answers to the questions you asked me outside the church in Eoforwic." Before I could respond, she kicked her heels into the ribs of her horse and rode away.

As I stood there in a daze, Ceolwulf appeared next to me. "So, Leofric. You drank well, you slept well, and you even got a farewell kiss from the comely maiden. Ready to die now?"

I watched her disappear into the forest, my insides quivering. If I survived this battle, I'd find her. "Ready as I'll ever be."

"Then let us hurry," Aethelraed said. "If we are to surprise Duke William, we must strike before he knows we are on the march."

We leaped on our horses and followed the rest of the mounted Anglo-Saxons, King Harold in the lead. Almost two thousand of us rode headlong down the path, two and three abreast, with thousands of footmen racing after us. The trail sloped downward for a distance, taking us along a ridge leading to another hill, and from there descending to the main road to Hastings. A glitter of sunlight reflected off something on the road ahead.

"Normans!" yelled one of the housecarls in the lead.

Ahead of us galloped about two hundred Norman cavalry. At the sight of us they veered off the main road and tore up the smaller path toward us.

"Ride!" Harold yelled. "We must not let them reach the high ground!"

We raced for the hill ahead, broken earth flying off our horses' hooves. One of the Normans pulled out a horn and blew on it three times. An answering call came from the south. William's army knew we were here; we had lost our chance at surprise. But we weren't going to lose the high ground. As the enemy galloped their horses uphill, Harold's forces rode with mad abandon to the crest. As each housecarl reached the hilltop, he jumped off his horse, smacked it on the rump to hurry it out of the way, then locked shields with the man next to him to create a small shield wall. The Normans veered off at the sight of this rapidly forming barrier, retreating to the bottom of the hill.

Reaching the crest, I dismounted, slapped my horse on its rump so that it would run away, and then took my place in the shield wall as other men came rushing to support us. So this was the site of the Battle of Hastings? It certainly wouldn't have been my first choice for a defensive position. The "high ground" that King Harold had rushed to protect looked like the bunny slope at a low-budget ski resort. Horses would be able to charge uphill with ease. The only thing protecting us was the forest on both sides, which would force the Normans to attack us head on.

As the sun crested the treetops, the rhythmic thumping of men marching sounded from the south. I'd been holding onto the slim hope that I wouldn't have to fight. No chance of that now. The Normans were coming.

Over the din of stomping feet, the jangle of weapons and horses became louder. Then the Norman cavalry appeared, emerging from the mist-covered road that lay to the south of us: hundreds of horsemen clad in chain-mail armor and carrying shields and spears. I bit my lip as I watched them. They looked so much stronger, so much more professional than our mix of housecarls and troops pulled from all over the south of England. Brightly colored banners suspended from spear shafts waved above them. A gold banner, flying higher than the others, caused a ripple of concern to spread among the Anglo-Saxons.

"What's that flag?" I asked Ceolwulf.

"That is the pope's banner," he spat, glaring at it with his one good eye. "He has given his blessing to the Normans in this battle. Although any pope who encourages Christian men to make war on each other is not worthy of the name." He watched the Norman horsemen move off the road and spread out at the bottom of the hill. "We must set ourselves for battle. I would have you fight alongside us, unless there is elsewhere you would be."

Other than back in my own time and safe in my bed, the only place I wanted to be now was with Ceolwulf and Aethelraed. Even though we were from different eras, I felt like we were all in this together. No matter how the fight ended, I wanted to be at their side.

I followed them over to the left flank of the hill, which would be commanded by Harold's brother Gyrth. Harold's brother Leofwine had the right wing, while Harold himself held the center, his two banners—the Fighting Man and the Gold Dragon of Wessex—fluttering in the breeze above him.

All around me, housecarls and other warriors rushed around, jockeying for position. There were so many men on the top of the hill now that we barely had room to move. "Where do I stand?" I asked Ceolwulf.

"Stay behind Aethelraed and me," Ceolwulf said as he jammed extra spears point first into the ground in front of him. "If either of us falls, you must take our place in the line."

I nodded and took my place behind them. All along our front lines were two or three rows of housecarls. Every one of them wanted to prove his bravery by being in the front of the line. Behind them, about ten rows deep, were the various local lords with their troops. Would these men be strong enough to hold against William and his thousands of Normans? And did I even want them to be? I either led my friends to their deaths or remained stuck here forever.

A knot formed in my stomach as I stared down at the Norman army gathering at the foot of the hill. As the men finished coming off the road, they divided themselves into three groups: archers, footmen, and cavalry. At the head of the Norman army rode a tall man wearing the same chain-mail armor and conical helmet as the riders around him. What set him apart was his weapon. Where others carried spears or swords, he held a short wooden staff in the crook of his arm. This had to be Duke William, the man I needed to ensure became King of England.

William separated himself from the group and rode forward twenty paces. He then turned his horse around to face his army. He was too far away to hear, but by the way his men raised their arms and yelled in approval, I figured he'd just given them some sort of rousing pep talk.

He thrust his staff high in the air, and a loud swell of noise came from the Norman lines. William yelled a few further commands, and the archers moved forward. Hundreds of them started walking slowly up the hill.

"Shields ready!" Gyrth yelled.

My knuckles cracked as I clutched my shield tight against my body. This flimsy piece of wood banded with leather was all that stood between me and the rain of arrows about to descend.

"Not like that, boy," said the housecarl to my left. "Put your shield down for now and rest your arm. When the time comes, hold your shield straight in front of you and make sure it touches mine and the shield to your right. That way, you will protect everyone, not just yourself."

I gulped and nodded. I'd never even played dodgeball before, so how was I supposed to know what to do when people took a shot at me?

"Relax, boy," the warrior added. "We have a long fight ahead of us."

The Norman archers proceeded to within two hundred paces of our lines and then stopped. They raised their bows and each nocked an arrow, drawing bowstrings back to their chests.

"Loose!" the archer captain yelled.

An ominous hiss whispered through the air as hundreds of arrows took flight, arcing for our lines like a swarm of locusts. On cue, every man raised his shield. Mine banged into place and I ducked my head low, waiting for the deadly points and praying that none snuck through and hit me.

A sound like hail pounding on picnic tables reverberated across the hilltop, punctuated by the odd cry as arrows snaked their way into gaps, pierced through armor, and found flesh. Men dropped to the ground, screaming and clutching at feathered shafts.

With most of King Harold's archers still on their way, we could fire back only a few arrows in response. Instead, we stood there and took the pounding. Barrage after barrage hit our ranks, and I winced each time I felt an arrow slam into my wooden shield. The partially healed wound in my shoulder screamed in protest, but I didn't dare lower my arm. One wrong move could mean death.

After what seemed like an eternity, the pounding stopped and a wild howling came from below. The archers had retreated down-hill, and in their place came the Norman footmen. Thousands of them advanced in a line, their spears raised to shoulder height. They marched slowly until they were about three hundred paces away, then began to quicken their stride.

The men closest to Harold began pounding their shields. "Out! Out! Out!" they chanted. The cry picked up until every Anglo-Saxon voiced it and the hilltop reverberated to their bellows of defiance. They were making it clear where William could take his army—and his claim to the throne.

Ceolwulf grabbed one of the extra spears lined up in front of him and handed it to me. "Your sword will be of no use now. Take this and stab at all who come near."

I grasped the six-foot length of wood in my right hand. I'd seen these spears in action at Stamford Bridge—their short metal tips could end a life easily. Hopefully I wouldn't have to use mine.

The Normans advanced to within one hundred paces of us, and the housecarls in our front rank raised their spears above their heads, ready to throw, with more jammed into the ground in front of them. I didn't have an extra spear, and even if I had, I wouldn't have thrown it; I didn't want to hit anyone. I'd stab at someone if it meant my own survival, but otherwise I was going to do my best to sit this one out. I wanted no more blood on my hands.

"Hold!" Gyrth yelled.

Fifty paces away now. I could make out individual faces among the Normans. So many grim-looking men determined to sweep us off our hilltop.

"Loose!" Gyrth shouted.

A hail of spears, hand axes, and large rocks flew from our lines and hundreds of Normans crashed to the ground. Their front ranks faltered, but the rest kept coming, racing doggedly uphill to attack us. King Harold's army then launched a second volley, killing and maiming more of the onrushing horde.

With a thunderous crash, the Normans smashed into our shield wall. Ceolwulf, Aethelraed, and the rest of the front row leaned forward with all their might against the attack and didn't give ground. On both sides of me, warriors stabbed out with their spears over the heads of those in the first row, trying to find any place to get a sharp point in and end a life. I stabbed with my spear, aiming specifically for hands or legs, any place that might wound a man but keep him alive.

The air resounded with the relentless thudding of spears hitting shields, men yelling taunts or howling in pain. So many Anglo-Saxons crowded the hilltop that I couldn't take a step, but my spear kept darting until it felt like a load of bricks in my hand. Thankfully I didn't kill anyone, but my stomach still churned at my actions. Whenever I aimed high, trying to poke a guy in the shoulder or arm, there was always someone else's spear sneaking in low for a thrust to the target's midsection while my spear distracted the victim. Each shocked and pained expression etched itself onto my memory, adding to all those already there.

The Normans numbered in the thousands, all of them well trained in battle and fully equipped for war. But the Anglo-Saxons were fighting for their homes with a ferocity that no Norman mercenary on foreign soil could match. No matter how hard the Normans pressed, our line did not give way. If a housecarl fell, the man in the line behind him pushed forward into the gap.

As the fight continued to rage, the clamor of combat grew even louder from the right side of our line, punctuated constantly by agonized screams. Clearly one side was winning, but which? The rod hadn't yet turned warm, so I was pretty sure it wasn't the enemy.

Then I saw a Norman running away from our lines—and another soon followed. Then a group of five. Then a group too large to count. Within seconds, the entire Norman left wing had turned and fled, abandoning their dead and wounded behind them.

A rousing cheer rose from our right, and over the heads of the men clustered around me, I could just make out Leofwine, the king's brother, jabbing his spear skyward. He started running downhill, pursuing the fleeing Normans. Housecarls and warriors from the right flank followed him, attacking the retreating Norman infantry. With axes and spears, the Anglo-Saxons stabbed and hacked at the fleeing men, killing even more as they continued downhill.

"Hold!" Harold yelled, his voice barely audible over the din of battle. "Hold!"

Men picked up the cry, relaying it down our ranks. "Hold the line!"

But Leofwine either didn't hear his brother or deliberately ignored him. While the center and left wings of Harold's army stayed firm on the hilltop, Leofwine and those under his command charged on downhill, away from us, slaying Normans as they went.

With half their line running, the remaining Normans started to retreat, leaving their wounded behind them.

Yaaaaaaaahhhhhh! We kicked butt!

I pumped my spear above my head, but my fist froze in midair. We weren't supposed to kick butt—we were supposed to lose. I might've done an awesome job at surviving, but I'd failed miserably in the saving-history department. And judging by the men around me, the battle could end right now. The Anglo-Saxon warriors watched the retreating Normans with hungry eyes. Some even took tentative steps forward from our lines. Others put aside their spears and picked up their close-combat weapons. Everyone shared the same thought—one solid charge right now could wipe out the entire Norman infantry.

"Hold!" Harold yelled again. He could also sense that his army was itching to run down the fleeing Normans.

Run! Damn it! Run!

I stood there unblinking, every brain cell trying to will the Normans to move faster. Any second now Harold could change his mind and send his army to finish off the withdrawing footmen. That would be it. I'd be stuck in this time period as Leofric for the rest of my life. History would be screwed up for eternity. And I'd have no chance of seeing Dad again.

A trumpet sounded from below, and the Norman cavalry came charging up the hill. In the center rode Duke William, spear in one hand, shield and reins clutched in the other. Leofwine and his troops either didn't see them coming, or they didn't care, as they continued to chase the infantry.

William's horsemen edged past the fleeing Norman infantry and slammed straight into Leofwine's men. Without the safety of the shield wall, Leofwine's troops now had little defense against the Normans. Housecarls and warriors alike fell under the onslaught.

"William is mine!" yelled Gyrth from somewhere to my right. He leaped forward, spear in hand, and raced for the chaos below us.

"Halt, Gyrth!" yelled Harold, but the man ignored him. Gyrth, the younger brother, the man who had no military victories to speak of, was aiming for glory today.

Gyrth's personal band of warriors chased after him, not wanting to miss out on the carnage, but no one else dared disobey the king's orders.

Gyrth launched his spear into the mass of Norman cavalry. It arced through the air, heading for Duke William. Every muscle in my body tensed as I watched its path.

Miss!

The spear fell short of William but sank into the neck of his mount. The animal bucked and whinnied in agony as William hauled at the reins, trying to regain control. The horse jerked sideways and the duke fell out of the saddle, disappearing from my view.

Seconds later Gyrth and his men joined in the carnage halfway down the hill, becoming lost in the confusion. From my position at the summit of the hill, I tried to figure out what was going on, but the battle was a wild mess. All I could tell was that many men were dying down there, and the rod at my back still hadn't warmed up.

"Duke William is dead!" a Norman knight suddenly yelled out.

His words sent a howl of fear among the Normans and the jumbled retreat turned into a rout. Cavalry and infantry turned and raced downhill, all thoughts for their own safety tossed aside. The Anglo-Saxons pursued them, killing relentlessly as they went.

William's dead?

I felt an ache in my chest as the hopelessness of the situation hit me. After all that I'd done, I'd failed. Game over.

CHAPTER 32

I was stuck in Anglo-Saxon England—forever. What was I going to
do? Settle down in some little cottage with Sam, trying to live a
normal life while dealing with the knowledge that we'd both failed
history? Was I doomed to be a farmer?

I looked up to see what Ceolwulf was doing. He stood there watching the battle below, a large smile across his scarred face. He turned
and saw me looking at him. "We have won, Leofric!" he cheered.

Beside him, Aethelraed shook his spear and began yelling at the
top of his lungs, while other housecarls banged their shields or bellowed their own shouts of victory.

I couldn't share in their celebration. Instead I lay down my spear
and shield and sat silently on the ground. Judging by the sun, I had
been in the line for about three hours. Now I dripped with sweat and
could barely lift my arms. I needed a rest.

Below, the battle continued to rage. With William dead, Leofwine's
men fought with even greater fury. No one could stand in their path.

In the middle of the carnage below, a soldier wearing full chain
mail jumped onto the back of a riderless horse. Spurring his mount

until its sides bled, the horseman sped after the fleeing Normans and pulled out in front of the pack of terrified cavalry and infantry. He halted his horse and tilted back his helmet to fully reveal his face. I couldn't make out the man's features because of the distance, but there was no mistaking the commanding manner in which he sat on his horse—William. He was alive!

A seed of hope grew within me. I might still make it out of here. The Battle of Hastings wasn't over yet.

The fleeing men instantly rallied around William, and in a moment reformed. Then, with William leading, they wheeled their horses around and charged Leofwine's troops.

The renewed Norman onslaught caught the Anglo-Saxons with no order, no discipline. Most of Leofwine's men had continued fighting, but others had already started celebrating their victory, so men were scattered across the hill. William's forces rampaged through these disorganized troops, trampling and spearing hundreds of them. Panic spread through the Anglo-Saxons, and they started running uphill in a desperate race to reach our lines, but they couldn't outrun the horses.

I took up my discarded spear and shield, racked by guilt as I watched the carnage below. The Anglo-Saxons were getting slaughtered. I should have been horrified, but instead I was … relieved. William was alive, so there was still a chance for me to set things right.

On the hilltop, men turned to Harold, looking for leadership. But the king didn't seem to know what to do. He rubbed his knuckles across his brow and paced in front of our lines. Every few seconds he'd stop and survey the ongoing bloodbath for a moment, then continue pacing. The men needed a king, but right now all we had was a man tortured by indecision.

Few of the men who had foolishly run down the hill returned to our lines. As the last fleeing straggler took a spear to the back and fell, I again expected the rod to go warm, but it remained cold.

"Unbelievable," I mumbled. Harold's forces were still on target to win this thing? How?

The Norman cavalry broke off their pursuit and returned to their own lines. A quiet descended upon the battlefield, with only the cries of the wounded and dying breaking the silence. Men lay everywhere on the hill. Some struggled to move, dragging themselves uphill or down, depending on which army they belonged to. I cringed seeing those who would probably be dead soon trying to get out of the way of the next attack.

"Collect the wounded!" Harold ordered, finally showing some decisiveness. "And find my brothers!"

Groups of men headed downhill to haul back our wounded while from the Norman ranks a band of foot soldiers ventured uphill to lug their own wounded away. The two groups avoided each other, observing an unspoken truce. The few survivors found among the bodies were carried behind our lines and bandaged up as best as possible.

Leofwine and Gyrth were dragged back up the hill as well, but they were beyond bandaging: Leofwine had taken a spear through the chest and Gyrth's skull had been nearly split with a sword. The rest of the dead remained where they'd fallen. No one would waste their strength moving them.

"Oafs!" King Harold railed at the sight of his dead brothers. "They only needed to hold the line." He moved along our defensive line, glaring at his remaining followers. "Do not chase those who are fleeing!" he scolded. "Look at what such folly has brought." He pointed to our dead lying farther down the hill. "We hold the line, no matter what. The longer we hold out, the more men will come to our cause. My ships have blocked the ports, so Duke William can get no more men from Normandy. We block the road as well, and he cannot send his men to pillage the countryside. If we sit tight and hold William here, he will starve and die. So hold the line!"

Hold the line.

My head shot up on hearing these words. That was the key to the whole time glitch. By holding the line, the Anglo-Saxons would prevent William from becoming king. But the Anglo-Saxons weren't supposed to win this battle.

I spat a long stream of spit into the dirt. Pinching the bridge of my nose, I exhaled slowly, trying to fight my rising feelings of guilt. Ceolwulf, Aethelraed, and the rest of the Anglo-Saxons were my friends. No, they were more than friends; they were my brothers. We'd fought and bled together on this battlefield, and now I had to figure out a way to get them rushing down that hill again.

The question was how? I was just one guy. I chewed my lip and looked down at the Norman troops. They milled about, trying to reorganize. They, too, had lost a lot of men, and huge gaps showed in their ranks.

Ceolwulf put his hand on my shoulder, startling me and breaking my train of thought. "You fought well, Leofric. Come share our food." He motioned to where Aethelraed sat on the grass a short distance from our line, chewing on a leg of mutton. Aethelraed was bleeding from a cut on his arm, and his shield looked like it was one hit away from becoming kindling.

"How can you eat?" I asked. "We're surrounded by the dead."

Aethelraed pointed with his leg of mutton at the bodies heaped near him. "What do you mean? They make the best companions when one is eating. No useless chatter, and they do not drink all the ale."

I waved away the offered food. "I can't eat." Not today. Not with corpses all around me. And, if the memories of this battle remained, probably not ever.

Ceolwulf nodded sagely. "A man never forgets his first battle. I could not eat after my first either." He pointed down the hill at the massing Normans. "But Duke William's men gather themselves and will come at us again soon. If you want to keep up your strength and stay among the living, you must eat."

Grudgingly, I sat down and took some of the smoked meat. I'd experienced bad picnics before, usually involving rain, annoying animals, or potato salad sitting too long in the sun. But sitting there on the blood-soaked grass, gazing upon dead bodies, and chewing tasteless meat while waiting for the Normans to attack definitely took the number-one spot as my worst picnic ever.

As I ate, I tried to figure out what the Normans might do next. My bet was on William sending his cavalry. We had already kicked their infantry's butts, and their archers had failed miserably.

I must have been reading William's mind because just then he shouted out some orders, and the cavalry moved ahead of the field.

Ceolwulf took a last swig of ale and tossed the ale skin aside. "The horsemen come now. Ten pennies says I kill more of them."

Aethelraed dragged his sleeve across his mouth to wipe away the mutton grease, then pulled his long-handled ax from across his back. "Let's make it twenty, you old goat. I feel lucky today."

Ceolwulf stabbed his spear into the dirt, passed his shield to the man behind him, and pulled his ax out as well. "Twenty it is." He stepped slightly ahead of our shield wall and stood waiting, ax in hands.

"Put me in for twenty also," said a housecarl farther down the line. "Winner takes all." He pulled out his ax and stepped in front of the shield wall.

Along the line, other housecarls also dropped their spears and shields and stepped forward, axes at the ready.

"What are you doing?" I asked Ceolwulf.

Ceolwulf rasped a whetstone along the blade of his ax. "William sends his horses now since his footmen have learned to fear us. Now we must make those horsemen fear us as well. Then the battle will be won."

"Just the few of you are going to stand up against their entire cavalry?"

"Aye. If we stay in the shield wall, the fight will rage for a long time. Their spears against our shields, with neither side gaining ground. Their footmen might regain their courage if that happens." He tested the blade with his thumb and nodded. "Our axes will make this battle much shorter."

"Five pennies says Uthraed kills the most," shouted one of the warriors near me.

"I'll take that bet," yelled a warrior near the rim of the hill.

Around me, men began shouting out bets on who was going to kill more. What was wrong with these guys? They were fighting for their lives, yet they were treating it like a game. Didn't they realize how serious this was?

Then it hit me. Yeah, they knew the importance of this battle, and that's why they were joking around. Every man here was prepared to fight to the death to achieve victory, so for many of them, it would be their last time ever to have fun with their friends.

I looked with newfound respect at the few housecarls who bravely stood between us and the Normans. They appeared oblivious to the danger, boasting about who would fight the best. And me? I had retreated to the shield wall, ready to wave my spear around like I was swatting flies, or maybe duck behind my shield whenever someone came too close. I wouldn't be able to change history. The guys out there were changing history. They stood up to the Normans, challenging them, making the enemy fearful of further attacks.

Don't do it, Dan.

There was nothing for me in the line. I was just another of the thousands of men holding on to a piece of ground. The guys in front of us were the heroes, the ones making the battle theirs. And if I wanted to change the outcome of this fight, it was time for me to start taking charge.

I dropped my shield and spear and unsheathed my seax and sword. "I'm in," I announced as I strode forward to take my place a few feet to the left of Ceolwulf.

Ceolwulf turned at my approach. "Go back, Leofric," he ordered. "No man can speak ill of your bravery. Leave this fight to us old men."

"I can't." And I meant it. I really couldn't go back to the shield wall. I needed to be here in front, no matter how much it terrified me.

Ceolwulf shook his head but said nothing further.

"Twenty pennies says the wolf cub pisses himself at the first charge," a warrior yelled.

Twenty? I'd bet at least a hundred on that.

CHAPTER 33

William's horsemen spread out into a line spanning the hillside, three rows deep. Each man carried a spear, a shield, and some other weapon like a sword or mace. On William's command, the cavalry began a slow walk uphill.

I licked my lips and tried to relax. If I was tense, I'd be slow. If I was slow, I'd be dead. No matter how hard I tried to relax, I couldn't—a forest of spears was heading my way.

Midway up the hill, William yelled an order, and the earth began to vibrate as his horsemen picked up speed. The men in our shield wall began banging their shields and shouting in an attempt to spook the animals. I didn't know about the horses, but my heart was beating so hard I felt it would knock a rib loose. The Normans were now three-quarters of the way up the hill, and every muscle in my body went taut. My mouth was dry, but sweat dripped down my brow. So many spear tips were aimed at me, and my shield was probably in someone else's hands.

"Loose!" yelled a warrior in the shield wall behind me.

A volley of spears flew over my head and fell into the oncoming cavalry. Gaps formed in the line where men and horses fell, but the rest kept coming—a thunderous wall of charging horses and razor-sharp spears.

Closer.

A few minutes ago, stepping out here had seemed like the bravest and smartest thing I could do. But now I cursed the Dan who'd decided to come forward. He was clearly a moron who was trying to get me killed. Every nerve of my being screamed *run*, but my feet stayed rooted to the spot.

Closer.

Ceolwulf leaped forward and sank his ax deep into the nearest horse's neck, bringing both horse and rider down. The Norman staggered to his feet, but Ceolwulf's ax cleaved through his helmet, splitting his skull. "One!" he yelled as he jumped back to his original position.

Aethelraed grabbed a spear thrust at him and yanked it out of the rider's hands. The owner of the weapon slumped forward in the saddle from the tugging motion, allowing Aethelraed to step in and strike a blow with his ax. "One!" Aethelraed yelled back.

"He is still horsed," Ceolwulf shouted. "You cannot count them if they yet ride."

Aethelraed hurled the Norman's spear back at him, drilling through the rider's chest and knocking him out of the saddle. "That better, you old goat? One!"

"One! And two!" yelled a housecarl over to my left.

All along the line, men shouted their kills. And me? No one attacked me. With my fancy sword and armor, they must have assumed I was just some noble's kid trying to prove he wasn't scared. Basically not worthy of their attention. Right beside me, Ceolwulf wasn't so lucky. Three horsemen closed in on him. One rider jabbed with his spear while trying to stay out of the range of Ceolwulf's ax while the other two approached from his left—Ceolwulf's blind side.

Aethelraed was busy on Ceolwulf's right. He couldn't help him, so that left me. I raced toward the closest Norman. He saw me coming and jabbed at me with his spear. I ducked under the thrust and sank my seax hilt-deep into the horse's belly. The horse reared in pain, sending the rider flying backward to the ground. The Norman lay there winded as I stood over him, my sword raised above my head.

He stared unblinking up at me, his eyes wide, expecting the death blow to fall.

What was I doing?

My blade trembled in my hands. I couldn't kill him.

At that instant, the man's eyes narrowed and his hand shot toward the knife at his belt. In a jolt of panic, I stabbed downward. My blade cleaved through his chain mail and sank into his chest.

I wrenched my sword from his body and jumped out of the path of the second rider's horse.

Wake up!

I didn't have time to question my ethics. I was in the middle of battle, and I'd die if I didn't start fighting back. As for messing up history, it was already messed up beyond recognition. Killing a few warriors couldn't make it worse. But it might, just might, make it better.

"One!" I yelled.

Ceolwulf's head whipped around and he saw the dead man lying at my feet. He gave a slight nod and then ducked under the spear thrust of the second attacker. His ax embedded itself into the attacker's side. The man fell off his horse and landed with a heavy thud at Ceolwulf's feet.

"Two!" he shouted before turning to the next.

I stuck close to Ceolwulf's left, protecting his blind side. We ranged across the front of our defenses, killing Normans whenever we could, and retreating momentarily to the safety of the shield wall when things got too tough or we needed to catch our breath. The kill counts increased, but the men yelling them out decreased. In some places the

Norman cavalry were directly attacking the shield wall, stabbing with their longer reach and probing for a gap through the locked shields.

Then, like the footmen earlier, the cavalry started retreating. First just one or two of them, and then the entire group of horsemen pulled away from the battle. A ragged cheer went up from our line as men yelled taunts at the fleeing Normans.

They retreated in a swirl of confusion. Some rushed all the way to the foot of the hill, while others halted at the middle or veered to the tree-covered sides. No one seemed to know what was going on. William and his nobles rode valiantly among all the scattered groups, calling men to them and trying to rally the defeated Normans.

My arms fell to my sides, and the tip of my bloodied sword scraped against the ground. I had failed to set history right—again. With slow, muscle-aching movements, I sat down and stared at the retreating horsemen. Part of me wanted to cheer and celebrate the Anglo-Saxons' success. Fighting beside these guys today was the first time I'd ever felt part of a team, like I actually had friends. But our victory was all wrong. We weren't supposed to win here. If I ever wanted to get back to my own time, I needed to get my side to lose.

With the back of my hand, I wiped the sweat from my brow. Getting the Normans to win here seemed impossible. We'd already battled them to a standstill for half the day, and as long as we held this high ground, we would continue pushing them back. If the Normans were going to have any hope of winning, they'd have to attack us when we weren't in an elevated position. But how? King Harold had forbidden the remaining army from running downhill. And his two brothers, the only ones who might be able to persuade men to ignore the king and do a mad rush downhill, were already dead.

I looked around at the surviving warriors in the Anglo-Saxon line. Most sat on the ground, exhausted from the hours of fighting, trying to snatch a few moments' rest before William rallied his troops to attack again. The only way to get this tired bunch to even think about charging downhill was to offer them a chance to end this battle right now.

My eyes zeroed in on Duke William as he rode back and forth over the hillside. He was the key.

I sheathed my sword and looped the sword belt over my shoulder. Then I collected my shield and three Norman spears lying on the ground, hopped over a horse's corpse, and scanned the slope. Hundreds of Normans milled around, getting in each other's way as they tried to decide whether they were going uphill or downhill. Could I make it to William?

Probably not. But it's my only chance.

I gripped the first spear and hefted it over my shoulder. Surprisingly, I didn't feel any fear. I was now staring down at the main mass of the Norman army, planning some suicidal attack to save history, and for the first time all day, I was utterly calm.

I took a deep breath and began jogging downhill. Behind me men both yelled encouragement and urged me to get back. I couldn't turn around, though. I'd either change this battle now or get used to being "Leofric the Failure" for the rest of my life.

I got within one hundred steps of William and launched my first spear in his direction. If I could hit his stupid horse so that it would dump him, then hopefully the Anglo-Saxons would rush down and attack.

The spear sailed through the air and landed woefully short.

Damn it!

A pair of Normans saw me standing out there alone, and they spurred their mounts toward me. My calm vanished, and that old familiar feeling of sheer panic jolted through me. I had only seconds left if this was going to work. I ran another ten steps and hurled my second spear, burying it into the leg of a Norman knight next to William.

Wrong target!

One spear left. Last chance. The horsemen were coming right at me. I threw myself to one side and rolled away from the trampling hooves of the nearest horse, feeling the air on my cheek as they kicked past my head.

With my eyes locked onto William, I leaped to my feet and hurled my last spear, then twisted sideways again to avoid the second horseman. From the corner of my eye, I saw my spear dig into the haunch of William's mount. The horse danced in a circle, kicking violently, and spooking the horses all around it. William tumbled from the saddle and fell to the ground.

Yes!

I paused for half a second, hoping to feel the jump rod growing warm, but it remained chill against my skin.

My spirits sank—for about the eightieth time today, I had failed.

The pair of horsemen had turned their horses and now approached from my right, their mounts kicking up huge clods of dirt as they thundered toward me. Waiting until the last second, I dodged to one side and rolled on the ground to get out of their way. As they blew past me, I jumped to my feet and began running back uphill. If I stopped moving, I was dead.

The rumble of hooves behind me warned that they were coming again. I threw myself to the side at the last second and a horse just missed trampling me.

I couldn't keep this up. My chest heaved as I gulped in air and my muscles protested each movement.

I scrambled to my feet again and ran, heading for a gap between the pair of horsemen. The rustling of my chain mail and the pounding of my heart in my ears blocked out all other sounds.

The ground trembled beneath my feet, warning me of another attack. I whirled around to see a third Norman almost upon me with no time to dive out of the way. He bent low in the saddle and swung his war hammer at my head.

With speed fueled by panic, I raised my shield to block the blow as I twisted aside. The hammer clanged off the edge of my shield and collided with my helmet, sending a blinding flash of pain through my skull. With my ears ringing from the blow, I fell to the ground, and something warm flowed from my forehead into my eyes.

Get up! Get up! Get up!

I staggered to my feet. The ground rocked beneath me, and everything seemed out of focus. I took a step forward and fell again to the ground, my shield flying out of my hand.

What's wrong with me?

I knelt on one knee and wiped at my eyes. My fingers came away red.

The earth trembled again. A horse was getting closer, but from which direction? I shook my head, trying to clear out the cobwebs.

I spotted a Norman horseman galloping toward me, his spear leveled at my chest. I froze in place, too groggy to move. Through the fog in my head, came the horrifying realization that I was going to die.

Suddenly an ax chopped through the Norman's spear shaft. The surprised rider reined in his horse and reached for his mace but was too slow. The ax's return swing cleaved right through his thigh, severing his leg just above the knee. The Norman tumbled out of the saddle, blood pumping from the stump of his leg.

"Run, Leofric!" Ceolwulf yelled.

He stood beside me, gripping his ax in both hands, ready for the next Norman to attack.

I pulled myself to my feet and managed to stay standing this time. "We're too far downhill," I panted. "We can't make it."

"Hold your tongue and listen for once. Run!"

I ran a few steps, my head getting clearer with each footfall. Behind me, I heard the clatter of horses, and Ceolwulf taunting their riders.

Two against one, and more Normans charging up the hill—
Ceolwulf didn't have a chance. If I kept running, I might make it
back to friendly lines. Might. Although, judging by how bad my lungs
heaved, there was a good chance I'd just pass out halfway up the hill.
And even if I did make it, Ceolwulf wouldn't. After all he'd done for
me, I couldn't just leave him.

I charged back downhill as a rider approached Ceolwulf from
behind. With all my energy I covered the few steps between us and
struck the horse's rump with the flat of my sword. A loud *thwack*
echoed across the hill and the animal reared, dumping its rider out
onto the ground. Before the Norman could react, I rammed my seax
into his throat.

"Do you ever listen?" Ceolwulf shouted. "I told you to run!"

The other Norman lay dead at his feet, but tons more were charging
up the hill toward us. My grip tightened on my sword and seax. There
was no way out of this. I was going to die here. But I was determined
to go down fighting.

A Norman came charging at Ceolwulf's blind side.

"Look out!" I yelled.

Suddenly an ax sailed through the air and embedded itself between
the rider's ribs, sending him crashing to the ground.

"Eight!" yelled Aethelraed triumphantly.

From behind me, a volley of spears flew through the air and fell
among the onrushing Normans, leaving only empty saddles wherever
they landed.

"Ten!" "Six!" "Nine!" came more triumphant shouts.

I turned around, and my heart swelled seeing the mob of housecarls rushing down the hill, axes raised and shields in hand.

Ceolwulf whipped his head up. "What are you doing here?"

"Saving you, you old goat," Aethelraed said. "And I lead you by
one now."

"Aye, you cannot take all the kills for yourself!" yelled one of the housecarls.

But we were now in the open. The Norman cavalry came galloping up the hill. There were maybe twenty of us and hundreds of them. We'd never make it back to the top of the hill in time.

Suddenly, the rod pulsed warmly against my back.

What the ... ? How?

Then I heard the savage howl of hundreds of men. I whipped my head around to see the entire left wing of the Anglo-Saxon line charging downhill. I fell to my knees and howled as tears streamed down my cheeks. After all the killing, I had finally fixed the time glitch. I could go home.

I was tempted to just say the words and get out of here, but there was one last thing I had to do. I had to save my friends.

"Run!" I yelled.

"Nay, Leofric," Ceolwulf shouted back. "I am too old and tired to run. Here I make my stand." He raised his ax and faced the huge wall of horsemen coming toward us.

"But you'll die here!" I shouted over the thunderous pounding of hooves.

"All men die. Few get to choose how or—"

But the rest of his sentence was drowned by the shouts of the Normans. They were almost upon us. Hundreds of them galloping at full speed against a few brave and foolish housecarls.

Goodbye, Ceolwulf.

"*Azkabaleth virros ku, haztri valent bhidri du!*" I yelled.

The horses and men slowed to a snail's pace as the world became bathed in white light. I shut my eyes against the glare, my last sight the spear point that would have killed me.

CHAPTER 34

The brightness of the time stream vanished, and I collapsed to the ground, blinded and exhausted. My fingers felt carpeting while my knees banged against hardwood. The jump rod had dumped me in a room, but where? And, more to the point, when?

With a grunt, I struggled to my feet and held my sword and seax at the ready, ears straining for any sound as my head spun from the dizziness of time travel. If someone attacked me right now, I was toast.

Slowly, the spots began to clear from in front of my eyes, and details of the room came into focus. A red Persian rug. Dark hardwood floor. A bookshelf crammed with history books. A brown leather couch. I tilted my head back and let out a long sigh. My trip through time was over. I was home.

As the last spots left my eyes, a scattering of gray-brown pottery shards on the floor caught my attention—the remains of the statue I had thrown at Victor. Beside them, barely visible against the rich walnut floor, was a huge dried bloodstain, right where Dad had collapsed. My brief moment of joy at being home evaporated; I needed to find him.

I started for the door, ready to rush off and search for him, but my hand stopped just inches from the doorknob. Running down the street dressed in medieval armor, bleeding from cuts and waving a sword, was not going to save Dad—I didn't even know where to start looking for him. Not to mention that, even though I knew where I was, I had no clue *when* I was. The broken pottery and the bloodstain proved that I'd arrived later than when I'd left—but how much later? A few hours? Days? Months? I needed to fight my rising panic and think things through.

With my senses fully alert for attackers, I flipped on the TV.

June 5, three days after the confrontation between Victor and my dad.

Date? Check. Next step: Secure the house.

I shut off the TV and crept from room to room, opening doors carefully and entering each room sword first. The clinking of my chain mail sounded alien here, but I kept the armor on. No telling whether someone had remained in the house. I searched closets, under beds, behind curtains, and in dark corners but found no one. In my father's study, papers lay scattered on the floor and the safe door was open. Victor must have trashed Dad's office after stabbing him. What else had he been looking for?

I locked the front door, set the alarm, and then headed upstairs, pausing in the doorway of my bedroom. It looked like a stranger's room; nothing felt familiar anymore. The unmade bed with dirty clothes lying on it, the posters of cars and swimsuit models on every wall, the pile of video games sitting under the TV—they all belonged to someone else. The boy who once lived in this room had died in Anglo-Saxon England.

And in my bathroom mirror, I didn't see the usual face with its cocky grin. Now a gaunt, bruised, and bloodied image looked back at me. I leaned in closer to the mirror and removed my helmet. It was dented where the war hammer had hit it, and that dent had opened up a huge gash on my forehead.

Great, that's going to need stitches.

I washed the blood off my face, then superglued the cut together. I didn't have time to see a doctor. I needed to find Dad.

Next I took off my Anglo-Saxon armor and clothing. My belt pouch with Sam's phone number in it fell to the floor.

Sam!

I needed to get in touch with her. I pulled the scrap of parchment out of the pouch and cursed. It must have gotten wet—the numbers were all smeared. I could only make out maybe four of the full ten.

Dejected, I stepped into a quick but amazingly warm shower to scrub off the weeks' worth of blood, sweat, and road dirt, then I put on jeans and a T-shirt, stuffed the few bucks on my dresser into my pocket, and headed back downstairs. The red light blinking on Dad's dinosaur landline phone caught my eye—messages. The first was from Dad's work, something about him not showing up and wondering if he'd forgotten to notify them about any vacation plans.

Delete.

One from Dad's teaching assistant at the university, wondering if he was okay.

Delete.

My breath caught in my throat as the third message began playing. *Daniel, this is Detective Johnson at the Eighth Precinct. I wish to speak with you in regard to your father. Please call me back as soon as you can. My number here is …*

My fingers flew over the phone as I punched in the number.

"Johnson here," came the response after just two rings.

"This is Dan Renfrew," I blurted. "Is my dad alive?"

There was a faint pause. "Yes," Detective Johnson answered, "but he's in bad shape. He received a—"

"Where is he?"

"He's getting the best care possible. But I really would like to talk to you, Dan—to get your side of things," Detective Johnson said. "Can you come down to the station?"

"No, I need to see my dad. Where is he?"

"You really should talk to us first."

"If you're not going to tell me where he is, I'm going to hang up and go find him myself," I barked into the phone. "I'll only talk to you *after* I've seen him. Clear?"

"All right, Dan. He's in the ICU at St. Vincent's. Can I meet you there?"

"Yeah, I'll be there."

Without waiting for his response, I hung up and called a cab. Dad was alive! But my joy at hearing he wasn't dead conflicted with new worry on hearing that he was in intensive care.

As soon as my ride pulled up to the emergency room entrance, I jumped out, paid the driver, and ran into the hospital. The woman at reception barely finished telling me directions to Dad's room before I took off. Rounding a corner, I knew instantly where to go—the room with two uniformed officers standing outside it.

"I'm Dan Renfrew," I panted. "Is my dad in there?"

The taller of the two officers flicked his collar walkie-talkie on and leaned his head into it. "Detective, the Renfrew kid is here."

Over the squawk of static I heard, "Tell him I'll be right over."

The officer motioned to a small waiting area next to the nurse's station, where a few padded chairs in cracked vinyl sat under an old TV. "Have a seat. The detective wants to talk to you."

I tried to peer around him to see into the room, but his body blocked the window set in the door. "Can I just see my dad?"

"Just wait for the detective."

"Why can't I see him?"

The officer raised his hands. "Look. I know you want to see your dad, but you'll have to talk to the detective first. Those are the rules. He'll be here in a minute."

My body was such a bundle of nerves, no way could I sit. I paced the hallway, my agitation increasing with every step. Why wouldn't they let me see Dad? What weren't they telling me?

Shoes slapping against the tiled floor announced the arrival of a man with thinning gray hair and a slight potbelly. He wore a blue suit jacket over a rumpled dress shirt, but the way he moved screamed cop.

"Dan Renfrew?" he asked.

"Yeah, that's me."

"I'm Detective Johnson." He motioned for me to take a chair across from him as he took a seat.

"I'm sorry to keep you away from your father, but I need to take your statement first. Can I ask you a few questions? You'll be able to see him once we're done." He pulled out a recording device, placed it between us, and looked at me expectantly.

"Sure."

"Where were you between the hours of ten a.m. and two p.m. last Thursday?"

"Wait …" The blood froze in my veins. "You think I did this?"

"No, not at all," Detective Johnson replied, but I could tell he was lying.

"I was at the mall until about one. Then I went home, where I saw some guy named Victor stab my dad. He's the one you want, not me."

Detective Johnson's eyebrows rose. "You witnessed the attack on your father?"

"Yes." I told him the full story of my day. Dad's mystery appointment. Hanging out at the mall. Meeting Jenkins, the mall cop. And then sneaking back home and witnessing the sword fight. I spent most of my time talking about Victor. I would never forget his face—it was etched in my memory forever. I went through as much of a description as I could, guessing height, weight, age, everything I thought was important. Throughout it all, Detective Johnson just nodded and kept silent.

"Would you be able to come to the precinct either today or tomorrow and work with a sketch artist?" he asked once I was done.

"Yes, but can I please just see my dad?"

"Of course. Just one more question." He sounded very relaxed, like he was trying to calm me down before making the kill. "Where have you been the past few days?"

I took a deep breath, desperately trying to buy time. Obviously, the truth was not an option. "I thought you said I wasn't a suspect."

"You're not," he said, but he didn't convince me. "I just find it a bit odd that you witnessed the whole attack and disappeared right after. And then we get an anonymous phone call telling us to send an ambulance around to your house."

Anonymous phone call? Did Victor call the cops?

Detective Johnson leaned forward, narrowing the distance between us. He glanced at my gashed forehead, bruised face, and battered hands. "Look," he said, his voice quiet so that only I could hear it. "It's pretty obvious someone's been beating the crap out of you. And, judging by the bruising, I'd say in the past week or so. Is this Victor guy a friend of yours? Someone who was trying to get your dad to lay off?"

"No!" I yelled, startling the staff at the nurses' station. "My dad has never hit me. He would never. I did get the crap beaten out of me, but it wasn't him. It was some kids at the mall. If you really want to know where I've been the past three days, I've been out on the streets. I'd just seen my dad get stabbed, and I knew this Victor guy was after me. I ran like hell—lost my phone and wallet in the process. I didn't dare go home until today."

"You should have reported this immediately."

"Yeah, I know," I replied. "But I was scared, okay? I had no idea whether my dad was dead or alive. And I'll have to live with that guilt for the rest of my life."

Detective Johnson seemed to be mulling over my story. "Okay, Dan, I think we're done here." He turned off the recorder and put it back in his pocket. "Come on, let's go see your dad."

I made a beeline for Dad's room. The two officers still barred the way, but at a nod from Detective Johnson they stepped aside. With my whole body shaking, I opened the door. Dad lay in the bed, tubes snaked into his arm and a breathing tube stuck out of his mouth. He looked deathly pale, and his skin seemed almost waxy. The only sounds in the room were the rhythmic whoosh and click of what I guessed was a breathing machine and the regular ping of his heart monitor.

I knelt by the side of the bed and grasped his cold hand. "I'm so sorry," I whispered. This was all my fault. I'd had the chance to save him, and I'd blown it.

A doctor entered the room, his lips tightly drawn. "Daniel?"

"Yeah?" I stood up.

"My name is Dr. Onakanyan. I've been looking after your father." He glanced at the clipboard in his hands. "He's suffered a major puncture wound to his chest. The blade pierced his lung and nicked his heart, resulting in severe blood loss. When the paramedics found him, he had already gone into hemorrhagic shock, which led to cardiac arrest. They managed to restart his heart and stabilize his fluids, but he slipped into a coma on the ride here. He has yet to regain consciousness. With the help of the respirator, he's been breathing, but only time will tell whether he'll pull through. And if he does wake up, we're still not sure he'll regain full brain function."

A steel band seemed to tighten around my chest.

"I'm very sorry, son," the doctor continued. "Do you have any questions?"

I shook my head, unable to look him in the eye. I heard him walk out, and the door closed behind him. I dragged a chair over to Dad's bedside and sat there just watching, hoping for a flicker of life. My entire body felt crushed by the weight of my sadness. I couldn't help him; I could only watch him and hope for a full recovery.

To pass the time, I began telling him everything that had happened to me: landing in Anglo-Saxon England, meeting Sam, Osmund, Ceolwulf, and Aethelraed; killing the rogue time jumpers; fighting at the Battle of Hastings; and saving history. I paid particular attention to Sam, describing her hair, her face, her smile. I kept talking and talking until I ran out of things to say.

He lay unmoving except for the rhythmic rise and fall of his chest. The sheer emptiness of the room began to press in on me. Outside were the sounds of life: gurneys wheeling past, nurses talking, doctors performing their rounds. The hands of the clock moved around in circles, but nothing changed. Time itself seemed to have stopped.

Somebody brought me a reclining chair, and I spent the night at Dad's bedside, waking up every hour as a nurse came in to check Dad's vital signs or change the IV bag. I was probably breaking some sort of hospital rule by staying overnight, but the nurses looked at me sympathetically and none of them kicked me out.

When the night nurse told me her shift was over, I knew I had to leave. I couldn't help Dad by sitting here; his life was now in the hands of the doctors. If I really wanted to help him, I needed to make sure the police found Victor.

CHAPTER 35

I got a bagel and juice at the hospital cafeteria and then headed to the police station to talk to the sketch artist. As the artist's pencil traced lines across the page, I pointed out corrections. The eyes were wider, the nose thinner, the eyebrows thicker. Detective Johnson came into the interview room and watched our sketch session with interest. As the minutes dragged, and Victor's face became better defined on the page, Detective Johnson began to look agitated. It was just a subtle indication at first. He'd cross his arms or tap his foot. But when I asked for corrections on the hairline, and the artist started drawing the hair up higher on the forehead, Detective Johnson rolled up his sleeves and leaned on the table, looking from me to the sketch and back. When I was finally satisfied that the image looked just like Victor, Detective Johnson was only glaring at me.

"Really, kid?" He held the picture up next to a copy of the morning's newspaper that he had with him. The artist's sketch matched the grinning photo on its front page. "You're telling me that Congressman Stahl is the man who attacked your dad? The way things are shaping up, this guy is going to be the next president. Why on earth would he bother with your dad?" He tossed both the newspaper and the sketch on the table. "I don't know what your game is, Dan, but you're wasting my time—and also the time of a lot of officers who want to catch the bastard who did this to your dad." He slammed his palms onto the table and leaned in so his face was close to mine. "Is there anything you want to change in this sketch?"

I barely heard his words. The photo on the front page of the newspaper stared up at me. It showed a man in a suit smiling as he shook hands with the ambassador from China. Same eyes, same face, same hair. There was no mistaking it. The man who stabbed Dad was Congressman Victor Stahl.

I sat there numb with shock. The archer hadn't lied. The rogue-jumper plot was bigger than just robbing history. Much bigger. Far beyond anything Detective Johnson would believe.

"That's the guy who attacked my dad," I insisted, stabbing the news-paper with my finger. "If you don't want to believe me, that's your problem." My chair scraped across the floor as I stood up. "You have my statement, and you have the name and picture of the guy who you should be arresting. I'm done here."

Without waiting for a response, I stormed out of the interview room, my mind reeling. What was Victor's ultimate plan? What did becoming president have to do with it? And most importantly, how could I stop him?

I emerged from the station into the sunlit street. People brushed past me, staring at their phones or chatting with each other. Everyone was blissfully oblivious to the threat coming their way. I wanted to run through the streets, warning everyone about Victor. Except no one would believe me. And the only thing I was likely to get for my efforts would be a visit from Victor and a blade in my chest, like Dad. So instead I hopped on a bus and headed home.

When I got back, there was a message from Dad's lawyer, calling me into his office. I stared at the receiver in my hands, doubt burrowing into my mind. Why would he be calling right after I visited the police? Had Victor been notified that I had positively identified him and this was some sort of trap to take me out? Or was it just a coincidence? Dad had told me to trust no one—did that include his lawyer?

I exhaled slowly as I dragged my fingers through my hair. This is what my life had become—a constant diet of doubt and fear and second-guessing.

I popped open my laptop and did a quick Google search to see if I could find any connection between him and Victor. The internet revealed nothing incriminating, but that didn't mean I wasn't going to be careful. I called for a cab, making sure to repeat the address and my name a few times so at least there would be a record of where I'd gone if this was a trap.

The cab dropped me off downtown in front of a large glass-and-steel building with *Morris & Rothstein* written in large letters on one side. So far so good. This was looking less like a trap and more like a legitimate visit to a lawyer. Even the name Morris kind of rang a bell. I was pretty sure he'd been over to our house a few times for dinner, or maybe just to hang out. If I remembered correctly, he and Dad had known each other since high school. Was he still Dad's friend, though, or was he in league with Victor?

The elevator took me to the twenty-third floor and into a lobby covered in wood paneling, with leather armchairs arranged around a low marble-topped table. The place reeked of money and importance. One thing it didn't look like was a trap.

An older lady in a gray suit, with her hair held back in a bun, sat behind a desk. She looked up as I approached, her face betraying a hint of annoyance before settling into a composed mask. "May I help you?" she asked.

"Hi, I'm Dan Renfrew. Mr. Morris asked me to come in."

She picked up the phone and punched a few buttons. "Mr. Morris, Dan Renfrew is here … All right, I'll send him right in."

She came out from behind her desk and ushered me along the hallway and through a large polished wood door with a nameplate reading *Henry Morris, Attorney.* I entered a spacious office with a wooden desk in the center. Behind it sat Mr. Morris, looking exactly like I remembered him. Still alert for danger, my eyes swept the room, scanning for anything out of the ordinary. Bookshelves filled one wall, and on another, floor-to-ceiling windows looked out over the city below. Nothing strange here.

Mr. Morris got up from his leather chair and clasped my hand in a firm grip. "Daniel, I'm so sorry about what happened to your father. Such dreadful news. He and I were … *are* great friends. To hear that someone attacked him in his own home just shocks me to no end." He waved me to a seat across the desk as he sat down.

I ignored the chair and remained standing. "How *did* you know about what happened to my dad?" I asked, not hiding my suspicion.

Mr. Morris blinked in surprise and then recovered. "I can see why you're suspicious, but I assure you I was not involved in your father's attack. I only know of it because the police contacted me, searching for you. They found my number on your father's phone." He motioned to the chair again. "Please. Sit."

Reluctantly I sank into the chair as Mr. Morris reached into his desk drawer and placed a large folder of documents in front of himself.

"Your father, prudent man that he was, left specific instructions in case he was unable to take care of you. Before we begin, your father asked that I give you this." Mr. Morris flipped open the folder and pulled out a simple white envelope with my name typed across the front.

He placed the envelope in front of me and then got up from his chair. "I'll give you some time alone," he said. Without waiting for my response, he slipped out of the room.

With trembling fingers, I tore the envelope open to find a single piece of note paper.

That's it?

I flipped over the sheet, revealing Dad's familiar handwriting.

Dan,

If you are reading this, I'm either dead or close to it. I don't know if I've been the best father, but I did try. You might resent how I kept you away from other kids and focused your education on things you found odd and boring, but please believe me when I say that it was all done with the best intentions. Throughout history, our family has had a great part to play in the shaping of the world, and I trained you to the best of my ability to inherit that role.

Unfortunately, I had to hide the true reason for all your training. There were forces at work that put my life in danger, and the only way to keep you safe was to keep you ignorant. I hoped that one day the danger would pass and I would be free to tell you of the great role you could play. If you are reading this letter, then it looks like my hopes will not come to pass.

I left instructions for Mr. Morris to sell the house. When this is done, take the money and move far away from here. Go to one of the remotest places imaginable, like the wilds of Northern Canada, the jungles of South America, or the mountain regions of Central Asia. I know this sounds crazy, Dan, but you have to believe me. War is coming, and you don't want to be near it.

You can trust Mr. Morris. He's been my friend since high school and will do anything to help you. Other than him, don't trust anyone!

You have always been the greatest joy in my life. I'm immensely proud of you and who you've become.

Love,

Dad

I sat for a long time with his note in my hands, reading and rereading the words. I finally understood why Dad had never taught me about time-jumping—he was trying to protect me. But this knowledge didn't make me feel any better. He should've trusted me. Maybe we could have fought Victor together. Maybe Dad wouldn't be lying in a hospital bed if he'd actually shared some of his secrets with me.

A tap on the door disturbed my thoughts. Mr. Morris poked his head in. "Are you ready to continue, Dan?"

I slipped the note into my pocket and nodded to him. He reentered his office and took a seat in the large leather armchair facing me. "I know that some of this may be confusing or difficult to understand," he began. "If you have any questions, please ask them at any time."

I had a ton of questions, but I was too stunned to put my jumbled thoughts to words.

Mr. Morris must have taken my silence as a sign to continue because he placed a long, multipage document in front of me. *Power of Attorney* was printed across the top. "This document gives me the power to act on your father's behalf, according to his prescribed wishes, which are contained in the subsequent pages." He flipped the page to show me rows and rows of detailed instructions, each one initialed by Dad. "According to his directions, I am to liquidate his various assets, including your current residence, and then consolidate them in low-risk investment vehicles for you to use at your own discretion. I have already consolidated some of his more liquid assets." He reached into his desk drawer and pulled out a bank card with a sticky note attached to the front of it: the PIN. "Here is a debit card to use so you can start extracting any necessary funds immediately." He tapped the card with a finger. "Please be mindful of your purchases. Until you finish school and find a job, the funds in this account will be your only source of money."

Mr. Morris raised his eyes to me, as if expecting some sort of response, but I merely nodded. I still couldn't believe Dad was selling the house out from under me. It was the only home I'd ever known. Where was I going to live? What was I going to do?

"Which brings us to the next item of business," Mr. Morris said. "Since you are only sixteen, with no close relatives, your father had already signed the necessary papers to appoint me as a standby guardian in case he became incapacitated." He pushed another document in front of me.

Of course Dad had a guardian all lined up. He was always more prepared than a troop of Boy Scouts. "What does this mean for me?" I grunted.

"As your appointed guardian, I am legally responsible for your well-being. Usually, this would require you moving in with me and my family. However, based on the somewhat peculiar directions that your father left, and when taking your own age into account, I think you might prefer to live in a place of your choosing. Either way, I will look after all your financial and legal affairs as a proper guardian should, until such time as your father recovers or ..." His voice cracked as his words trailed off. For a few seconds, he said nothing, then he took a deep breath to compose himself. "Sorry," he said. "I still can't believe this happened to James in his own home. Who would do such a thing?"

Victor Stahl would. "I don't know," I muttered.

"Going back to what I said previously," Mr. Morris continued, his composure now restored, "before you make a decision, please make sure you fully understand what being on your own entails. You'll have to buy your own food, cook your own meals, wash the dishes, do your laundry, vacuum the house, pay bills, and do everything that an adult would. So think carefully before you decide. If you need some more time to think things over, I understand."

Living with some guy I barely knew or being on my own? Talk about a no-brainer, especially considering the way I'd spent the past few weeks. "No offense, but I'm good on my own. Do I have to sign anything?"

"No. Not for this decision. And, if you wish to change your mind at any time, my door will always be open to you."

"So what now?" I asked.

"You merely need to determine where you will live, and I, as your guardian, will sign all the necessary papers."

Where to live? Good freakin' question. I wanted to live at home, where I'd always lived, not in the "jungles of South America" like Dad had suggested. "Did my dad give you any specific directions on *where* I had to move?"

"No. He always spoke so highly of you to me. He trusted your decision-making in this matter."

All right. That was one thing in my favor. I knew Dad would be super disappointed to find out I'd ignored his warnings and stayed put, but I didn't care. I restored history at Hastings by fighting, not by hiding in the back of the shield wall. There was no way I was going to run and hide now, while the rogue jumpers did what they wanted to the world. If Victor was running for president, the election wouldn't be for another year, so I still had time to stop their insane plot. And to do that I had to be in the heart of things: close to the airport, media, and everything else New York City provided. And this part of the state had one other thing that some little hick town in the middle of nowhere didn't—millions of people to hide among. "Is there anything else?" I asked.

Mr. Morris took a business card off his desk and scribbled a phone number on the back. "I know that this is tough on you, Dan, but I'm always here to help. You already have my office number, and that's my cell." He slid the card across to me. "If you ever need anything, just give me a call. It's the least I can do."

I mumbled my thanks, pocketed the business card and the debit card, and headed home. So that was it. I was pretty much an orphan now. The house felt so big and so quiet, and yet there still lurked that creepy feeling of violation, of knowing that Victor had been inside my home. I went into Dad's study and rifled through his papers, looking for anything at all that he might have left. All I found were lecture notes for his classes, some papers about his next book, and a few newspapers. Nothing of interest to me. Whatever secrets Dad had hidden from me, he'd kept them in his head.

I went to my room and flopped on the bed, my sword tightly gripped in one hand. Tears flowed down my cheeks and sobs racked my chest. This was all so unfair. I had done everything to save the past, but now my present was falling apart. Dad was in a hospital bed, my house was going to be sold out from under me, and I had no clue how to stop a plot to take over the world. If Dad had actually left me some information, I could have done something, but as it was, I was just lying there, useless.

Wait … I'm not completely useless.

I sniffed back my tears and crossed over to the pile of Anglo-Saxon clothing and armor that I had tossed on the floor earlier. Gingerly I picked up the jump device.

Yup, there was one thing I could still do.

I clenched the rod in my fist. One day it would turn cold again. And when it did, I'd jump back through time and find some more of these rogue jumpers. They'd have answers, and they'd give them to me, even if I had to hunt down and kill every last one of them.

EPILOGUE

My little condo was cold that morning. As always, it felt empty. No smells of breakfast cooking. No sounds of Dad hammering away on his computer, typing up his lecture notes. Just an oppressive silence. Dad's furniture and books occupied most of the small space, along with all the artifacts he'd collected over the course of his life. Suits of armor, medieval weapons, ancient pottery, and tapestries crowded the walls, leaving few gaps for the paint beneath to show through. It was like living in the world's smallest museum, but it made this place feel like home.

The three months since I'd returned from the Battle of Hastings had passed like a whirlwind. Putting our old house up for sale, packing everything into storage, finding and buying this new place, moving in. Somewhere in that chaos I also had my seventeenth birthday, a totally depressing event that involved take-out Chinese for one and movies I watched alone.

Being truly on my own for the first time made me realize how much Dad used to do for me. Of course there were all the daily chores that Mr. Morris had warned me about. But there were also big things.

I had to get myself a new phone and set up accounts with utility companies. I registered at the local high school as a senior. I filled out a ton of forms and stood in endless lines to replace all the ID that Sam had made me burn. I got a credit card. Basically I took a crash course in being an adult.

Through it all, I kept visiting Dad every day. His condition hadn't improved, and the doctors held out little hope, but I still made sure to spend time at his bedside—talking to him was the only constant left in my life.

As for Victor, the case against him was going nowhere—all the fingerprints and hair samples that had been gathered at the scene had "mysteriously" disappeared, and the neighbor's house had been broken into and their security camera stolen. I didn't know if Detective Johnson was in on it, but someone in the police force was definitely making sure that nothing tied Victor to the attack on Dad. So Victor was still out there, a constant threat.

I knew it wasn't over between him and me—he wouldn't be happy until he got Dad's jump device, and he didn't even know I'd picked up an extra. So for now I tried to appear as nonthreatening as possible. When he and his men came looking for me, they'd find what I wanted them to see—a simple kid who was getting on with his life.

With hardly a sound, I crept to the master bedroom—my room. My days in England had definitely left me a quieter person—I didn't stomp around the place anymore. From the closet I grabbed my suitcase and packed a few days' worth of clothes: T-shirts, jeans, underwear. On top of these I laid a dress shirt, tie, pants, and one of my dad's suit jackets. I hated dress clothes, but if all went well, I'd need them. I lugged the bag into the living room and pulled my Anglo-Saxon armor and sword off the wall, wrapped them in towels, and stuffed them on top of everything.

With one last look around, I locked the condo door, took the elevator to the lobby, and stepped out into the September sunshine, where my ride to the airport was waiting.

The pilot came on with a crackle to announce that we'd be landing in fifteen minutes. As I looked out at the low mountains of Virginia spread before me, their valleys shrouded in cloud and mist, all I could think about was that I couldn't get off this plane soon enough. I'd been pretty much a recluse for the last few months, hiding out in my apartment during the day and only venturing out late at night to buy food or to visit Dad. This was the first time I'd been cooped up with other people, and it made my skin crawl. So many discussions going on about stupid things like how cramped the seats were, the high price of gas, or how rude the TSA agents had been at the security check. Sam had been right: once you jumped through time and saved the world, you didn't really belong in the present anymore. I listened to these people and shook my head at their complaints. They wouldn't have survived a day in Anglo-Saxon England.

About two hours after we landed, my Lyft driver dropped me off at the only motel in the town, a place with about ten units strung together in a row that looked badly in need of a paint job.

I checked into the motel and took a hot shower to calm my nerves. All I'd been thinking about during the entire trip here was everything that could go wrong. Did I have the right address? What about the date, was it the right one? Even though I'd spent weeks on the internet, looking up names, property records, addresses, and all sorts of other things, I still could have made a mistake.

After my thoroughly nonrelaxing shower, I changed into my suit and somehow managed to knot my tie so it didn't look completely terrible. On top of this, I pulled on my armor and belted the sword at my side. I checked myself one more time in the mirror and then left the room. A man in faded jeans and a cowboy hat was waiting in the parking lot. "Well, I'll be damned," he said. "You gotta be Dan."

"Yeah, that's me."

"I'm Billy." He spat a long stream of tobacco to one side and looked me up and down, an amused grin on his face. "You know it ain't Halloween, right?"

"Yeah, yeah," I muttered impatiently. "Did you get everything like I asked?"

"Of course," he said. "Come with me." He led me to an old Ford pickup at the far end of the parking lot. From the trailer attached behind it came the sound of a horse shuffling its feet as we approached.

"Easy, Winston," Billy said, and the animal quieted down.

We both hopped into the truck, and Billy drove for about five minutes along a curving tree-lined road before turning down a dead-end street. There, he parked the truck at the side of the road and then led a horse out of the trailer. The animal was beautiful—completely black except for a white blaze on his nose. "This is Winston," Billy said. "He's already saddled and fed, so he'll be in a good mood. Make sure you treat him well, and I'll pick him up in an hour. At the high school, right?"

"So far. I'll text you if the plan changes."

He passed me a bouquet of white roses from the truck's back seat. "Don't forget these."

I took the bouquet. "Thanks."

"Good luck, kid. I hope it works out for you." He touched two fingers to the brim of his cowboy hat, then hopped into his pickup and drove off.

Luck. I'd need it.

I climbed into the saddle and with gentle nudges guided Winston along the street. Run-down houses on huge, forested lots dotted both sides. My goal stood at the other end of the street, second-to-last house on the right—a small bungalow with an overgrown lawn and a roof patched in places with blocks of different-colored shingles.

I gripped the reins tightly in my sweat-slicked hands as the clip-clop of hooves echoed down the street. I felt like hundreds of eyes were fixed upon me, so many witnesses to what could become a fall-flat-on-my-face failure of epic proportions.

Come on, Dan. You handled a Norman cavalry charge. You can do this.

I tied Winston to a tree and approached the house. *Please be home.* With the flowers hidden behind my back, I walked up the path.

A light was on in the living room, where a slob of a man in a stained undershirt sat watching TV. One pudgy hand was wrapped around a can of beer; the other was covered in a cast.

I opened the rusty screen door, and with a shaking finger I rang the bell.

"Get the damn door!" the man yelled.

I heard footsteps and I stood there in nervous anticipation, barely remembering to breathe. After a few seconds, the door swung open, and my heart soared. Sam was there, dressed in baggy school sweats, her hair tied in a ponytail, looking every bit as gorgeous as I remembered.

"H-h-hi," I said as my stomach tied itself in knots.

Sam's eyes widened. "You're alive!" She wrapped her arms around me and held me tight. "I was so worried about you. Why didn't you text or call me?"

"The numbers got smudged." It felt so good to have her in my arms. "I missed you, Sam," I said quietly, my mouth only inches from her ear.

"I missed you too." She gently pushed me out to arm's length so she could look at my face. "That's new." With her fingertips she traced the scar across my forehead.

"Norman war hammer. It almost killed me."

"Sounds horrible."

"It was." There was so much I wanted to say to her, but nothing would come out.

She cocked her head to one side. "How'd you find me?"

"Well … Google, and a lot of time calling the wrong people. I must've called half of Virginia trying to find you."

Sam's eyes suddenly narrowed. "What's with the armor? Is something wrong?"

I whipped the flowers out from behind my back. "Sam, you're the most beautiful woman I've ever met," I began, reciting the words I had practiced probably a hundred times already. "You fought by my side, saved my life, made me laugh, and saw me cry. I know it was only a few weeks, but I feel like I've known you for a thousand years. Will you go to the homecoming dance with me?" With a flourish, I pulled two tickets out of my jacket pocket and held them out to her.

Sam looked at me with disbelief. "You randomly show up on my doorstep on the day of the second-biggest dance of the school year, hoping I'll be free to go on a date with you?" She raised her hands out to her sides, palms upward, and shook her head. "The dance starts in an hour. If you figured out where I live, you had to have figured out my phone number. Why didn't you call me weeks ago?"

In my head, showing up on the day of the dance dressed in armor and riding a horse had seemed like the most romantic thing ever. Like something you'd see in movies, where the guy performs such a grand gesture that it sweeps the girl off her feet and into his arms. Except this wasn't a rom-com—this was reality.

"Yeah, I guess it's pretty lame." I sighed, my shoulders slumping. "I'm sure somebody asked you weeks ago. He's probably going to show up at any moment." I stared at her feet. "Well … I guess I'll go now. It was great seeing you again, Sam. I'm glad you're okay." I turned to leave.

"Still a newbie, aren't you?" she asked.

I spun around to face her. "Huh?"

"Does it look like I'm getting ready for a dance?" She waved her hands toward her legs. "I'm wearing sweatpants. And look at my hair! I told you about the losers at my school. No one around here is sweeping me off my feet." She smiled at me—a warm, loving smile that made my pulse race. "But here you are on my doorstep, my knight in almost-shining armor. With flowers too." She took both my hands, then pulled me close and kissed me. Deeply, passionately, like she had on the hill outside Hastings. My entire body was electrified by her touch, and I worried for a second that my knees might give out.

Finally Sam broke the kiss. "I have to get ready," she said, her face flushed. "Wait for me out here," she said, grimacing over her shoulder at the man in the chair. "Trust me."

And as I stood there, I realized I could. No matter what.

A few minutes later, Sam came out in a floor-length dark green medieval gown, its wide sleeves and deep neckline trimmed in silver ribbon. Her gold necklace bore a small ruby pendant that nestled in her pale cleavage. Her hair flowed over her shoulders like a fiery mane.

"Wow," I said breathlessly.

"You like it?" She spun around in a full circle.

"You look like a queen," I said.

"Thanks. I kept it from a previous jump. Renaissance Italy."

With my toe, I nudged my sword and chain mail, which I had taken off while she'd been inside and were now lying on the front step in a little pile. "Can you stash these inside somewhere?"

"Awww ... You took the armor off. You should have kept it on. It was cute."

"No way," I snorted. "I already had one guy laugh at me today. I'm not having your whole school laugh at me."

She tucked my gear inside and then, arm in arm, we walked down the path to where Winston waited. I helped her into the saddle and then took my place behind her, reaching around her to hold the reins.

Finally, I had her in my arms, and I wasn't planning on letting go this time. I put my chin on her shoulder, inhaling the strawberry scent of her hair. "I won't leave you, Sam," I whispered.

She put her hand over mine. "I know."

We rode along the rural highway to her school, our bodies swaying in unison in the saddle. At Sam's high school, the parking lot was crammed with pickup trucks and small, older-model cars. Girls in short dresses and guys in ill-fitting suits hung out next to their vehicles, smoking or drinking from plastic cups. All eyes turned toward us as we approached. Conversations died down until the only sound was the clop of Winston's hooves on the asphalt.

"What a loser," a guy snickered.

"Shut up, Brad," his date said. "Why can't you be romantic like that for once?"

I ignored them both and helped Sam out of the saddle, then tied Winston to the bike rack. Sam crooked her arm into mine, and together we walked through the front door of the school—a knight and his lady. Someday soon I'd find out what Victor's plans were, and how to stop him. But tonight was just for me and the girl of my dreams.

HISTORICAL NOTES

Dan may be a fictional character, but the history he visits is very real. The events depicted in this book occurred in England during the late summer and early fall of CE 1066. On January 5 of that year, King Edward the Confessor of England had died without an heir. Realizing that the country needed a king, the leading nobles of the land chose Harold Godwinson, Earl of Wessex, the richest and most powerful man in England, to be the next ruler. He was crowned on January 6 but had little time to enjoy his kingship. Before the year was over, he faced two massive challenges to his rule. The first was an invasion in the north of the country, led by Harold's brother Tostig and Tostig's ally, King Harald Hardrada of Norway. King Hardrada had his own weak claim to the English throne based on an agreement his nephew had made with Harthacnut, the king of England before Edward. Together Tostig and Hardrada landed a large fleet of ships near the modern-day city of York, which was called Eoforwic at that time. Hardrada's and Tostig's forces, numbering roughly eight to ten thousand Vikings, easily defeated the local forces sent against them at the Battle of Fulford, on September 20, 1066.

When Harold Godwinson heard of this threat in the north, he gathered his army and rushed from London to confront the invaders. By September 24, they had reached Tada (modern-day Tadcaster) where they spent the night. As for Hardrada and Tostig, they had split their troops, assuming that there was no one to threaten them. One portion of the Viking army stayed with their ships at Riccall, while the others remained in the vicinity of York, waiting for the city to send them tribute and hostages.

On September 25, 1066, Godwinson and his Anglo-Saxons fell upon this group of unarmored men at a place called Stamford Bridge. The Vikings fought for their lives, and a long battle ensued, but without armor the Vikings had a hard time protecting themselves. Tostig, Hardrada, and most of that northern group of Vikings died. The group of Vikings at Riccall, who had been guarding the ships, heard of the slaughter and rushed to join the battle. But since they were running in full armor, most of the troops were exhausted by the time they reached Stamford Bridge and fought poorly. The end result was that almost all the Vikings who had landed in England were killed. Of the three hundred boats full of troops that the Vikings brought to England, only twenty-four returned home. This was the last major battle the Vikings ever fought, effectively ending the Viking age.

After the battle, Harold and his forces went to the city of York to celebrate their incredible victory. There, on October 1, while in the middle of celebrating, Harold was informed that a large army of Normans led by Duke William had landed at Pevensey in the south of England on September 28. William, a distant cousin of Edward the Confessor, had his own claim to the English throne, stating that Edward had promised him the throne earlier.

Harold gathered up as many troops as he could from his northern battle and rushed south, arriving in London around October 6. He remained in London for a few days to gather more troops. However, on hearing that William's forces were ravaging English territory, Harold marched his army south to meet them. The two forces met at Hastings on October 14, 1066.

From a strategic standpoint, Harold had many chances to win the Battle of Hastings. He could have waited a few more days for more troops to show up. He could have kept his men united at the top of the hill so they would have been able to fend off the Normans' attacks. But he did neither, and his forces were cut down. After a daylong battle, the Normans defeated the Anglo-Saxons, killing Harold Godwinson and his brothers Gyrth and Leofwine. With the cream of Saxon nobility dead on the battlefield, Duke William claimed the crown of England, ending hundreds of years of Anglo-Saxon rule in England.

This novel is heavily indebted to many sources. For the Battle of Stamford Bridge, my main sources were *Harald's Saga*, written by the Icelandic poet Snorri Sturluson about 130 years after the event, and the *Anglo-Saxon Chronicle*, a book compiled by Anglo-Saxon monks who provided yearly summaries of significant events that happened in England during Anglo-Saxon times. (The chronicle contains entries dating as far back as the Roman conquest of Britain, but these were taken from earlier sources. From the late ninth century onward is when the chronicle was actively maintained by the monks.) These two sources provided many details about the Viking attack on York, King Harald Hardrada's bravery in battle, the lone Viking on Stamford Bridge, the deaths of Tostig and Hardrada, and the arrival of the Vikings from Riccall.

For the Battle of Hastings, I had to use various Norman sources, as the *Anglo-Saxon Chronicle* had very little to say about this momentous event in English history. My first source was *The History of William the Conqueror*, written by William of Poitiers, the personal chaplain to William the Conqueror (Duke William, as Dan knows him). Although not present at the battle, this biographer would have had direct access to the accounts of men who were there. The other source I referenced was the Bayeux Tapestry. This massive piece of embroidery, which is more than 230 feet long, was woven just a few years after the Battle of Hastings and depicts the entire history of events leading up to the battle as well as the battle itself, all in needlework. It's like viewing one long cartoon strip of the conflict, complete with captions explaining each scene. The tapestry was most likely commissioned by William the Conqueror's brother Odo, who was present that day.

The Battle of Hastings is truly one of the most important battles in the history of Western civilization. Without that victory by Duke William and his army of French-speaking warriors, there would be no French influence on the language, so English would have most likely remained much closer to German or Icelandic, as it had been previously. In addition, without the Normans' strong ties to their large land holdings in France, the centuries of power struggles between England and France that began during William's reign would never have happened. These struggles lasted until 1453, when the French decisively defeated the English at the Battle of Castillon, effectively ending the Hundred Years' War and leading to England losing their last territorial possessions in France.

If William had lost at Hastings, the complete history of Europe would have been rewritten. The British Empire might not have existed, and more than a thousand years of history, culture, and exploration would not have unfolded as they did.

PLACE NAMES

Throughout the novel, I used the contemporary Anglo-Saxon names for towns and cities.

Skarthaborg = Scarborough

Tada = Tadcaster

Torp = Thorp Arch

Acum = Acomb

Eoforwic = York

And when Gunnar the Viking speaks of Miklagard, he is referring to Constantinople, which is modern-day Istanbul.

ACKNOWLEDGMENTS

When I first started writing, I thought it would be a solitary event like you see in the movies—just me, alone in some dark corner of my house hammering away at a keyboard for weeks and months on end and then finally emerging with a brilliant manuscript that would instantly be turned into a bestselling novel and a movie. Those delusions got shattered quickly. The reality is that this book never would have been published without the generous contributions of time and effort by many family members and friends over the years. I am deeply grateful for all their help along the way.

In particular, I would like to thank my beautiful, vivacious, charming, brilliant, hilarious wife, Pam (*Hey! Who inserted all these adjectives in here, Pam?*) for her love and support during my writing journey. She is one of the first to read my chapters and has always been quick to point out any ways to improve the story or phrasing. I would also like to thank my wonderful kids, Leah, Arawn, and Calvin. So many times they shared with me the books they brought home from the library, and this became my introduction to the world of YA literature. Talking to them about the stories they liked and the characters that moved them inspired me to write this book and series.

A special thank you goes to all the previous and current members of my critique group who have read my chapters over the course of years, particularly Cryssa Bazos, Tom Taylor, and Gwen Tuinman. Their encouragement, suggestions, and feedback pushed me to make countless revisions and improvements that only made the story better.

I would like to thank Peter Lavery and Heather Sangster, who edited the earlier versions of the manuscript and helped bring it to a point where I could confidently send it out to agents.

Maya Myers has my extreme thanks for all the work she's done on the final versions. Her detailed editing and countless suggestions improved the book on so many levels.

My agent, Lloyd Kelly, deserves thanks for introducing me to Imbrifex Books and the incredible publishing team of Mark Sedenquist and Megan Edwards. I am wholeheartedly grateful to Imbrifex for taking me on as a new author. I never knew how much additional work would be involved in getting my manuscript to a finished product, but Mark and Megan have been there to guide me along at every step of this amazing publishing journey.

Most of all, I would like to thank you, dear reader, for joining me on this time-travel adventure.

Coming in September:
THE CELTIC DECEPTION
A Jump in Time Novel, Book 2

CHAPTER 1

I stood in the hallway outside my condo door, a backpack full of schoolbooks hanging from my shoulder. At the top corner of the door, almost invisible unless someone was intentionally looking for it, was the piece of clear tape I had stretched across the door and the frame before I'd left for school. It was now split neatly in two—someone had broken into my place. Not that it surprised me. I always knew Victor Stahl would come after me one day. Powerful men like him make sure to clean up all loose ends. And since I'd been the only person to witness him savagely stabbing my dad four months before, I was one big loose end.

My hand hovered over the doorknob. Expecting this day didn't mean I was ready for it. Victor was ruthless, and he wouldn't hesitate to snuff me out if I even looked at him the wrong way.

If only I could call the cops. But the cops had been completely useless in investigating the attack on my dad. I'd flat out told them that Victor was the guy who'd stabbed him, and they'd done nothing. They'd either been bought off to look the other way, or they didn't believe me because I was just some dumb seventeen-year-old with no evidence to back up my story, and he was a congressman. No, the cops couldn't help—I'd have to handle this myself.

I took a deep breath and opened the door. Whistling to mask my nervousness, I tossed my backpack on the floor, hung up my coat, and headed for the living room. Even though I'd been expecting him, bile still rose to my throat when I found Victor sitting on my couch. He wore a dark-blue pinstriped suit, and his neatly trimmed black hair was streaked with gray. He sat casually, like he owned the place, his right arm resting on the seat back.

He looked up at me with his dark soulless eyes. "Master Renfrew, so good to see you again." He used a disgustingly friendly tone, as if his breaking into my house was a normal event and we'd just ignore the fact he'd left Dad in a coma and sit down to tea.

I glanced behind me, making sure my escape route was clear.

It wasn't.

Another man in a suit stepped out of the kitchen and crossed his arms over his chest, blocking my path to the door. This guy was built like a wrestler, with beefy arms, a thick neck, and an indifferent scowl that made me feel like a bug about to be squished. Somehow, none of my carefully thought-out plans had accounted for Victor bringing help.

"W-what are you doing here?" I stammered.

Victor shook his head in disappointment. "Now, Daniel, is that any way to treat a guest? I simply came to visit you and see how you are. It has been months since we last spoke."

Spoke? Was this guy freakin' serious?

The last time we "spoke," he'd just finished plunging a sword into Dad's chest. And the only speaking we'd done then was him barking orders at me. I curled my hands into fists to control the tremors of rage coursing through me. Every inch of me wanted to grab one of the medieval weapons displayed on the wall and ram it through his chest. I'd never make it, though. Victor was a great swordsman, and he'd brought muscle. I wasn't going to get out of this mess by fighting—I had to play it cool.

Victor waved toward one of the armchairs opposite the couch—as if it was his house, not mine. "Please, sit. We have so much to talk about."

I perched on the edge of the chair, legs tensed, ready to bolt.

"So, Daniel, you left rather abruptly during our last meeting. Please tell me where you went."

"Why should I tell you anything? You tried to kill my dad."

"Ah, yes," Victor sighed, "a very unfortunate occurrence that I truly regret. How is your father? Has his condition improved? I send flowers every week."

I felt like puking. How dare he ask about my dad? "Call the hospital if you want to know how he is," I snapped. "Now can we skip the chitchat and get to the part where you tell me why you've broken into my place?"

"Daniel, Daniel, Daniel," Victor sighed, like a disappointed school-teacher. "I merely came here to have an amicable discussion about a few matters of importance. If your father had sat and listened to reason, he would not be in the hospital now. Unfortunately, he chose to cause problems." Victor leaned forward, his eyes narrowing. "Are *you* going to cause problems, Daniel?"

As if to emphasize the question, the thug in the suit cracked his knuckles. "No!" I shook my head rapidly. "No problems."

"Good. Now if you answer a few questions to my satisfaction, I will be on my way." He steepled his fingers. "What happened while you were off in the past?"

"I have no clue what happened," I said. "One minute I'm in my living room, watching you and Dad fighting … then Dad throws me some weird metal rod, I say this dumb rhyme that he'd taught me since I was a kid, there's a blinding flash of light, and, poof, I'm back in England in 1066. And amazingly I can speak and understand the language!" Victor nodded. Clearly he was buying my story so far, which he should, since it was the truth. All my life I'd thought Dad was just some nerdy history professor. I had no clue that he belonged to a secret community of people who fixed glitches that appeared in the time stream and threatened to alter history. So when I accidentally teleported myself to medieval England, I'd stumbled around completely clueless for the first little while.

Now came the hard part—lying through my teeth about the rest of my time jump and hoping that Victor didn't catch on. "I hid out in the village of Torp with a guy named Osmund," I continued. "I spent a few days there, picking cabbages and sleeping in the church ... and then the rod suddenly warmed up and I could bring myself back home."

Victor stroked his chin thoughtfully, assessing my words. "Did you happen to encounter any other time travelers?"

You mean the two who got themselves killed while trying to kill me, or the one I can't stop thinking about?

"Don't think so," I said. "How would I know if I met one?"

Victor pointed to the tattoo on my right forearm—a black four-pointed star in a circle that I'd had for as long as I could remember. "All the community members bear that mark. Did you see anyone with this same tattoo?"

"No," I lied.

"Interesting," Victor responded, which he managed to make sound exactly like *I don't believe a word you're saying*. He gave a slight nod to the man by the door, and the thug walked over and stood behind my chair. I couldn't see him, and I couldn't hear him, but I could feel the menace radiating behind me. My hands began to tremble, and I gripped the armrests.

"Now, Daniel," Victor continued. "You have to forgive me if I do not have the utmost faith in everything you tell me. These are difficult times, and not everyone can be trusted." He leaned forward. "*Can I trust you?*"

I swallowed hard and a trickle of sweat ran down my back. Victor wasn't a man who played games. This was a guy plotting to unleash a wave of global destruction that would kill billions, all so that he and the other time jumpers allied with him could take over the world. I meant absolutely nothing to him. "Y-y-you can trust me," I stammered.

He smiled, but his eyes remained cold, dark—reptilian. "Excellent! I hate it when people are dishonest. Nothing disappoints me more." He brushed the sleeve of his suit jacket and his gold cufflinks glinted in the light. "Now, Daniel, since it seems I can trust you, I want you to tell me what you feel about me."

This was a test, clearly, but what was the correct answer? Did he want me to say that I forgave him for stabbing Dad and that I hoped we could become the best of friends? Big nope. "I hate you," I said. "I hate your face. I hate your suits. I hate that you're in my house threatening me. I hope you get hit by a bus."

Victor clapped his hands and laughed. "See, Drake? I told you that young Daniel here was an honest boy. He would never lie to us."

"I still don't trust him," said the man behind me. "We should kill him."

"Wait!" I howled. "I'm telling you the truth!" I darted my head around, looking for a place to run. Drake had put the lock chain on my door so even if I did get past him, there was no way I could get through the door before he caught me.

Victor tapped his lips with a finger. "That *would* be easier. But I am sure young Daniel here can be persuaded to be agreeable." He nodded at me. "Do you think we can come to an agreement, Daniel?"

"Yes."

"Very good." He held out his hand to me. "Give me your time-travel device."

I wiped my hands on my pants, trying to remove the sheen of sweat that covered them. I couldn't give up my jump rod. Dad had taken a sword to the chest rather than surrender it to Victor. "Why do you want it?" I asked, trying to buy some time.

"For a simple reason. The members of our community should not be killing each other. There are so few of us left, and we perform such a vital task that it is sheer folly to continually shed blood among our ranks. However, I also believe that those who strive for greatness should not be hindered by those with small minds. The best way to stop you from causing any further problems is for me to take away your time-travel mechanism. If your father had only listened to this uncomplicated reasoning, he would not be in the hospital now." He waved his hand dismissively. "The choice is yours, as I do not believe in forcing people to do things. You can either bring me the mechanism willingly—and my associate Drake and I will be on our way—or we will have to resort to measures that you will find much less palatable." He smiled at me. "I can assure you that no matter which path you choose, you will no longer be a threat to us and we will still have the device. The choice is yours." He leaned back and drummed his fingers on his knee, like he was waiting for a train on a sunny day.

My heart pounded. This is what it all came down to: Victor wanted the jump rod, and he was going to take it, no matter what. Drake's meaty hands clamped down on my shoulders, keeping me firmly in my chair. His thick fingers were right beside my neck. All he had to do was squeeze and I'd be dead in seconds. "I'll give you the rod," I said, my voice coming out as a squeak. "Just leave me alone."

"But of course," Victor soothed. "You will be free to lead a happy life. You can continue going to school, get a job, or do whatever other mundane things you had planned. Now go get me the mechanism."

Drake removed his hands from my shoulders and, for half a second, I thought about bolting, but I knew I'd never make it. I didn't trust

Victor, and I definitely didn't trust Drake, but I'd always known this was the only way to get Victor off my back. I went over to the TV set. Underneath it sat a bin containing all the gear for my video games. I dug around in the pile of extra controllers, attachments, and cables, and pulled out a metallic rod about the length of a pencil and slightly thinner than a banana. It was hexagonal, like a pencil, and divided into six segments. Strange glyphs were etched into each face.

"How very clever, Daniel," Victor said. "Hidden in plain sight. See, Drake, I told you the boy was smart. It would have taken us hours to find the device hidden there." He stood up from the couch and smoothed out the creases in his suit jacket before walking over to me and taking the rod from my hand. "Now, Master Renfrew, I do hope this concludes our business. You will find that I am a very fair man to those people I can call friends." He wrapped his hand around my wrist and slowly squeezed. I'd never felt such a tight grip; my bones felt like they were going to snap. I gasped and he yanked me even closer. "But never, *ever* go against me, Daniel."

He turned toward Drake. "Shall we leave now? I am sure young Daniel here has other plans for the evening." He picked up his overcoat from the arm of the couch and headed for the front door, with Drake following like an obedient dog.

I slammed the door behind them and locked it. With my back leaning against it, I took several slow deep breaths to calm myself. I just wanted to smash something. Victor had broken into my house and nearly killed me. I felt so … violated. How could he just do whatever he wanted? I screamed as I pounded my fist against the wall. I wanted to kill him. I wanted to stop his insane plot. I wanted to make him pay for hurting my dad.

My shoulders slumped as my rage fizzled out of me. Who was I kidding? I'd never get to Victor. He was rich and powerful, and I was just some dumb seventeen-year-old who lived alone, barely surviving.

I sagged to the floor and pulled out my phone. Vid call? I texted. A few seconds later an answering text came back: OK when? 10 mins.

I couldn't stay here—the place reeked of Victor. What had he done here while he was waiting for me to come home? Had he installed spy cameras? Bugged my rooms? I wasn't going to feel safe here for a very long time. At least not until I had ripped the place apart and made sure I wasn't being watched.

I took my phone and coat, applied a new piece of tape to the front door, and headed out into the street. Dusk had already started to fall, and the autumn wind had a chill to it. I turned a few corners and ended up at a coffee shop with free Wi-Fi. I got a doughnut and picked a small table near the back, where I could watch people but not be easily watched. I pulled out my phone. Within seconds the screen lit up, and Sam's mane of red hair and lightly freckled face appeared on screen.

"Hey," I said casually, as if the mere sight of her didn't take my breath away and twist my insides all up in knots.

"Hey. What's up?"

"Victor came to my house today."

Her green eyes widened. "You okay?"

"I've been better. He didn't hurt me, but he took the jump device."

She leaned closer to her screen, eyebrows raised in a question she didn't need to voice.

I shook my head. "I told him I never got out of the village I landed in. He asked me a few questions about his missing guys, but I played dumb. And he seems to still have no clue that you exist."

"Thanks." She smiled in relief. "Did you get any information out of him?"

"No. He asked all the questions; I could only answer. He brought some muscle with him, too. I'm lucky they didn't kill me."

Sam's brow creased with concern. "You sure you're okay? You look pretty upset."

"Of course I'm upset! The guy broke into my house, pushed me around, and I couldn't do a thing. I felt so powerless."

Sam nodded sympathetically. "We'll get him."

"How? The guy can do anything he wants."

"You know how. Our only chance is to jump again."

An ache formed in my stomach. I hated time-jumping. On my first and only experience, I'd been stabbed, put on trial for murder, had my skull almost caved in with a war hammer, and fought on the front line of one of the most important battles of medieval history. Except for meeting Sam, nothing good had happened to me while time-jumping. But unfortunately, Sam was right: there was no other way to stop Victor. He was too strong, and we were nothing. "Yeah, yeah," I grumbled. "Do you have any idea when the next glitch might happen?"

"Nope. Like I told you in England, it's totally random. One could happen next week—or next year. We just have to be ready to jump out whenever it happens."

"Fine," I muttered.

We talked for about half an hour, then I packed up and headed home. To my relief, the tape across the door frame wasn't broken this time. I spent the next few hours ransacking my apartment, looking for any surveillance equipment Victor might have planted. I tossed books off shelves, ripped armor and weapons off the walls, and flung cushions to the floor but found nothing.

When I was finally satisfied that the place was clean, I went into the laundry room and pulled the large box of detergent off the shelf. With one hand I dug deep into the soapy powder like I was searching for the prize in a box of cereal. My fingers closed around a metal rod exactly like the one I had given Victor. A smile snuck across my face.

No matter how much I hated time-jumping, I hated Victor even more. And with this other jump rod, I was ready to go back in history as soon as the next time glitch came around.

THE CELTIC DECEPTION: A Jump in Time Novel
by Andrew Varga will be in bookstores and
wherever fine books are sold on September 5, 2023.

ABOUT THE AUTHOR

Ever since his mother told him he was descended from Vikings, Andrew Varga has had a fascination for history. He's read hundreds of history books, watched countless historical movies, and earned a BA with honors from the University of Toronto with a specialist in history and a major in English.

Andrew has travelled extensively across Europe, where he toured some of the most famous castles, museums, and historical sites that Europe has to offer. During his travels he accumulated a collection of swords, shields, and other medieval weapons that now adorn his personal library. He is skilled in fencing and Kendo—the Japanese art of sword fighting. He has also used both longbows and crossbows, built a miniature working trebuchet, knit his own shirt of chain mail, and earned a black belt in karate.

Andrew currently lives in the greater Toronto area with his wife Pam, their three children, and their mini-zoo of two dogs, two cats, a turtle, and some fish. It was his children's love of reading, particularly historical and fantasy stories, that inspired Andrew to write this series. In his spare time, when he isn't writing or editing, Andrew reads history books, jams on guitar, or plays beach volleyball.

Connect with the author online:

andrewvargaauthor.com

@AndrewVargaAuthor

@ andrewvargaauthor